D0460323

"MAKE LOVE TO ME, RICK. HERE. NOW."

Karla's voice was pleading. "I need you to make love to me one last time."

Rick held her gently as he gazed into her eyes. The meeting of their lips was as explosive as the first time they had kissed. But now their passion was tinged with sadness....

With a fluid movement he slipped her sweater over her head. Karla shivered with bittersweet desire as he stroked the rounded flesh above her bra. Their movements soon became urgent, their surroundings forgotten in their burning need.

When finally he entered her, Karla cried out his name. That one word expressed the vast love and sorrow she had inside....

WELCOME TO...

SUPERROMANCES

A sensational series of modern love stories
from Worldwide Library.

Written by masters of the genre, these longer,
sensual and dramatic novels are truly in keeping
with today's changing life-styles. Full of intriguing
conflicts, the heartaches and delights of true love.
SUPERROMANCES are absorbing stories —
satisfying and sophisticated reading that lovers
of romance fiction have long been waiting for.

SUPERROMANCES
Contemporary love stories for the woman of today!

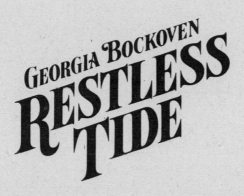

Georgia Bockoven
RESTLESS TIDE

A SUPERROMANCE FROM
W🌐RLDWIDE

TORONTO · NEW YORK · LONDON · PARIS
AMSTERDAM · STOCKHOLM · HAMBURG
ATHENS · MILAN · TOKYO · SYDNEY

To John, for being my "Rick"
and Nancy, for being my "Maggie"

Published October 1983

First printing August 1983

ISBN 0-373-70082-2

Copyright © 1983 by Georgia Bockoven. All rights reserved.
Philippine copyright 1983. Australian copyright 1983.
Except for use in any review, the reproduction or utilization of
this work in whole or in part in any form by any electronic,
mechanical or other means, now known or hereafter invented,
including xerography, photocopying and recording, or in any
information storage or retrieval system, is forbidden without
the permission of the publisher, Worldwide Library,
225 Duncan Mill Road, Don Mills, Ontario, Canada M3B 3K9.

All the characters in this book have no existence outside the
imagination of the author and have no relation whatsoever to
anyone bearing the same name or names. They are not even
distantly inspired by any individual known or unknown to the
author, and all the incidents are pure invention.

The Superromance trademark, consisting of the word
SUPERROMANCE, and the Worldwide trademark, consisting of
a globe and the word WORLDWIDE in which the letter "O" is
represented by a depiction of a globe, are trademarks of
Worldwide Library.

Printed in Canada

CHAPTER ONE

A SENSE OF FOREBODING had plagued Karla Fleming all day. What started out a mere trickle of apprehension in the morning had, by late afternoon, turned into an unshakable feeling of gloom. Finally, after she had charged one customer at the Artists' Co-Op Gallery twice for the same item and then neglected to charge the next customer anything, she stopped trying to convince herself the feeling didn't exist.

When the usual late-afternoon lull struck, and she realized the only footsteps on the highly polished oak floors were hers, she gave up all pretense of normalcy and nervously began to pace around the shop. She ended her wanderings at the front door, where she paused and pulled aside the Open sign to stare absentmindedly out the mullioned windows. She watched as a sailboat, carrying a billowing rainbow aloft to catch the wind, adroitly maneuvered its way into the harbor. Behind the sailboat, the deep green, forest-covered hills of neighboring islands absorbed the early-afternoon sun, while tufts of clouds overhead reflected it. The composition was tailor-made to sell cameras, but today its ethereal beauty failed to penetrate Karla's pensive mood or lighten her sense of unease.

A sudden chill that had nothing to do with the temperature made the hair on the nape of her neck brush uncomfortably against her cowl collar. Hugging herself for warmth, then running her hands briskly down her arms, she sighed and pressed her nose against the cool glass. Marten's Cove was a town still in the lethargy of waking from a long winter's sleep. The wooden sidewalks that now held only an occasional stroller would soon fill with jostling crowds of tourists eager to spend their money for a memento of their vacation.

Impulsively Karla reached up, flipped the sign in the window to Closed, and locked the door. Within five minutes she was out the back entrance and down the stairs. As she slipped behind the wheel of her pickup truck, she suppressed a twinge of guilt over her unusual behavior by vowing that several days in midseason she would stay open longer—even though she knew none of the artists whose work she sold would object if she didn't.

While she mechanically drove the three meandering miles around the island to her cabin, she managed to convince herself that the sudden onset of nerves was nothing more than an early reaction to the tax audit the business was scheduled to undergo in a few weeks. Certainly nothing a long soak in the tub with a steaming mug of herb tea wouldn't cure.

As Karla rounded the last bumpy curve in the gravel road, her gaze automatically went to the rustic log cabin she called home. Bordered on three sides by a grove of Douglas fir with colorful madrone interspersed, the snug bungalow faced west to witness the spectacular Puget Sound sunsets. Compact, airy and functional, the diminutive two-bedroom dwelling had become her own small piece of heaven on earth. It had been a refuge from the hell she had gone through three years before, a place where she had withdrawn from the world to heal her almost terminally deep wounds.

Her house was the last one on the little-used island road, and the only one in this particular rock-strewn cove. Its isolated location had given her the privacy and solitude she had needed when she'd first arrived on the island, two things she had since come to cherish.

As Karla parked the pickup in the driveway she heard the faint ring of her telephone. She hesitated before slamming the truck door, strangely relieved that she was too far away to answer before the caller would hang up. Slowly making her way to the front door, she absently nudged a fir cone with her toe until it rolled off the cedar deck and into the cushion of fern and pine needles below.

Once inside the sunlit living room, she tossed her purse and sweater onto a chair, then stepped out of her black leather heels and headed for the kitchen to start water boiling for tea. Tea, regardless of the brand or brew, had become her self-prescribed tranquilizer for times of stress. There was something curiously comforting about wrapping her hands around a warm, oversize mug and burying her nose in the fragrant steam.

While filling the kettle, she suddenly remembered that several artists who sold their wares through the shop were to be featured on the local afternoon TV program that day. She backtracked to the living room and turned on the old, seldom-used black-and-white set she had inherited from the former owner.

Karla spent a couple of minutes fiddling with the knobs, trying to adjust the snow before deciding she would have to settle for just the sound. Disappointed, she straightened up and sighed. "At least I won't miss it entirely," she said aloud.

She stared at the faint figure of the talk-show host and tried to make out how many people were sitting on the couch next to him. Frustrated, she wondered if a swift kick would do anything for the set. Maybe it wouldn't help the reception but venting her pique on the one-eyed monster might do something for her mood.

Karla let out a deep breath, turned and headed back to the kitchen to put the teakettle on the stove. Before she had retraced five of the ten steps, however, her world collapsed around her like a house of cards in a windstorm.

The devastating words rang out clear and sharp

and cruel, well modulated by an obvious broadcast-school graduate. They were a surefire "teaser" to get people to tune in to the early-evening news on Puget Sound's only locally owned channel.

"Race-car driver Rick Fleming maintains his fragile hold on life after being involved in a spectacular five-car crash this afternoon during the Baxter Colsen Memorial Race at Riverside Motor Speedway. This story and more when...."

The rest was lost in the deafening sound of her heartbeat as Karla clung to the kitchen doorframe for support. Her legs felt as though she had just risen from a cramped position, painfully tingling their protest at being asked to hold her upright. Her vision began to recede in undulating waves that finally engulfed her, and she collapsed on the floor.

The punishing, persistent ring of the telephone swirled through Karla's fog of unconsciousness, yanking her from the comforting bliss of nothingness to the world she had briefly escaped. She pulled herself to a sitting position and immediately grabbed for her head, trying to ease the blinding ache that sliced through her temples like a flaming sword. Tenderly, with her left hand, she examined the bump where she had struck her head in the fall. With her right, she reached up and groped for the wall phone, pulling the receiver off its hook by swinging the cord.

"Yes," she hesitantly whispered into the mouthpiece, unable to trust her voice with anything louder.

"Karla? Is that you, Karla?" The deep, impatient male voice didn't wait for a reply. "This is Steve McDonald, Karla...I'm afraid I've got some bad news for you."

She could hear a nasal quality in his tone and immediately wondered if he had been crying. *Oh, God, no,* she screamed silently. There could only be one reason for Steve McDonald to shed tears. She felt a severe pain in her chest. Rick must be dead.

Karla fought an urge to hang up, to simply deny the truth by refusing to hear it. Instead she woodenly asked, "How is he, Steve?"

He paused. When he finally spoke he ignored her question. "He wants to see you. I think you had better hurry."

"Oh, Steve, I can't." Her words were barely audible. "I can't come there to watch him die. There isn't a piece of me left that's strong enough to do that. Not again. I just can't."

"You're stronger than you think you are, Karla," he said, an urgent plea in his voice. "If you would just see him! He lies there, fighting to stay awake, waiting for you to get there. He won't say anything except, 'Get Karla for me. Please get Karla.' I've been trying to reach you all afternoon."

No matter how desperately her mind told her to protect herself from this final devastating loss, she knew she would go to Rick. She would lose her hard-won battle for self-preservation. Her fragile hold on the "ordinary" life she had built for herself here on Quiller Island would be gone forever.

And when it was all over, when Rick was laid in a small rectangle of earth beside her brother, Bobby, she would be left a shell. Her essence would die with him as surely as day ends when the sun is gone. Everything afterward would be as artificial as illumination at midnight.

"I'll come, Steve," she finally said. Deep down she had known all along that should anything ever happen to Rick she would go to him. Almost to herself she added, "Now, I just pray I won't be too late."

Karla glanced at her watch. The last ferry would be gone before she could get back to Marten's Cove. "Steve," she said, her voice strong and clear now that she had made her decision, "the only way I can get off the island tonight with any kind of speed is by seaplane. Could you—"

"Have the pilot take you to Bellingham," Steve interrupted. "I have a friend there who will fly you on to Seattle. When you get to Seattle, go to the United terminal. I'll make sure there's a ticket to Los Angeles waiting for you."

Even after they had worked out all the details, and Karla knew she should start getting ready to leave, she couldn't bear to break the connection. Her intuition warned her not to ask, but the words rushed out anyway. "Is he really bad, Steve?"

"Just hurry, Karla," he replied. "Get here as fast as you can." The words echoed hauntingly after he'd hung up.

AFTER THE NUMBING PHONE CALL and the frantic arrangements to get to Bellingham, Karla was thankful the noise of Steve's friend's single-engine aircraft was loud enough to preclude conversation. It allowed her to retreat into the private world of her thoughts without seeming rude. In addition, it let her escape any further reminiscences, well-intentioned though they were, of what a terrific guy Rick Fleming had been. The soliloquy had started as soon as she'd met the pilot, an ex-race-car mechanic, at the dock. The praise, delivered as if Rick were already dead, was almost unbearable for Karla to listen to.

As often as she had dreaded it, she could not imagine Rick lying broken and bleeding on a hospital bed, with transparent tubes pumping artificial life and promise into his inert body. She couldn't picture him attached to a battery of machines that frantically worked to keep him alive but were also primed to unemotionally indicate that the battle had been lost. She couldn't visualize him in an intensive care unit, filled with a hundred odors that combined to create one unforgettable perfume of death. In fact, she couldn't see Rick at all. The face that kept intruding into her thoughts was not Rick's. It was Bobby's.

Karla had spent five long days in a hospital watching her younger brother die. All the attendant emotions were indelibly impressed on her memory. He, too, had been a casualty of the race—of the indomitable spirit that compelled certain men and women to chance everything in their pursuit of a mystical perfection Karla couldn't understand. They were the risk takers. The ones who arrogantly demanded that life give them more than the ordinary.

And, Karla thought, because she had been a sister to one and had fallen in love with another, she was one of those mortals who waited and hoped and prayed that they would return safely. For Bobby, the wait had been short—only twenty-three years. For Rick, it seemed she would have to be satisfied with a measly gift of thirty-four.

Dammit, thirty-four years was not long enough! The sparkling lights of the towns below disappeared into soft unfocused blurs as tears filled Karla's eyes, slid down her cheeks and landed one by one on her tightly clasped hands.

As they neared Southern California and the airport, Karla noticed that the sky over the Los Angeles hills still held the deep black of night without a hint of the coming day. When she landed she found that Steve had met her plane with a police escort. After a perfunctory exchange, he took her arm and guided her into the waiting car.

Once inside she forlornly smiled a welcome, a sad greeting for an old, once close friend. Immediately she felt his hostility toward her, a seething hostility that was a lingering remnant of their emotion-packed parting three years earlier. Steve had accused her of selfishly destroying Rick by leaving him when he needed her the most.

Though they were nearly the same age, the two men were almost complete contrasts. Everything about Steve was oversize, from his broad, muscular body to his huge hands. A stranger would find him stern looking, with an unapproachable air about him—until he smiled. Then, for anyone astute enough to notice, the true nature of his personality was revealed.

Karla could remember being a little frightened by Steve's size and noncommittal stare when she'd met him. But it hadn't taken her long to discover that his taciturn, abrupt behavior covered a deep underlying shyness. After that she'd made it a point to spend some time with him whenever she went to the track. Within weeks Rick had laughingly told her that she had managed to wrap his blustery chief mechanic around her little finger. She and Steve had become close, intimate friends over the years, a fact that had made their bitter parting even more painful.

Within minutes they were careering down nearly

deserted streets on a top-speed race to the hospital. To Karla the trip seemed to have a touch of black humor. How ironic it would be if they were killed rushing to Rick's side, when he lay dying because of a race-car accident. She shook her head in despair when she realized her agony was developing a bitter edge.

They were dropped at the emergency entrance, and although she nearly broke into a run to avoid them, two enterprising reporters intercepted Karla before she could get inside.

"Mrs. Fleming...do you agree that race-car drivers have a death wish?" An eager-looking young man in a rumpled corduroy jacket shot out the question as he blocked her way.

"Is that why you left Rick Fleming three years ago?" his older-looking companion added.

Karla shielded her face from the incessant probe of a camera and its electronic flash. "Please let me pass," she begged, knowing full well her words would fall on deaf ears.

"Tell me, Mrs. Fleming, how does it feel, knowing your husband is inside this hospital dying?" The man in the corduroy jacket hunched closer.

Steve McDonald bulldozed his way between the photographer and the reporters, sweeping Karla with him. Within seconds they were walking down the hospital corridor on their way to intensive care. When they neared the unit the first thing that struck Karla was the smell. It was as piercingly familiar as if she had inhaled it just yesterday instead of nearly four years ago.

They were in the core of the massive building, a windowless, frighteningly sterile area where everyone moved, talked and even smiled with an intensity found nowhere else in the hospital. A nurses' station, filled with all the marvels of the electronic age, was the hub of the complex, and a series of glass-walled rooms radiated out from it like spokes. Karla noticed with dread that one room was different from the others. Its curtains had been closed so that only the nurse sitting behind the flashing machines could see in.

Karla's heart thudded heavily against her chest, and she drew her blue cashmere sweater tighter. With certainty she knew that that room was Rick's. She caught her breath. He must be terribly injured—or already dead.

Her footsteps quickened. Stifling a sob, she pulled away from Steve and rushed to the door, suddenly afraid that she was already too late. Rick must not, he could not, die thinking she didn't love him.

She pushed open the door, fear her only companion as she walked into the small room. A nurse in an incongruously bright yellow uniform, with a happy-face button pinned on her chest that said, I Gave—Did You? rose from a chair and stepped out of the way. Karla moved toward the bed in a trance. Everything in her focused on the still form lying beneath the green nubby-textured hospital spread.

Shiny chrome bars had been pulled up to form sides to the bed. The thought flashed through her mind that as an infant Rick had probably slept in a crib. Now it seemed he would also die in one.

Beyond the bars, lying amid a jungle of tubes and suspended jars was Rick...her Rick. She sobbed in relief. He was still alive, though frighteningly pale. His long thick lashes and finely arched eyebrows looked like bits of coal that had been stuck on a snowman's face.

Tentatively, with shaking hands, Karla reached out to run her finger along the jagged abrasion that covered the left side of his face. The years they had been apart disappeared with her touch. Undenied now, the love they had shared flowed through her unchecked, giving her the strength to smile as she leaned past the railing and softly pressed her lips to Rick's forehead. Slowly his eyes opened.

"Hi, angel," he whispered, his greeting as familiar as if they had but parted yesterday. "I knew you would come."

She had to strain to hear the labored words. She bent closer to be sure that he could see her as well as feel her presence, so that he would know as directly and as intimately as possible that she loved him.

"I love you, Rick," she said. "If you die, when you die, my soul and my heart will go with you."

"Stay with me, Karla...."

She ached when she saw the effort it took him to speak. A part of her wanted to press her fingers to his lips and tell him to save his strength. But another part of her selfishly longed to hear his voice for as long as she was allowed. To savor the sweetness of his words and to tuck them away in a corner of her being, where she could forever cherish this small part of him, a memory against the endless years she would live alone.

"Please stay with me, Karla...."

How could he think that she wouldn't? "I'll be here, my love," she said. She touched him as she spoke, her fingers caressing the remembered contours of his face as though she could absorb and share his pain.

He stared at her. His eyes demanded that she look at him. "I promise you...." He paused to catch his breath. Patiently he waited for the strength to continue.

"I promise you that I won't die. I won't leave you."

Karla smiled through her tears. How desperately she wanted to believe him. She let her finger trace the outline of his full lower lip, then she leaned over to kiss him. As she did so her heavy, honey-colored hair tumbled free from the pins she had hurriedly used to hold it away from her face.

She quickly reached up to tuck it behind her ear.

"Leave it," Rick said slowly. "You don't know how I've missed having it on the pillow beside me or—" His voice faded until Karla had to hold her breath, afraid the slightest sound would make her miss his next words "—or softly caressing me when we make love."

He had slipped away from her, but this time it was only sleep that claimed him. Karla gently covered his face with hesitant kisses, then sank down into the chair beside the bed. Her hand reached through the bars and lightly clasped his. She leaned her head against the cold tubular aluminum and prayed for a miracle.

Finally she fell into a light sleep and dreamed the dreams of a drowning person. Her life with Rick whirled before her like film on an editing machine—months passing in a blur, then moments becoming single frames and standing out in sharp focus. She relived the zaniness of their first meeting, then skipped on to the agony of her brother's death. Her mind recoiled at the additional pain and went back to the happy perfection of the earlier memory. . . .

Seven years ago, Karla had just graduated from Washington State University with a master's in business administration. She had been invited to spend two weeks at her aunt and uncle's home in Las Vegas before she had to report to her new job at IBM in Los Angeles. After the years she had spent in rainy Washington, she was looking forward to fourteen days in the dry Nevada sun.

Karla scanned the airport lobby for her silver-haired aunt, whose six-foot height should have made her stand out in any crowd. It was so unlike Aunt Maureen to be late for anything that Karla felt a nagging sense of unease when she was unable to find her in the throng. Then she shook her head in irritation and chastised herself. She was almost twenty-three and still hadn't abandoned her childhood habit of jumping to dire conclusions whenever someone wasn't on time. She forced herself mentally to go over a dozen logical reasons why her aunt could be late, then she calmly maneuvered her way to the baggage-claim area. She would wait until her luggage arrived. If by then her aunt still hadn't appeared, she would call.

As she made her way through the crowd, she blew a dangling wisp of hair back from her forehead, positive that if she didn't get out of some of her clothing soon she would suffocate. After the cool climate in Washington, even the air-conditioned terminal seemed infused with the undulating waves of heat she had glimpsed rising from the asphalt outside. Although her pantsuit was a lightweight linen, she had forgotten that *anything* with long sleeves was inappropriate for this desert climate.

Shouldering her way through the crowd, she began to juggle her purse, overnight case and camera bag in an awkward attempt to get out of her jacket.

"Can I help you?" a male voice offered.

Karla looked up to see a tall, dark-haired man blocking her path. He had deeply chiseled features that were further accentuated by a lopsided grin. Karla bristled when she noticed the almost arrogant self-confidence that surrounded him. She had had enough of overblown male egos in college to last her a lifetime. She knew by his assured bearing that he anticipated his magnanimous offer would readily and gratefully be accepted.

She groaned inwardly. The last thing she needed right now was an airport lothario. She stared at the mirrorlike sunglasses that covered his eyes, seeking a more positive clue to the motivation behind his altruistic offer. Instead she found her own weary, disheveled appearance—giving her yet another reason to feel annoyed.

Fleetingly, sarcastically, she wondered why he wore the glasses inside the building. What was he trying to hide? Or could it be that someone had told him how attractive and mysterious he looked in them, and so he wore them everywhere? Regardless of the reason, she wasn't in the mood to put up with a self-styled Romeo, handsome or not. Especially one who had nothing better to do than pick up stray women at an airport.

After another look at herself in the twin mirrored disks, where her rumpled appearance was unmercifully duplicated, she doubted that he could be interested in her as a pickup. Unless he liked his women on the disheveled side. More likely he was one of the airport thieves her aunt had warned her about, the ones who preyed on incoming tourists. Either way, she wanted nothing to do with him.

"Thanks, anyway," Karla said, her assessment of his personality, plus her worry and the heat, making her words even more abrupt than she had intended. "I can manage quite well by myself."

"Suit yourself." He shrugged and stepped out of her way, capitulating so easily Karla was a little surprised.

She readjusted her load, moved past him and found a low railing where she could lean back and take some of the pressure off her feet. While she waited for her suitcases she closed her eyes and thought about the last few weeks. They had been fantastic but hectic, with little sleep separating the days. She'd had to get ready for graduation, study for finals, find places for what seemed like dozens of relatives to stay and arrange to maintain contact with scores of friends she knew she would probably never see again. Through it all Karla felt she had grasped and caught the gold ring but had fallen off the merry-go-round in the attempt.

She opened her eyes and noticed that the tall, chiseled featured man had followed her. He now stood beside her, his hands comfortably tucked into the back pockets of his jeans. Surreptitiously Karla glanced at him. He was even better looking than she had first thought. His hair had a casual look, as if he had driven to the airport with the windows down and had used his fingers to comb the wavy black strands into place once he got there. The offensive glasses had been removed, and she could see his eyes were a deep, nearly black brown. They were framed by thick black lashes that curled softly and naturally the way she tried to get hers to do every morning. Now that she could see his eyes, she knew with a certainty that she had misjudged him. No one with eyes as guileless as his could possibly be guilty of the crimes she had been indicting him for. Sheepishly, grudgingly, she acknowledged that he had probably simply offered her some friendly assistance, for which she had responded by snapping at him like a bear with a toothache.

Well, she wondered, her curiosity suddenly aroused, if not a lothario or a pickpocket, then who? His skin had the tanned ruddiness of someone who worked outside. She looked down at his worn, toe-curled cowboy boots and guessed him to be either a local rancher or...judging from the lean, well-developed muscles of his arms and thighs, perhaps he was a construction worker.

Karla kept expecting him to say something, *hoped* he would, in fact, so that she could apologize for her earlier rudeness. But he remained

silent as he stood beside her and watched the infinite variety of luggage arrive on the belt. She tried
to think of an opening line of her own, but somehow everything she came up with sounded suggestive.

After a while she started to get the feeling she was
being stared at, and she looked out at the milling
crowd to see several people whispering and pointing in her direction. Self-consciously she glanced
behind her, wondering what could be drawing so
much attention. Behind the railing a steady stream
of passengers moved by—nothing at all out of the
ordinary.

Several more uncomfortable moments passed
before Karla realized that the man standing beside
her was the object of all the commotion. She
glanced at him again. Oh, come now, she thought.
Sure, he was a handsome guy—she'd give him that
much—but he wasn't *that* spectacular.

Finally, consumed with curiosity, she said, "You
seem to be attracting quite a bit of attention."

"What?" He blinked, as if forcefully coming
out of a daydream.

"Your presence seems to be hindering the
smooth flow of traffic," she carefully articulated.

"Oh?" he said, obviously uninterested. "I
hadn't noticed. I'm afraid my mind was wandering."

"Does this happen to you often? The attention, I
mean, not the wandering mind." Karla was fasci-

nated with the casual way he accepted people's staring and pointing at him. Perhaps she had misjudged his occupation yet again. Las Vegas was a show town as well as a gambling mecca. . . .

She felt completely out of the swing of things, having spent the years since high school either holding down several jobs at the same time to earn money for college or with her nose buried in a book, trying to earn her master's degree as quickly as possible. It would be fun, she thought, to tell her aunt that she had waited for her luggage with a celebrity. Now, if only she knew who he was.

"Aren't those your bags?" he asked, interrupting her reverie.

Karla's eyes opened wide as she recognized her new Hartman leather suitcases. "How did you know that?" she gasped.

"Your aunt told me you would probably be using them. If only because they had given you the set for graduation."

"My aunt?" she sputtered.

He gave her a conspiratorial wink. "It was pretty obvious you were, ah, a bit cranky after your flight and that you very definitely did not want to have anything to do with me." He shrugged helplessly. "I didn't want to force myself on you."

Karla stared at him. He was grinning at her with a smug satisfaction that ignited her already short fuse. She knew she was being baited, that he had control of the situation, but she plunged ahead anyway. Hot, tired and more than a little embarrassed by her rude dismissal of him earlier, she was in no mood to play games.

"So instead of telling me who you were, you just let me think you were a thief, or—" she tried to think of something appropriate "—or some garden-variety pickup artist?"

His eyebrows rose in mock horror. "Where I come from a simple offer of help doesn't automatically place you in such disreputable company."

With little effort, he was making her feel like an idiot. "Where *I* come from," she said, "manners come before amusement."

"Touché!" A slight bow of his head accompanied the word. He grinned at her as if he was thoroughly enjoying their confrontation. Finally, responding to the fury in her manner, he chuckled. "Come on now, don't be angry. It's such a monumental waste of energy." He lifted her bags, carrying the three heavy pieces as if they were empty.

Karla glared at his back as she struggled to keep up with his long stride. "It seems to me," she grumbled, fuming at his cavalier behavior, "that you could have told me who you were in the beginning."

He stopped so abruptly that she almost ran into him. "How about if I tell you now? Then can we call a truce?" Without waiting for a reply, he set her cases down, took her overnight bag from her, set it beside the luggage, then grasped her hand in his. "Richard Allen Fleming, at your service. Your wish is my command."

He shook her hand vigorously, then reached up to clasp her shoulders. Before she knew what was happening, he had leaned over and was giving her a lusty kiss. Almost as quickly, he broke the contact and smiled at her with that same boyish, lopsided grin she had witnessed earlier. He looked immensely pleased with his peace offering and as if he expected her to be just as delighted.

Karla twisted herself free from his grasp. "My aunt must have been out of her mind to send you to pick me up," she raged. She had to make a conscious effort to keep her voice below a shout; they were already drawing an embarrassing amount of attention.

Richard Fleming threw his head back and laughed. Incredulously Karla watched his strange reaction to her words and shook her head in amazement. She refused to admit that the deep throaty sound had an infectious ring that appealed to her despite her anger.

"I'm simply following your delightful aunt's orders, Miss Thompson. She said you had been dutifully struggling through school for umpteen years and that this was a well-earned vacation. And wouldn't I see to it that you had an especially good time since, although I'm an ancient five years older than you are, I'm closer to your age than anyone else around.''

''I've never met a man with such a gigantic ego. Is that kiss supposed to last me for two weeks or do you have other entertainment planned?'' She didn't give him a chance to answer before she shot out, ''And as for our being close in age, I'm afraid I passed you up years ago.''

''Ouch!'' He grimaced in mock pain and reached for her shoulders again.

''If you so much as touch me,'' Karla hissed through clinched teeth, ''I will give you an embarrassing ache to remember me by.''

Smiling and calling her bluff, he firmly grasped the firm flesh of her shoulders.

''I like you, Miss Karla Thompson,'' he beamed. ''I like you very much. But then, your aunt said I would, and she's rarely wrong about anything.''

''Oh, I wouldn't say that. She's made at least one mistake that I know of—and it was a dilly. She sent *you* to meet me.'' Karla made a grab for her luggage, but Rick easily beat her to it.

''No truce, huh?'' he grinned.

''I'll consider it,'' Karla spat, ''at the first sign of snow.'' She stomped out of the terminal and hailed the nearest cab.

CHAPTER TWO

KARLA COULD STILL FEEL THE WARMTH of Rick's touch on her shoulders. It was several moments before she realized it was Steve's hand that rested where Rick's had been, and that he was gently trying to wake her.

"Karla, it's morning. Why don't you come down to the cafeteria with me to get a bite to eat?" he asked.

Karla responded to the warmth in his voice like a sailor seeing his home shore after a long voyage. She looked into Steve's eyes and could see that the coolness and hostility she had felt earlier were gone. In their place was the love she remembered. She couldn't guess what had caused the transition, she only knew that a weight had lifted from her heart, and it felt wonderful.

Her hand still held Rick's, the fingers melded in a contact she was afraid to break. "I'm all right, Steve. I don't think I could eat anything, anyway Perhaps you could bring me back a cup of tea, though."

"I understand how it is, Karla, but you've got

to move around some to keep the muscles working. How about if I stay here while you take a short walk? If Rick wakes up, I can tell him you'll be right back.''

"I promised him I wouldn't leave." She spoke slowly, her heart breaking with the undeniable truth of what she would say next. "It really wasn't too much for him to ask—and it's all I have to give.''

Steve patted her arm and told her he would be right back with the tea.

Rick's lean body lay exactly as it had when he went to sleep. Only his skin had changed. It had grown impossibly white, as if drained of all blood. His high prominent cheekbones and strong jaw now created hills to the valleys of his sunken eyes and the hollows of his cheeks.

Karla refused to believe she was sitting beside Rick to watch him die. But she dared not let herself hope that he would live. She forced herself into a limbo of existing only for the present as she continued to watch the barely discernible rise and fall of his chest.

The day nurse came into the room and moved with quick, economical steps around the bed, checking the bottles and tubes and pointedly avoiding Karla's eyes. Karla swore to herself that she would not ask, that she didn't need to have confirmed with words what she could already see for herself. But a feeble ray of hope, encouraged by a desperate longing, forced the words out.

"How is he?" She spoke low enough that the nurse could pretend she hadn't heard. Perversely, knowing better, she spoke again, only louder. "How is he?" She was unable to keep the plea from her voice.

The nurse still wouldn't meet her gaze. It was the most devastating thing she could have done to Karla's tiny ray of hope. Her cryptic reply of "no change" passed almost unnoticed as Karla fought to swallow the bile she felt burning her throat.

She spent the rest of the day in a trance, her fingers locked with Rick's, her eyes riveted to his softly moving chest, his still face. Steve came and went, and she heard snatches of whispered conversation between the doctors and nurses who drifted in and out of the room like waves on a beach at low tide.

"...incredible that he's lasted this long...."

"...amazing...."

"...just a matter of time...."

And then, "We're going to have to go back in — he's bleeding internally."

Suddenly the room erupted in a flurry of motion. Karla was shoved aside as orderlies and nurses rushed to unhook bottles and carry them beside the moving bed. Frantically she tried to accompany them, but strong hands held her back, effectively blocking her attempt.

Karla pleaded with her captors to let her go, trying to make them understand how important it was that she be allowed to stay with her husband, but they held her with unrelenting arms.

"Rick," she screamed over and over. Her cries echoed off the walls like ricocheting bullets. Fear and pain built within her until it became suffocating, and for the second time in her life, her mind recoiled in self-defense. She felt herself spinning in a vortex of faces—doctors, nurses, Steve, Rick— until they spun so fast she could no longer recognize them. The voices around her faded until they sounded as if they were coming from a great distance. Finally she could hear them no more and, blessedly, she found herself back with Rick in Las Vegas.

DESPITE RICK'S LAUGHING PROMISE to behave himself, Karla insisted on taking a taxi to her aunt's house. He agreed begrudgingly and deposited her suitcases on the pavement. She thought she had seen the last of him when he drove by in a bright red Porsche, smiling and waving at her. Karla considered a number of appropriate return gestures, but discarded them all as demeaning. She also had a strong feeling that any disparaging response she made would only further delight his perverse sense of humor.

The cab pulled into traffic and was headed for the airport exit before the driver glanced in his mirror and said, "Where to, lady?"

Karla gave him the address, then settled back in

the hopelessly sprung seat. She leaned her elbow on the door's armrest and stared at suburban Las Vegas, trying to erase the image of a tall, obnoxious stranger. On first meeting Richard Fleming had managed to push every one of the buttons guaranteed to infuriate her. Instead of banishing his memory, her efforts only brought him more vividly to mind, so she stopped trying.

Instead she pointedly listened to the running monologue the driver was delivering about Las Vegas and the current shows in town. Before long Karla began to wonder if he had been hired by the casinos as well as the cab company. When there was a pause, she asked if it was true.

He glanced at her in the mirror, and Karla had the feeling she was being quickly, but carefully, inspected for any possible underlying motivations behind her question. Then, apparently satisfied that she was innocent, he confided that he was given free tickets to the late shows at several casinos in exchange for the promotion. He was allowed to do anything he wanted with the tickets, he said, and selling them provided a nice extra income.

Karla shook her head, amused at the cloak-and-dagger atmosphere that had entered the cab. She wondered if everyone in Las Vegas had something going on the side. To her, all of Nevada seemed like a giant adult-amusement park, a little bit of never-never land, Oz and Lilliput rolled into one giant state, where the majority of people made their living doing things that were illegal almost everywhere else. A place where day and night melded together to the tune of spinning wheels, ringing slot machines and the soft thud of dice rolling on a carpet of green felt.

As she watched the city pass by the square of her taxi window, the only thing familiar was that air of unreality. Karla slipped into her own thoughts, ignoring the driver's continuing chatter. Everything had changed so much since she'd last been here, four years ago. Everywhere she looked, new construction had altered the landscape. It wasn't until the cab left the freeway and started down a quiet stretch of desert road that anything stirred a memory. But as the countryside grew more and more familiar, she began to get excited. The unpleasant incident at the airport was nearly forgotten.

In the distance Karla spotted an Appaloosa mare with her foal. The two animals stood next to the road, confined by a split rail and barbed-wire fence. Karla was so enchanted by the nursing colt that she swung around to watch it as the cab sped by. It was then that out of the corner of her eye she spotted a bright red Porsche following about a quarter of a mile behind them. By the time her aunt and uncle's sprawling adobe home came into view a few miles later, her mood was as black as the asphalt.

The cab paused at the entrance and waited for the iron gate to swing open, then pulled onto the long circular drive. In the distance Karla could see the front door open and Aunt Maureen step out onto the porch. The elegant woman looked like an island of sanity, a refuge from the sea of lunacy Karla felt she had been unceremoniously dumped into.

As soon as the taxi stopped, Karla was out the door and into her aunt's arms. They held each other in a crushing embrace, unable to express with mere words how much they had missed being together.

"Oh, Karla, how beautiful you look! Every time I see you I'm amazed all over again. How did a stunning creature like you ever come out of such plain pioneer stock as our family?"

"Aunt Maureen, you tell the best lies of anyone I know. If I hadn't caught my reflection at the airport—" she winced at the memory her words evoked "—I might almost believe you."

Karla felt the weight of the world slip from her shoulders when she was around her aunt. Although the rest of the family considered this gray-haired lady something of a rogue, to Karla she was special. Maureen was the one member of their far-reaching family who had encouraged her to fly when others would have had her walk. From the time Karla had been toddling around in fluffy white pinafores—immensely impractical for a little girl who, later, loved to climb trees—her aunt had told her to set her goals high. Maureen had even insisted on helping her financially in college. Karla's own parents had refused to help her get a degree in something as "unfeminine" as business administration.

Their happy chattering was interrupted by the sound of Rick Fleming's footsteps on the driveway. He stopped to help the taxi driver unload the last of the luggage, then looked up at Karla and nonchalantly said, "You want to pay the gentleman so that he can get back to work?"

It was the final, infuriating straw. His pointing out the obvious, as if she were a child who needed to be told to mind her manners, made Karla nearly choke with anger. What right did he have to follow her? To embarrass her in front of her aunt? She glared at him as she fumbled through her purse.

The driver mumbled his surprised thanks at her generous tip and quickly left. It was as if he could feel the tension growing and wanted to be out of range before an explosion occurred.

Karla ignored her aunt's inquiry about why she'd taken a taxi and turned to face Rick. "Just what the hell do you think you're doing, following me out here?" she seethed, finally losing control of her temper.

Her aunt, who had turned and started into the house with a piece of luggage, gasped in surprise.

"Karla! Rick has every right to be here; this is where he lives. He's our houseguest."

Feeling like a complete idiot for the second time that day, Karla absorbed the totally unexpected news. With shock she realized that she was so angry she wanted to punch Rick Fleming's finely chiseled nose. And, vindictively, she knew she'd enjoy watching it bleed. In a few short hours he had purposely let her make a fool of herself over and over again. With astonishing ease he had managed to turn her normally pacifist nature militant.

Rick was standing with his hands tucked in his back pockets. He was grinning at her. In a voice loud enough only for her to hear, he said, "Once we get over the rough spots, this is going to be a terrific week. I have a feeling I'm going to enjoy it more than I've enjoyed anything in a long, long time."

To Maureen, who stood transfixed at the door, he said, "Don't be mad at Karla; I deserve whatever she cares to dish out. I'm afraid I let my baser side out of its cage today, and your niece was the victim." He bent down to get the remaining bags. "I plan on making it up to her, though—I've made reservations for tonight at Caesar's Palace." He looked at Karla and winked. "Scout's honor, I'll be on my best behavior."

Karla summoned a withering stare, normally guaranteed to stop all but the most tenacious pursuer "I don't think I'll go anywhere tonight, Mr.

Fleming; I'm really exhausted." She said this loud enough for her aunt to hear.

Rick chuckled, as if he knew what was coming next.

"Nonsense, Karla," Maureen interrupted. "You're here to kick up your heels before settling into that new job of yours. I can't think of anyone more appropriate to do it with than Rick. You can take a nap this afternoon. By tonight you'll be fit as a fiddle."

She was trapped. Her aunt had decided that Rick was the man to show her a good time, and Karla knew it probably would take a negative report from the FBI to get her to change her mind. She muttered a disgruntled, "All right," and headed into the house, vowing to get out of her "date" one way or another if it killed her.

Karla followed her aunt into a bedroom comfortably furnished in warm desert colors, with deep rust carpeting and eggshell-white walls. An original Remington sketch, one of Karla's favorites among the four her aunt and uncle owned, was centered on the wall above the sitting area. A sliding glass door looked out onto the patio and pool and provided her with a private entrance to her room, should she care to use it.

Maureen helped Karla unpack, each taking the opportunity to catch up on the news of their extensive network of aunts, uncles, cousins, nieces and nephews. Finally Karla brought the subject around to Rick again.

"Tell me, Aunt Maureen," she said casually, "how did you happen to meet someone like Rick Fleming?" She had to fight to keep the question from sounding like an accusation. "He seems a little strange even by your magnanimous standards."

On her way to the dresser, Maureen stopped in midstride. She turned to face Karla, a puzzled frown on her kindly face. "I can't imagine what happened between you. Rick is one of the nicest young men I know. I was so sure you two would hit it off splendidly."

"I don't think that's the exact word I would use to describe our relationship so far," Karla mumbled under her breath, then said louder, "How long have you known him?"

"Oh—" she gazed at the wall for a moment, her mouth pursed in thought "—I think it's been about four or five years since he began using your uncle's law firm. But you'd have to check with Roger about that to be sure. All I remember for certain was that Roger was greatly impressed with Rick. Whenever Rick stopped by or phoned he would talk about him for a week. Then one day he invited him home for dinner. Rick's been a friend of the family's, as well as a client, ever since. He has a boat at Lake Mead that he lives on sometimes, but most often when he's in the area he stays with us." She turned back to the dresser. "I only hope Michael and Paul turn out as well."

"How are my wild cousins?" Karla's voice lightened.

"Due to arrive home from their respective colleges at the end of the week." She sighed as she placed the last of Karla's undergarments in the drawer. "I had no idea when they were obnoxious teenagers that I would miss them so much when they went away to school. Sometimes the silence almost kills me. It's going to be such fun to have you all here at the same time again. Rick, too. The boys adore him, and he treats them like favorite younger brothers." She spoke with a smile in her voice.

Karla could see that any complaints she harbored about the arrogant, overbearing Rick Fleming were going to fall on deaf ears in this household. From the sounds of it, not even her rowdy cousins could be counted on for support.

Maureen pulled Karla's skimpy new bikini from one of the side pockets of her suitcase. "Wow!" she said appreciatively. "With your figure and this little number, I'll bet you have to use a club to keep the men at bay."

Karla smiled. "I don't know; I haven't worn it yet."

"Why don't you put it on now?" Maureen's innocent smile belied the mischievous gleam in her eyes. "A swim will do you a world of good. Then after lunch you can take a nap, and you'll be refreshed for your night out with Rick."

The scenario sounded delightful, Karla thought, right up to the last part. . . .

Finished with the unpacking, Maureen went to prepare lunch. When she had gone, Karla walked over and picked up the brief swatches of white material that were her new swimsuit. She couldn't quite summon the same feeling of adventure she'd had when she had impulsively purchased it. Now, looking at the tiny bundle resting comfortably in the palm of her hand, she realized she would probably never wear it where anyone could see her. She put the suit into the drawer and pulled out her old standby, a one-piece suit she had worn when she was on the diving team at school.

The water was deliciously cool in contrast to the nearly one-hundred-degree heat of the surrounding air. The pool was large enough that Karla managed a few good laps before she decided she would rather loaf than exercise and pulled herself up onto a floating air mattress. She snuggled her rear end into the cushion, leaned back with a contented sigh and lazily closed her eyes.

"You'd better be careful your first day out. This desert sun can be treacherous." Rick's voice shattered her peaceful daydream.

Karla partially opened one eye and scowled in the direction of his voice. *My gosh,* she mentally gasped. It was a good thing he had been fully clothed at the airport. Dressed in the brief suit he had on now, he might have caused a riot. She had to give him that much, she grudgingly admitted: he was an incredible example of the male of the species. Even relaxed, his lean arm, chest and leg muscles were well defined. He had the powerful thighs of a sprinter and the all-over tan of a swimmer—or, she thought disparagingly, someone who spent a lot of time lounging around a pool.

"I've never burned in my life." She wiggled around on the mattress until she managed to turn over onto her stomach, hoping her obvious disinterest would preclude further conversation. Hearing a small splash, she opened her eyes to see Rick floating beside her. He reached up to grab the side of the mattress and began to propel her slowly around the pool.

"Maureen tells me that it was quite an achievement for you to get the job you did at IBM."

Karla propped her chin on her hands and looked at him. She sought some sign of mockery, but his face showed only sincere interest. At his urging she started telling him about her new job and was surprised at the astute questions he asked.

"Then when you've worked your way up to the head of your division, will they let you transfer, along with your title, to another division where there's still room for advancement, or are you going to have to switch companies?" he asked, his feet lightly splashing behind him as he pushed her air mattress around the deep end of the pool.

She told him what the recruiter had said and what she had managed to discover on her own. The conversation moved to the particular problems women were facing in the higher echelons of industry. Karla was flabbergasted at his knowledge.

"Are you a personnel manager for IBM running around in disguise?" she asked, only half teasing.

He laughed the same infectious way he had at the airport, but this time Karla joined in. "No, nothing so reasonable, I'm afraid," he said. "I drive race cars."

Karla blinked. She'd never met a race-car driver before. "What kind of car do you drive?" she asked, wondering how she could sound as bright about his field as he had about hers.

"This year I'm sticking to Formula and Champ cars. I tried to plug into some stock-car races last year, but it was just too much, and I didn't do as well as I wanted in any field." Rick noticed her confused expression. "You don't know much about racing, do you?"

"Not a great deal," she admitted. "If Yves Montand or James Garner didn't do it or race it in *Grand Prix*, I don't know about it."

Rick smiled. It was the same lopsided, appealing grin she had seen earlier, and she found she was being drawn to him despite her resolve to remain aloof.

"That puts me in pretty exclusive company," he said. "I'm not sure I can compete."

"What's this? Do I hear modest words coming

from Richard Allen Fleming, the man who fells women with a single kiss?''

Rick cupped his hand and sent a spray of water in her direction. "I can't understand what went wrong," he said. "I've used that approach a hundred times. You're the first one who's managed to resist."

"It's all that Washington rain. I'm impervious to a sun-belt Don Juan." She reached up to wipe away a drop of water dangling from the end of her nose. "So tell me about these cars that you race."

"What would you like to know?"

"Oh, what they look like, where you race them—things like that."

"Do you know what the Indy 500 race is and what kind of cars are there?" He waited for her to nod before going on. "Well, that's one kind of racing I do. The other is like the movie you mentioned. Only I hate to disillusion you by telling you that my life is not nearly so glamorous."

"That's too bad." She smiled without any sympathy and propped her head on her hand. "That must be an incredibly expensive hobby, what with the traveling and all. Isn't the Grand Prix thing all over the world?"

Rick stared at her, as if it was his turn to figure out if she was serious. "It's a little more than a hobby," he said dryly. "I do get paid for what I do."

"Sorry...but I did admit that I don't know much about race cars. Or, it seems, their drivers."

"You're a delight, Karla," he said, reaching over to tweak her nose. "I knew you didn't give a damn about who I was, but I had no idea just how unimpressed you really were." He sent another spray of water in her direction as he swam away.

"Tell me now—I promise I'll be impressed." Karla gave him her most serious look but was unable to keep the laughter from her eyes. She earnestly crossed her heart to emphasize her words.

"Not on your life." He pulled himself out of the pool with a seemingly effortless and totally graceful movement, then reached for a towel. "You would just fawn all over me. I've had enough of driver groupies to last me a lifetime. Believe me, it's better this way. You just keep on acting like I'm a big fat zero, and we should get along famously."

"No problem," Karla laughed and eased into the water. "No problem at all."

Maureen stepped through the French doors leading to the kitchen. "I hate to interrupt, kids, but lunch is ready."

After ravenously consuming a huge shrimp and crab salad, Karla excused herself, saying she was going to take a short nap. She slept the afternoon away, however, not stirring until Maureen tapped lightly on the door and reminded her she had to get ready.

As she prepared for her date with Rick, she dis-

covered she was actually looking forward to it.
The biggest clue was that she tried on three of her
new dresses and was unhappy with all of them.
She finally settled on the one she had started with.
It was floor length, made from a soft, forest-green
silk, and was so simply cut that it used the unfet-
tered body beneath for its design. The only jewelry
she wore was a fine gold chain and small hooped
gold earrings.

She was stepping into her heels when she heard
a light tap on the door. "Come in," she called, expecting her aunt to enter. When no one came in or
answered her invitation, she went to the door and
opened it. It was Rick.

His eyes lighted up when he saw her, to Karla's
delight. She backed up and twirled around for his
inspection. The slight flare of the skirt made a soft
circling embrace around her ankles and clung
seductively to her thighs.

"Stunning," he said in open admiration. "Simply stunning."

"Why, thank you, sir," she said flirtatiously,
batting her eyelashes. "I take it that means you
approve?"

A slow, sensuous smile lifted the corners of his
mouth. His eyes stared directly into hers. There
was no mistaking the message. Karla felt a lump
form in her throat. A shudder of reciprocal desire
washed over her, making her legs feel weak. She
knew that Rick was aware of what had just hap-

pened to her—of how she had reacted to the mere implication of his look—and, surprisingly, she didn't care. Something inside her cried out to play Eve to his Adam. Without even being aware of it, she had discarded the normal, almost frigid reaction to men she had painstakingly developed in school to avoid complications. Probably at the same time she'd received her diploma.

Well, if she was ever going to "kick up her heels," she thought, looking openly into Rick's beckoning eyes, she could do worse than the man standing in front of her.

THE SHOW AT CAESAR'S PALACE was a Hollywood revue. Karla thoroughly enjoyed it. Afterward, when she told Rick that this was the first time she had been to Las Vegas since she'd gotten old enough to enter the gambling houses legally, he took her on a grand tour of the clubs.

Everywhere they went they drew attention. At first Karla thought it was fun, but by the time they'd left the strip, the excitement had worn thin, and she found herself desiring anonymity again.

"How terrible it must be to put up with that constant attention on a day-to-day basis," she said as they drove through the black tunnel of a desert night on their way home.

"Some of it you get used to, some of it's actually fun, but mostly it's an annoying sacrifice of your privacy." He glanced in her direction, a teasing gleam in his eyes. "Can you imagine what would have happened if I'd reached over and kissed you and run my hands over those magnificent breasts of yours the way I've been wanting to do all night?"

Karla could feel the heat of a blush on her neck and face, and she turned to look out the window, trying to hide her reaction from Rick. She didn't want him to know how unsophisticated she was or how easily his words had affected her. As lightheartedly as she could, she said, "Yes, I can imagine what would have happened quite easily. I would have hit you."

Rick's voice dropped to a low caressing tone. "Because you didn't want me to, or because we were in public?" He reached down, found Karla's hand and raised it to his lips. His tongue made a slow sensuous circle on her palm.

Karla caught her breath. "I think I'll pass on that one." She could hear his soft chuckle, then felt a light kiss on her hand before Rick returned it to her lap.

He knew! She hadn't fooled him at all. Her naiveté was as obvious as the freckles on her nose.

They traveled the remainder of the way home in an easy silence. When they arrived, the house was dark except for the standard night lights. "Do you have a key?" Karla asked.

Rick shook his head. "I take it that means you don't have one, either?"

"No." Karla thought for a moment. "I hate to wake them," she mumbled and tried the door again.

"Are you sure you locked the sliding glass door in your room?"

Karla tapped her forehead with the palm of her hand. "I didn't even think about it. It's open unless Aunt Maureen locked it."

Hand in hand they groped their way along the unlighted path and around the house until they reached the door to Karla's room. Then she stood on the step and lightly kissed Rick's cheek. "I had a marvelous time...thank you."

A slow smile spread across his face. "You're welcome. I enjoyed myself, too."

When he made no motion to leave, Karla nervously shifted her weight from one foot to the other and said, "Well, good night. I guess I'll see you in the morning."

The amused smile still lighted Rick's eyes. He let go of her hand and reached up to run his fingers through her hair, pulling the long golden brown strands away from her ears. Then, holding her head firmly locked between his powerful hands, he slowly leaned over and kissed the hollow under her left ear. With maddening skill his lips moved the short distance to her ear, where he stopped kissing her and said, "Karla—my room doesn't have an outside door. If we're not going to wake up the household, either I'm going to have to sleep out here on the patio, or you're going to have to let me come in through your room."

Karla was still reeling from the effects of his kiss. At the moment she didn't want him to move anywhere, let alone leave her. She reached up and placed her trembling hands on his chest as if she were about to push him away, but her hands continued their journey until her arms were encircling his neck. She moved closer so that their bodies melded together, her softer flesh yielding and molding to his harder surfaces.

At once his hands left her hair and moved down her body, stopping at her waist and pulling her closer still. Their lips met. The tension that had existed between them all day exploded like a tidal wave that had at last found a shore. Blood coursed through Karla in a flush of passion that blocked out everything except Rick and the feel of his body against hers.

Her mouth opened, inviting his exploring tongue to seek its deepest recesses. Then, tentatively, her tongue touched his lips. He coaxed and led and encouraged her, and when finally she delved into the sweet taste of his mouth she heard as well as felt a rumbling moan of desire rise powerfully within him. Rick's hands moved up her sides and pressed into the fullness of her unbound breasts. This time it was Karla's turn to moan aloud. Her building need frightened her. It was a force she had never experienced. Always before she had had supreme control over her emotions. Now she could feel that control slipping from her grasp as easily as a cold wind finds a crack in a door.

It was as if the sound of her longing was a warning signal to Rick, and he slowly, reluctantly, broke the contact their lips made. He looked deeply into Karla's eyes, and she could see the confusion he was experiencing as plainly as if he spoke it aloud. The message she sent back was clear. She wanted him as much as he wanted her. He closed his eyes. A deep sigh escaped his lips. With gentle insistent pressure, he pulled her head toward him until it rested on his shoulder.

"It's too soon," he whispered into her hair. "Dammit, it's just too soon. This shouldn't be happening."

SLOWLY KARLA BECAME AWARE of the soft ding of a bell somewhere in the distance. Muffled words followed the sound before there was quiet again. She opened her eyes and looked at her surroundings. It took a minute for her to realize that she was in a lounge area, probably somewhere deep in the bowels of the hospital.

She rolled over and buried her face in her hands—she was back in the real world again. She started to get up, but quickly sat down on the edge of the couch again as a wave of dizziness struck her. A compelling need fought through the dizziness, a need to find Rick and explain why she had not stayed beside him. Irrationally, she had felt that she need only keep her promise to stay by his side, and he would live.

But she had already broken her promise. It didn't matter why, it had been broken. She must get to Rick and explain. She staggered across the room. The door opened onto an empty corridor, which ran in both directions before veering off to form another jog in its maze. The bottom three feet of the walls were a dark brown, the top and ceiling a noxious tan. Crazily, Karla wondered how they had managed to paint the division so perfectly without the slightest waver. She looked down the hall in both directions. Each was identical, giving no clue as to which way she should go. While she stood there, frozen with indecision, Steve McDonald came around the corner. She caught her breath with the pure joy of seeing him and ran into his arms.

He held her tightly, crooning soft sounds into her hair and awkwardly patting her back with his big hands.

"Where is he, Steve? I want you to take me to him." When Steve only continued to hold her, she added softly, "Please!"

"Rick's still in surgery, Karla."

"How long—"

"It's been a couple of hours now. I just went down to check. I was on my way back to waken you and make you eat something."

"I'm really not hungry, Steve."

"Dammit, girl, you're going to eat if I have to sit on you and force-feed you myself."

Steve's uncharacteristic anger and the picture he had painted brought a feeble smile to her lips. "All right, I'll eat," Karla relented, "but not in the cafeteria. Help me find the operating room, and let me wait there," she bargained. "Then I'll eat whatever you bring."

He held her away from him and looked down at her. Slowly, sadly, he shook his head. "I'm sorry, Karla," he said softly. "I should have left you up there in Washington; I shouldn't have asked you to come down here. But with Rick calling out for you as he did, I just had to do what I could for him. I hope you understand."

In answer Karla stood on her toes and kissed his stubbly cheek. "I love you, Steve McDonald. I know that you love Rick as much as I do and that you really didn't have any choice." She saw tears fill his eyes.

"Yeah," his voice cracked, "I guess you could say that. Rick's always been special to me."

Steve slipped his arm around Karla's waist and took her down to the second floor, where they followed a black line painted on the tile until they came to a pair of wide swinging doors, each bearing a sign that said No Admittance—Authorized Personnel Only. He left her there and went to find something for her to eat, telling her he would return shortly.

Karla collapsed onto a turquoise molded plastic chair and watched the men and women in their green unisex uniforms and paper booties come and go, exchanging the latest hospital gossip, oblivious to her presence. She leaned her head against the wall, closed her eyes and let her mind drift back to a happier time.

ON THE ALMOST IMPOSSIBLY BRIGHT MORNING of her second day in Las Vegas, Karla had stretched her long, lanky body between cool cotton sheets, luxuriating in the pleasure of waking naturally instead of to the blare of her clock radio. Her hand touched the extra pillow, and she drew it to her in a teddy-bear embrace, resting her cheek against the cushiony down. A Mona Lisa smile gently curved her mouth as she thought about yesterday and what a kaleidoscopic day it had been. Marveling at her delight and happiness, she snuggled closer to the pillow. Once again her aunt had been right; Rick Fleming was one terrific guy. Unpretentious, intelligent, exuberant, debonair, eclectic, he embraced life more fully than anyone she had ever known. He was a glaring contrast to the intense, single-minded men she had met in college.

Karla's tongue touched her lips, unconsciously seeking any lingering taste of Rick's mouth that might still be present. She smiled, then sighed at the memory her action provoked. A blush warmed her cheeks when she remembered the intense yearning she had felt in Rick's arms. She wasn't embarrassed by the feeling; she'd been experiencing similar longings since her teens. No, it wasn't the rumblings of passion that bothered her, it was their magnitude and her inability to control them. If Rick hadn't stopped their ardent encounter last night, would she have stopped him? Would she have wanted to?

The thought perplexed her. She had always been far more circumspect than she had behaved in his arms—had prided herself on it. Rick probably thought—oh, God. She moaned and buried her face in the pillow. She could just imagine what Rick thought.

A knock on the door roused her from her mortifying reflections. "Come in," she called, her voice muffled by the pillow.

There was a slight pause before the door opened, and Rick's head appeared. "Are you decent?"

"Not always." She could feel a private, unbidden smile curving her mouth. "But I'm okay now." In a muted grumble meant only for herself, she added, "As long as a thought really isn't a deed, I'm okay."

Rick's eyebrow quirked. "Want to explain that?"

He must have the hearing of a stalked stag, Karla thought. "Not on your life!"

"Are you sure?" Rick grinned enticingly. "Sounds like a promising topic."

Karla could feel her cheeks turning crimson again. Incredible behavior for someone who had gone through two semesters of human sexuality without so much as one blush. As if sensing her unease, Rick changed the subject.

"I have to go into town this morning. Do you want to come along? I'll be tied up with an interview for about an hour, but afterward we can do whatever you'd like."

"I'd love to. What time?"

Rick glanced at his watch. "Can you be ready in forty-five minutes?"

Karla tossed back the covers and hopped out of bed, making sure her threadbare but prim nightgown adjusted itself to cover everything it should. She went to the door and carefully stood at an angle behind it so that as much of her disreputable gown as possible was hidden. "I'll be ready in thirty."

"Mmm, I'm impressed. Mind if I watch?" He looked suggestively at her hand, which held the front of her gown closed.

Karla caught her breath. His teasing suggestion conjured up a flood of unspeakable images. "If you watch, that voids the guarantee." She tried to keep her voice light, but failed.

Rick smiled and leaned forward to kiss her on the nose. "See you in half an hour."

Karla showered and dressed in her new pale yellow batiste suit, one of the items of clothing she had purchased with the graduation money her parents had given her. Half jokingly they had called the gift, "funds to purchase a work trousseau," subtly hinting that they despaired of her ever needing any other kind.

She stood back and examined herself in the full-length mirror. "Not bad," she murmured. "Not bad at all."

Tucking her tan clutch purse under her arm, she stepped into her heels, then went looking for Rick. She found him in the kitchen with her aunt, reading the morning paper and drinking coffee.

Rick looked up as Karla entered. Slowly he lowered the paper. His gaze traveled the length of her, as if memorizing every curve, every line. His mouth formed a silent O. She could see a glint of admiration in his eyes, but there was more stunned surprise than anything else. Clearing his throat, he pushed back the chair and stood up. Now it was Karla's turn to stare. He was dressed as casually as she was formally, wearing walking shorts, a T-shirt and sandals.

"Ah...I guess I'd better go and get dressed," he said, his struggle for appropriate words obvious in his hesitation. "I didn't expect you to get ready quite so fast."

Karla stilled. Last night, like a sunflower to morning, she had been drawn to Rick's incredible sensuality. Today, she was delighted to discover, she could bask in the warmth of his personality by

choice, because she also liked him. She understood completely what he was trying to do. He was
willing to spend the day in a stifling coat and tie
just to save her embarrassment.

She leaned against the doorframe. "It seems as
if one of us is overdressed, Mr. Fleming," she
said, letting her gaze wander once more over his
lean, muscular frame. She almost lost her control
of the situation when a sudden, unbidden shiver of
attraction brought a flush to her cheeks and a
radiating warmth to the pit of her stomach. "It's
thoughtful of you to offer to change, Rick," she
stammered, "but it will only take me a minute to
get out of this and into something more appropriate."

"No, don't. You look lovely just as you are."

"And you look sensible. I'll be right back."

Karla glanced at her aunt before turning to
leave. Maureen's elbows were propped on the
table, and she held a coffee mug suspended between her hands. The mug hid her mouth, but
Karla could see that her eyes were lighted with an
amused smile that could only be described as self-
satisfied. Karla wondered if she was thinking of
giving her a well-deserved, "I told you so."

She changed into a pair of white shorts, a red
tube top, and a navy blue short-sleeved blouse that
she tied at the waist. Rick rewarded her efforts
with a soft low whistle, a quiet, intimately seductive sound that sent a chill down her spine.

"Ready?" he asked as he reached out to take her arm.

Karla nodded.

When they passed the Appaloosa and her foal on their way to town, a secret smile played at the corners of Karla's mouth.

"Are your thoughts for sale?" Rick asked.

"I don't know...." Her smile became a grin. "What am I bid?"

Rick glanced at her, a wicked gleam in his eyes. "I'm not sure you would appreciate the first offer that comes to mind, so how does lunch at the Derby Room sound?"

Karla wanted to tell him she'd like to consider the alternative but decided to play it safe instead. She had already learned she couldn't match his easy repartee. Their suggestive verbal sparring left her far too vulnerable. "Lunch it is."

She reached over to adjust the air-conditioner control before settling back again in the nut brown leather seats. *This kind of luxury could easily become addicting,* she thought as she glanced at the molded interior. The car fitted around both of them with the detailed richness of a forty-thousand-dollar glove. A far cry from the Volkswagen Bug she had nursed through college.

"Well?" Rick prodded.

Karla jumped. "Well, what?"

"Are you going to tell me about the thoughts that prompted that mysterious smile?"

She laughed. "Sometimes I have the attention span of a three-year-old." She hesitated. "I'm not sure if I should tell you now or wait until you've fed me. You may be disappointed in your purchase."

"Try me."

"I was just remembering how angry I was yesterday when I turned around and saw you following my cab. And now here I am, less than twenty-four hours later, blithely, eagerly, accompanying you into town."

Rick winked. "Makes life interesting, doesn't it?"

"If not interesting, at least far from dull." They had reached the freeway, and in the distance Karla could see the world-famous row of Las Vegas's most prestigious casinos. Their lights still blinked and flashed in a futile attempt to compete with the brightness of the desert sun, making what was sparkling and magical in the darkness of night seem garish and tacky in the glare of day.

Karla turned away from the depressing sight. "So tell me about your interview," she said, a mischievous glint in her eyes. "Does this mean you've given up racing and are looking for a steadier job?"

Rick swung his head around to look at her. A slow smile spread across his face, exposing perfect teeth that were nearly bridal white against his deeply tanned face. "So the little lady likes to dish it out, too," he drawled, then laughed. "You're a rare woman, Karla Thompson. I have this peculiar feeling that if I'm not very careful, you're going to have me wrapped around your little finger.''

"Fat chance. I'd wager a lunch at the Derby Room that no one has ever had any more control over you than you gave them." The truth behind her words caused a sudden sharp pain in her chest.

"I've been accused of being cold-hearted and single-minded before, but never with such finesse." Rick grimaced in mock pain. "How did I manage to climb so high in your esteem?"

"It must be your wild but winning ways," Karla bantered.

"You've been reading my press releases. Actually, I'm a sloppy sentimentalist who wears his heart on his sleeve."

"Hmm, is that anything like having a chip on your shoulder?"

"Stop! You win." Rick laughed and reached over to cover her hand with his. His fingers curled into her palm, brushing her bare leg in an unconscious familiarity that made her heart swell with pleasure.

KARLA REMEMBERED THE INCIDENT several days later as she waved goodbye to her uncle, who was leaving for work. That was the last time Rick had touched her in such a spontaneous way, she realized grimly. The rest of that day, and every day following, he had carefully avoided not only any intimate contact between them, but also any extended time alone together.

Karla had lain awake nights reliving that ride into Las Vegas, trying to understand Rick's sudden, subtle change toward her. She had finally broken down and asked Maureen if she had noticed any difference in Rick's behavior. But her aunt had merely listened politely, shrugged and said that she hadn't noticed a thing. Her tone had implied that she thought Karla was imagining things.

Karla watched her uncle's Mercedes disappear down the road to town before she sighed in frustration and punched the button to close the driveway gate. She was alone at the house for the first time since she had arrived. Suddenly, surprisingly, since it had been her own choice, she discovered she felt disconcerted by the absolute quiet.

It was the servants' day off. Rick had informed her that after an early-morning meeting with some "tire people," he was going to be tied up with her uncle in legal matters the entire afternoon. And Maureen had a luncheon at the Mesquite Club, which, despite her aunt's urgings, Karla had decided not to attend.

In a moment of reckless abandon, she decided to spend her solitary time beside the pool outfitted in her Band-Aid bikini. As she slipped into it she found she was again looking forward to some time alone—felt, in fact, that she needed it to sort out her feelings.

Karla walked around the room gathering the paraphernalia she would use for her day beside the pool. As she stepped through the sliding glass door and ambled toward the padded chaise longue, only the soft slapping of her sandals disturbed the hushed desert air. She was alone with her thoughts—thoughts that contrasted violently with the serenity of her surroundings. Like a hurricane around its eye, all of those thoughts centered on Rick Fleming.

Every waking moment seemed to center on him, she thought grimly. Most of her sleeping ones, too. She could no more dismiss him from her mind than she could deny to herself that she was falling in love with him. But, she lamented, the timing was so wrong! Even more important, the *man* was wrong.

Karla had spent her high-school and college years carefully planning her life. If love was to enter, it was supposed to do so with someone in the business world. Someone who shared her goals; someone who'd be a part of the demands her career would put on her and therefore would understand them. Rick was none of these. He was a free spirit with a Gypsy's soul. His roots were like those of the phalaenopsis orchid, capable of clinging to almost any surface, then easily rerooting in another. Karla's own roots were deep and definitely earthbound. Rick's and her differences were so profound that neither of them would be able to change without severe, possibly catastrophic, damage to the magical essence that made them each what they were.

Why, then, was she letting herself fall in love with Richard Allen Fleming?

Letting herself, she thought in disgust. As if she had any choice! It had been so easy avoiding entanglements with other men. Why was it different with Rick? Especially since he hadn't given her the least encouragement in the past week.... Anything that *did* happen between them would be temporary, and therefore, in the end, bound to be painful.

Did she really care, Karla wondered. Surely knowing Rick's love, for no matter how long, was worth any short-lived pain that might come from their parting. He was the only man she had ever felt this way about. What if there were never another? She might live her entire life not knowing....

Karla turned over onto her stomach, tucked her hands under her head and rested her cheek on them. From that position she could see the gate, and she stared at it blankly, wishing Rick would walk through it. A second later he actually did so, making her gape in surprise.

Dressed in light brown slacks that clung to his thighs as he walked, he moved across the distance between them with an easy stride. Karla watched in silent admiration. He was supremely in tune with his body, exuding a glow of health that was incredibly seductive. His saffron yellow shirt was open at the neck, revealing a triangle of softly curling black hair. His jacket and tie he carried slung over his back, hooked on two fingers.

"Sorry," he apologized, noting her stunned expression, "I didn't mean to frighten you. The meeting broke up early, and I thought I'd see if you wanted to ride over to Lake Mead with me while I check on my boat." He pulled a webbed lawn chair across the cement patio and sat down beside her.

Karla felt trapped. Thinking about her minuscule bathing suit, she groaned inwardly. He might as well have caught her in the nude, she thought, blushing furiously. Other than a few strings, the only thing covering her backside was a small, strategically placed swatch of cloth.

When she didn't answer immediately, Rick's eyebrows drew together in puzzlement. "Is something wrong?"

Karla jumped. "Why?" she asked defensively.

"You haven't answered me, and it really isn't that tough a question. A simple yes or no will suffice." Casually he reached over, picked up her suntan lotion and snapped open the lid.

"I'd love to go to Lake Mead with you," she said in a rush, "but you'll have to give me a little time to get ready."

Rick leaned over and began to spread the lotion across her back. His strong fingers massaged the creamy fluid along her spine. "I'm in no hurry. There's plenty of time."

"Still, I think I should start getting ready now," she said, unable to keep the tension she felt out of her voice.

"What's wrong with you, Karla?" he asked in an exaggerated Texas drawl. "Why, you're acting as nervous as a rookie driver at Indy."

Karla ignored his homespun metaphor. She was having enough trouble just thinking straight with Rick's hands traveling across her back...down to her waist...then gently, slowly along the edge of her suit bottom.... Witty conversation was miles beyond her. At each touch, her nerve endings exploded, making her yearn for more. The feeling was glorious, yet at the same time torturous. Did he know what he was doing to her? Did he have any idea how torn apart she felt? Had he been able to detect how hard and fast her heart was beating?

Finished with her back, Rick's hands moved down to her legs. The lotion provided a lubricant so that his hands could press her flesh intimately, yet move smoothly, effortlessly down the length of her long thighs, past her knees and to her feet.

"Nothing is wrong," she finally stammered, abruptly pulling away from him. She sat up, forgetting her earlier shyness and how little of her anatomy her suit covered. "Yes, dammit, something is wrong. I don't understand what's happening between us. Why have you been so cool toward me this past week? You've been treating me like an uncouth cousin you've been sentenced to show around town."

Rick sat back in the chair, stretching his legs out in front of him. He came directly to the point. "I assume you're asking why there hasn't been a repeat of that first night when we damn near made love at your door?"

She hadn't anticipated such bluntness and was at a loss for words. She nodded in answer.

"I think you already know why." He paused and rubbed his hand over his eyes. "But then, maybe it would be better if it was out in the open."

Rick leaned forward, rested his elbows on his knees and reached for her hand, which he held loosely between his own. "You're woman enough to know what effect you've had on me, Karla I'm a wreck every time we're together." He chuckled mirthlessly. "Even though I haven't acknowledged it until now, I want you to know how grateful I am that you've been strong enough to ignore every damn signal I've been sending. Believe me, it's put me off in no uncertain terms." He looked down at her hand. "What a wonderful way for me to pay back your aunt and uncle for their incredible hospitality, whisking their favorite niece off to bed for a romp."

What was he talking about? What signals? Karla quickly skipped over their days together. She'd never spent a more circumspect time with anyone.

"Rick, if you were sending signals, I never received them." Impulsively she reached up to brush a lock of hair from his forehead.

"Dammit," he barked, "don't touch me, Karla."

She jerked her hand away, stunned by the harshness of his voice. Then anger replaced her surprise. "Oh, it's all right for you to rub lotion all over my body, but I had better keep my hands to myself, is that it?"

Her rage made her reckless. Without considering the consequences, she crossed the short distance that separated them and eased herself onto Rick's lap. The fluid movement brought her mouth within inches of his and her breasts enticingly close. Rick stiffened. Karla felt as well as heard his sharp intake of breath. Purposely she ignored his less-than-enthusiastic response to her presence and began to unbutton his shirt. When she could slip her hand inside, her fingers explored the mat of hair covering his chest, and her mouth reached up to capture his.

She lost the role of aggressor immediately. Rick's tongue moved possessively against her lips, demanding entry. When she responded, he ravished her mouth with a hunger that left her stunned. The force, the raw desire, the unbridled anger of his kiss frightened her, and she began to pull away, only to find that his hand was entangled in her hair, that he held her captive in a firm embrace.

As though sensing her fear, he became gentle, methodically coaxing her, with practiced ease, to react to him. Finally he released her.

"Don't start something you're not prepared to finish, Karla," he said, glaring at her. "As far as I'm concerned, tease is a four-letter word."

What had gone wrong? Why had he reacted to her advances with anger and labeled her a tease? Karla dropped her gaze to the top buttonhole of his shirt. She was afraid he would see the tears that had sprung to her eyes. The last thing she wanted was for him to feel sorry for her.

Rick let out a deep, pent-up sigh. "God help me, Karla," he groaned. "I'm so tired of fighting it. I'm tired of denying...." His fingers touched her chin, raising it gently. Slowly he bent forward until their lips met, this time in an almost chaste kiss.

Karla reached up and wrapped her arms around his neck. He felt the same way she did; he'd as much as told her so! She wanted to cry with joy. Her body, her mind, her soul sang with harmony, with the rightness of being with him. This was a celebration of life that she had denied herself for almost too long, and like a starving person at a banquet table, she hungered for everything all at once.

She pressed herself against him, suddenly anxious to know at last the ecstasy she had lain awake these last nights dreaming about. But he refused to be hurried. He broke their kiss and let his mouth slowly wander over her face, absorbing the feel and taste of her—lingering at the corners of her eyes, the tip of her nose, then nibbling tenderly at her earlobes until she felt she would go mad with wanting him. Down her chin and onto her neck his lips moved, finding and touching secret, sensitive spots she had never known she had.

When he sat back to undo the tie that lay between her breasts, the backs of his fingers brushed her highly sensitized skin as he worked, sending shuddering waves of desire through her. Once the tie was undone he pulled aside the material that covered her now erect, throbbing nipples. Her breasts were aching for his touch. It was a sweet, anticipatory pain that she knew his hands would assuage.

But they didn't. Instead they moved to her waist, and she felt herself being lifted. Rick set her back on the chaise longue, then lay down beside her. The heat of the day combined with the heat of their bodies to make the air around them as torrid and as tension-filled as a tropical storm. Karla was oblivious to everything except her growing need— for Rick to touch her, to kiss her, to. . . .

Rick's hands began an upward journey that made her catch her breath with expectation. When finally they reached her breasts, she wanted to cry out at the relief they brought. Unbidden, a deep moan of pleasure escaped her lips. The sound was like an aphrodisiac to Rick, and he responded in a throaty whisper.

"My God, Karla, you're everything I've lain awake nights imagining you would be." His mouth moved possessively along her chin. "Your lips...." Fleetingly he tasted her mouth. "Your skin...." His fiery trail moved to the hollow of her shoulder. "Your breasts...." Slowly, tantalizingly, with featherlike kisses his mouth traced a path down from the smooth skin at the base of her throat.

Karla's heart raced with anticipation. When finally his seeking mouth captured the areola and its centered peak, a rush of elation pierced her with an unimaginable sweetness.

Her back arched, and she pressed her breasts wantonly into his claiming mouth. Her fingers tangled in his hair, pulling him closer still. Her mind and body reeled in the vortex of the new, unfathomable sensations she was experiencing.

But she wanted more—the feel of his bare flesh against hers, the fulfillment of the promise his touch aroused.

She slipped her hands beneath his shirt. Hesitantly, unsure her action would bring him pleasure, she sought the small mounds buried in the curling hair of his chest. When, unerringly, she found the rigid flesh, she began to make slow sensuous circles with her fingertips. Rick tensed, and she knew a moment of panic, an instant of fear that she had done something wrong. But then she felt a low moan rumbling through his chest and heard him calling her name.

"Karla..." he gasped. "Karla, Karla...." Her name became a litany of pain, of ecstasy echoing through her senses. She knew she had pleased him. The knowledge was intoxicating. She withdrew her hands and began to unbutton the last closure of his shirt, which had grown into such an irritating barrier between them. Rick leaned back and looked at her, his eyes no longer veiled with reserve but filled instead with undisguised desire for her. With nimbler fingers he finished what she had started, and his shirt joined her bikini top on the chair. Karla reached up and ran her hands across his chest, then to the back of his neck, where she applied a gentle pressure that drew him to her again.

The meeting of their bare skin was yet a new sensation. The slightly abrasive quality of the hair on his chest against her nipples shattered what little reserve she had left. She breathed raggedly, aching for something she had never known, with a need that was almost unbearable.

Disjointed thoughts whirled through her mind, surfacing, then being pulled under in waves of passion. But one thought kept working its way into consciousness—a thought that would not be denied. She tried again and again to ignore the inner voice, which warned her to tell Rick this would be her first time. It didn't matter, she tried to tell herself, but always the voice refused an easy answer. Beyond what she *wished* were true, she knew Rick would care. She could not, would not, risk it.

"Before we go any further, Rick, I have to...I have to talk to you." Her voice was a husky whisper that contradicted her words.

"I'm listening," he murmured. His tongue lightly traced a line from her temple to the hollow behind her ear.

"Please, Rick," she breathed. "Please stop. I can't talk, I can't even think when you're doing that." She felt a tension, a wariness in his movements as he pulled away and propped himself on his elbow, looking down at her.

"You're serious, aren't you?"

Her voice was choked by a sudden fear. She nodded.

"Well?" Rick asked in a soft but guarded monotone, as if experiencing his own nameless fear. "What is it?"

How should she begin? Never in her wildest fantasy had she pictured herself apologizing for her lack of experience. How could she tell him, and in the same voice assure him she desperately wanted him to make love to her. *And* that she honestly had no intention of asking for any commitments. How could she say all that without sounding like a prude who'd turned into a harlot?

Karla felt like an idiot. She couldn't think of any way to even broach the subject. Finally she just blurted it out.

"Dammit, I'm a virgin!" Softly, shyly, she added, "I just thought you should know before we went any further."

Rick stared at her, at the impassioned revelation written on her face. After a moment he let out a deep, eloquent sigh. A warm smile curved his mouth as he lay back against the cushion and drew her on top of him. He touched her cheek, then her chin, then the soft folds of her eyelids as if he was memorizing the feel of her. Lastly he reached up to tuck an errant golden curl behind her ear. "Why?" he finally, simply asked.

It was not the reaction she had anticipated, nor the one she had feared. Maybe a "Sorry lady, but I don't mess around with virgins," or "That's a minor problem." Never "Why!"

"Why!?!" she threw his question back at him.

"Yes, why?" he repeated in the same level tone.

Flustered, she thought for a moment before answering. "I guess because I've never met anyone I wanted badly enough. Affairs seem to require so much drama and clandestine behavior." More truthfully, she could have said that she'd never wanted anyone to have that much power over her.

She looked into Rick's steady gaze and swallowed, seeking the nerve to go on. "Until now," she whispered, looking down at her hands, splayed so possessively and familiarly across the broad expanse of his chest. How vulnerable she felt.

Rick reached up to lace his fingers through her hair. In a low throaty tone, he said, "I've never been paid a higher compliment. Thank you."

He held her face between his hands and looked into her eyes. Tenderly he kissed her. "I'm grateful you stopped this from going any further."

Karla's heart sank. The day had been filled with new sensations; had not only awakened passions but had taught frustration. She was shocked by the enormity of her feelings—a rage that made her want to strike out at Rick, while at the same time she desperately wanted him to make love to her. Barely able to speak coherently, she murmured, "Stopping was not what I intended."

"Impulsive cravings shouldn't have such permanent consequences."

Karla pushed herself away from his embrace and sat up. "Is that what you think my wanting you was? An impulsive craving?" She looked at him incredulously, her eyes wide in disbelief.

He didn't answer right away. Instead he tucked his hands behind his head and stared at a hawk circling overhead. His eyes were still on the bird when at last he said, "Perhaps it isn't what I think—more what I fear."

He turned to face her. She could see torment and frustration in his eyes, but there was something else too—something she couldn't identify. "I would hate to have you ever think you'd made a mistake, here, with me," he said. "I wouldn't want you to regret that it had happened."

Karla didn't know whether to laugh or to cry. As she reached down to touch his arm, she silently acknowledged to herself what she had been trying to deny since that first crazy day. As impossible, as improbable as it was, for better or worse she was most definitely in love with Richard Allen Fleming. She had spent only a week with this man, whom she had hated on sight, and he had managed to turn her world upside down.

CHAPTER THREE

KARLA MECHANICALLY CHEWED the chicken-salad
sandwich Steve had brought, then forcefully
swallowed, washing the last bit down with some
milk. If she sat very still, she thought, she might
just keep the tasteless mess down. After a while
she realized she wasn't trembling quite so
badly and, with a sheepish grin, thanked Steve
for being so persistent in his efforts to make her
eat.

Steve found another chair, and they waited together in the cold hallway for word about Rick's
surgery. The long silences that followed were
broken periodically by snatches of thoughts
spoken aloud, some bringing replies, others
needing none.

"When I went after your sandwich, I checked
the waiting room. There's still quite a crowd in
there," Steve said as he stood up to pace the narrow confines one more time. His attitude toward
her was still slightly strained, but far warmer than
it had been earlier.

Karla pulled her legs up, wrapped her arms

around them and rested her chin on her knees. "Who are they?" she asked.

"Oh, mostly race-car people. There's some fans and a few stringers who work for racing magazines, but mostly people from the track. Jerry Benson's been by several times. So have Tully and Monroe. They were involved in the wreck," Steve went on to explain, "but none of them got hurt too bad. Just Rick and Cory Adams."

"How is Cory doing?" Karla immediately asked. This was the first she had heard of the other drivers in what the television announcer had called a "spectacular" five-car crash. Cory Adams had been a good friend of hers and Rick's when they were together. With his face-splitting grin and "good guy" personality, he was a favorite among racers and fans alike. Karla hated to think his wife would be suffering the way she herself now suffered. She patiently waited for Steve to answer. When he didn't, she slowly lifted her head from her knees and looked at him.

"Good God, girl," he said miserably, "I don't know if I'll ever learn to keep my mouth shut."

Karla's face paled. "Cory's dead?" she asked hoarsely.

"He died at the track hospital before they could get him transferred." Steve rubbed his forehead as if he could erase the weariness that furrowed his brow. He came over to sit beside her again. "There's something else I suppose I should tell you. You're going to find out whether I do or not, and it might be better coming from me rather than someone else.''

He reached over, slipped his arm across her shoulders and drew her to him in an awkward embrace. Karla let her head rest comfortably against his barrel chest and waited with a sense of trepidation for him to begin.

"There's this girl. . . .''

Her heart slipped a beat as she waited for Steve to clear his throat before he continued. "I wouldn't even bring this up except you're going to run into her sooner or later, and you should know what's what when you do.'' He ran his hand nervously up and down her arm until the fine hairs of the cashmere in her sweater stood straight up, filled with static electricity.

"You can't imagine how crazy lonely Rick has been since you left him, Karla. I don't think God ever meant for a man to love anyone as much as Rick loved you—'' angrily he corrected himself "—*loves* you, dammit. He near lost his mind without you around, Karla. I never felt so sorry for anyone in my whole life.''

Karla felt an insidious hand of doubt clutch her heart. Could she have made a mistake? Was it possible the choice she'd made was the wrong one? She couldn't believe that. She mustn't believe it. She had to continue to believe she'd never really had a choice. How could she go on otherwise?

"What about the girl, Steve?" she prodded gently, anxiously, afraid of the answer, yet having to know.

Steve sighed. He stared blankly at the beige wall opposite them. "Her name's Mary. Mary Davies." His voice was a monotone. "Rick's known her a long while. He took her out a couple of times about a year ago." Almost painfully he added, "I guess she's never been able to convince herself it's all over."

"She must have had some encouragement," Karla said barely above a whisper.

Roughly Steve sat her up and looked angrily into her eyes. "Don't you go building more than there is. It was you he asked for, and it's been you that's near drove him insane with loneliness these last three years. If he tried to find someone to help ease that ache, then you have *no* right to complain." He saw the pain in Karla's eyes and softened his anger to a frustrated growl. "Dammit, girl, you should have been with him. Then there wouldn't ever have been anyone else."

Karla didn't want to tell him why she had left. She had never said the words aloud before, but now they demanded expression. She must make Steve understand. Perhaps if she did, she herself would understand again the feelings that no longer seemed to form cohesive thoughts in her mind.

"If I had stayed, Steve, there wouldn't be anything left for Rick to love. After Bobby died, a piece of me died every time Rick got into a car. And if you remember,'' she said, smiling weakly, "Rick's way of mourning Bobby's death was to drive in every race he could find. He was so adamant about it I almost started to believe all the five-cent psychiatrists who insist race-car drivers have a death wish. Finally I realized that Rick was desperately trying to prove just the opposite, that someone could participate in racing for the love of it and be passionately in love with life, too. But I still found it impossible to erase the memory of Bobby's crash."

She laughed derisively before continuing. "I even developed a long list of arguments to try to help me think objectively about the whole thing. They ranged from comparative statistics of football deaths and injuries to the number of people who die on highways each year. I even found a chart somewhere showing the fatality statistics for professional firemen. They were all worse than for racing, and no one accused any of them of trying to commit suicide. But none of my rationalizing did me any good. I still spent every race day, and the day before it, vomiting. I was terrified every waking moment.

"Even if I stayed home from the track, I almost passed out if the phone happened to ring. And it never got better." Tears were streaming unchecked down Karla's cheeks and falling gently on her chest, where they glistened like tiny diamonds in her sweater.

"Instead of thinking Bobby's death was a fluke, I became convinced it was only a matter of time before the same thing would happen to Rick. When I realized I was creating a self-fulfilling prophecy, I knew I had to leave. Although I managed to keep it hidden most of the time or to blame my strange behavior on other things, it eventually became impossible to pretend that my paranoia wouldn't spread to Rick. I knew that if he ever got into his car feeling my doubts, it would take away his edge, and that I would be the cause of whatever happened. The thought nearly drove me over the edge." Karla reached up to wipe away the tears with the back of her hand.

"Why didn't you tell Rick any of this?" Steve's voice betrayed his skepticism.

"What you really mean is, why did I tell him I was leaving because I had stopped loving him, don't you?" she asked woodenly.

"Yeah, something like that. He never really came right out and told me what happened. All I know for sure is what he told me one night after you left. He got stinking drunk and kept asking me what went wrong, what he did to make you stop loving him. He suspected it had something to do with Bobby's dying and it being his fault, but I told him he was crazy. No one ever thought for a minute that he was responsible for what happened to Bobby. He couldn't have loved that kid more if he'd been his own brother.''

Karla winced. She had gone over and over her reasons for leaving Rick. The farther away that day grew, that day when she had so cruelly told him she no longer loved or cared for him, the more trouble she had remembering how terribly frantic she had felt at the time. She only knew she had believed, with every fiber of her being, that she would be the cause of Rick's death if she stayed. And that the only way she could show her love was to let him go in such a way that the break would be irrevocable. Why, where, how had all grown fuzzy since then. Only the pain had continued, never lessening.

Karla looked at Steve with tear-swollen eyes. ''At the time—'' she choked on the words, realizing how empty they sounded ''—at the time I thought it was the greatest gift I could give.''

Once again he pulled her into the circle of his arms and mumbled into the cushion of her hair, ''Seems like I'm always apologizing to you, Karla. Think I'll ever learn?''

Before she had a chance to answer, she felt him tense. She followed his gaze and found the reason for his anxiety. Through the crack in the door she could see a gurney being wheeled down the corridor toward them. She jumped up and peered through the window. It was Rick.

She managed to catch a quick glimpse of his

face as they wheeled him through the door. Although still deathly pale, there was a slight tinge of color in his cheeks.

The orderly pulling the head of the gurney glanced in her direction, then called out to the other two attendants to stop. He looked at her conspiratorially and said, "He's awake, ma'am, if you'd like to say something to him real quick."

Afraid to trust her voice, she simply nodded and stepped over to the bed. Leaning over, she breathed a kiss onto Rick's forehead and whispered in his ear, "I'm here, Rick—I love you."

Out of the corner of her eye she saw him try to raise his hand, and she reached down to place her fingers gently in his. She walked beside him as they moved through the corridors and elevators on their return journey to the intensive-care unit.

Once back in the room, Karla found that someone had brought a more comfortable chair for her to sit in. It had cushions and padded arms and was big enough for her to pull up her legs and snuggle against the back. When all the bottles were installed on their hooks, everything had been checked and attached and Karla was finally alone with Rick, she pushed the chair over to the bed, reached through the bars and twined her fingers with his once again. It was like a transfusion into her soul to be able to touch him. The warmth of his fingers reassured her, letting her know that he was still with her.

She watched as his breathing settled into the steady rhythm of sleep before she leaned her head back and dozed. She fell into a deeper sleep than she had planned and awoke with a start when she heard a soft rustling in the room.

The night nurse smiled at her and went back to hooking up a new iv. Karla untangled her legs and stiffly got to her feet, grimacing as she tried to straighten up. She could remember feeling this stiff only one other time—after she'd spent a night in Rick's Porsche. She smiled at the memory. They had broken down in the middle of nowhere late one night and had spent a funny, miserable twenty-four hours trying to get help.

Attempting to stretch the kinks out, Karla hobbled around the room. As she did so she caught her reflection in the window and was stunned to realize how terrible she looked. She glanced at the nurse and softly asked if she would stay with Rick for a few minutes while she ran to the bathroom to splash cold water on her face.

When she returned she discovered that Steve had brought her a tray of food, which contained several of her favorite things in a mismatched gastronomical feast. There was a deli corned-beef sandwich, a container of Chinese won-ton soup and an order of barbecue ribs. For dessert he had included a piece of fresh strawberry pie.

She smiled and shook her head. Remembering how much better she had felt after the lunch he

...ad made her eat, she took a bite of the sandwich. Ten minutes later she was amazed and a little ashamed to realize she had eaten everything on the tray. She started to get up to take the tray to the nurses' station when she found Rick staring at her. He smiled, and her heart melted.

"Hi," Karla said softly. She pushed the chair aside so that she could stand next to him. "How do you feel?"

Slowly he formed the words. Karla leaned close to hear them. "With...my fingers."

She choked back a sound that was a cross between sobbing and laughter. "Oh, Rick," she chided, "that's really beneath you." She smiled through her tears. Looking into his eyes, she saw him grow serious again. He started to speak and she strained to hear.

"Karla, I want you...I want you beside me... always. Not just for now...always." She heard the plea in his voice, and saw it in his eyes. The need, the pain he felt were as strong as her own. The years they had been apart were a cancer. Would the two of them be granted the time to attempt a cure?

Karla leaned farther over the railing. She knew that everything she did could be seen from the hallway, but the only person who mattered was Rick. She was sure he would understand. As completely, as thoroughly as she could, she kissed him. When she finished she looked into his eyes

and saw his acceptance of her pledge to be w
him—always.

"When I get out of here..." he said slowly,
pausing frequently to catch his breath, "I would
love to go boating with you."

Karla blushed deeply at the seemingly innocent
statement. She reached up to smooth back his
hair. "It's a deal," she murmured huskily. "Now
get some rest or you'll never be up to it." She
winked suggestively, and he smiled.

She was no longer afraid to let Rick sleep. Somehow she knew and believed he was going to live and
that their promises to each other were more than
mere words spoken to ease the passage of life.

She pulled the chair back to the bed and settled
herself into the cushions. She smiled at his sleeping form and blushed all over again at his words.
If one of those magical machines monitoring
Rick's state had the power to read minds, she
thought, basking in her joy, it would undoubtedly
have just registered a TILT.

RICK'S BOAT AT LAKE MEAD had turned out to be
somewhat more than Karla had expected. It was a
sleek, luxurious cruiser, compactly outfitted with
galley, head and separate sleeping quarters. When
her cousins, Michael and Paul, returned home
from college, they all enthusiastically made plans
to spend Rick's last day in Las Vegas aboard the
boat.

he plans fell through, however, when word ar-
ed the next morning that Roger's father had
uffered a stroke. The entire family caught a plane
for Minneapolis, leaving Rick and Karla alone.

"I think it would be better if we forgot about
going out on the boat," Rick said thoughtfully as
Karla waved goodbye one last time to her depart-
ing aunt, uncle and cousins.

She didn't immediately answer him, waiting instead until they had walked through the parking
lot and were about to get into her aunt's station
wagon. Then she leaned against the door, barring
his way as he reached to unlock it. "Why can't we
go out on your boat today?"

Rick placed a hand on either side of her and
leaned against the car, pinning her in place with
his arms. "I think you know why," he said in a
low, gravelly voice.

"Because you're afraid of me," she goaded.

"Look, Karla," he said impatiently, "let's not
play games. You know damn well what will happen if you and I spend today alone on my boat."

"Yes, I do. Or at least I hope I do." She tried to
make her voice teasingly seductive, but the words
came out sounding more like a feeble attempt at
humor.

"Dammit, Karla," he said, grabbing her shoulders and pulling her out of the way, "behave yourself. You don't have any idea what you're doing
or what you're talking about."

"Why don't I? Because I'm a virgin?" She spat out the word as if she had created a new obscenity. In frustration she kicked a pebble across the parking lot. It bounced along the asphalt, then clinked to a halt against a shiny spoked hubcap. She whirled back to face him. Pleadingly she looked into Rick's eyes. "How could you possibly think that that could make me want you less, that my feelings would be any less sincere?"

"My God, Karla," he groaned. "You have no idea what you're doing to me." Hungrily he took her into his arms. She thrilled at his deep exploring kiss, knowing he had capitulated at last.

They stopped by the house to pick up Rick's car and their suits before heading for the lake. By the time they were actually on the water, it was nearing noon and the outside temperature had risen to over ninety degrees. Rick had slipped into a quiet, thoughtful mood and went about getting the boat ready as if Karla weren't along.

He started to climb out on the dock again to release the final tether that held the boat, then hesitated and came back to Karla. Standing directly in front of her, he reached down to tuck his hand under her chin. Slowly he raised it until she looked directly into his eyes. She saw a battle raging there and feared for a moment that he was going to take her home. Finally, painfully, he said, "Are you sure, Karla...are you absolutely sure?"

Without hesitation she replied softly, "Yes, I'm sure."

He kissed her on the forehead. His mood seemed to lighten perceptibly as he shouted orders for her to tuck this and to stow that as they got ready to cross the sparkling blue waters of Lake Mead. It was as if her words had lifted a crushing burden from his shoulders.

"Where are we going?" she shouted over the sound of the powerful engine and the rushing wind.

"To a cove I found a couple of years ago. It's a little tricky to get into, so few people try. We should have plenty of privacy."

While she stared into the foaming blue white water of their wake, Karla fleetingly wondered if she *was* sure of what she was doing. She knew she had fallen in love with Rick, but she also knew he didn't reciprocate the feelings. As much as she wished it were different, she had no intention of trying to manipulate him into loving her. She sincerely doubted that that could be accomplished with Richard Allen Fleming, anyway. Any man as successful at avoiding entanglements as he had obviously been must have built an impenetrable shield around his heart. As much as she'd like to deny it, she could understand why he'd done so. He lived like a Gypsy. The only thing that could be said to even resemble his home was this boat. And he liked his life-style the way it was. Why shouldn't he?

She knew she was heading down an emotional one-way street and that there was nowhere to turn around. She glanced up at Rick. The wind was blowing his hair back from his forehead and filling his shirt like a balloon. He looked young and vital and utterly free. She knew that if she told him she'd changed her mind, he would take her back. And then what? She sighed.

She had always scoffed at love stories, calling them mere biological needs laced with flowery words. She laughed at herself. It was certainly poetic justice that she had been afflicted with such a gigantic dose of the disease. Somehow, as she watched the graceful man before her, she knew he would be her lifelong obsession. There might be others after Rick, but none would ever claim her heart the way he did. With a startled, pained gasp she realized again that she would probably have to spend the rest of her life with only these few days as memories of the man who would forever hold her heart. . . .

She jumped when the boat suddenly stopped. She looked around to see if something was wrong, then glanced up. Rick was moving toward her.

"I thought you said you were sure," he said angrily.

"What?" Karla asked, confused.

"I've been watching you," he said, bending down in front of her and taking her hand.

Karla laughed in relief. His deep concern for her

feelings only made her love him more. "Rick, would it convince you that I know what I'm doing if I stand up, take off all my clothes and attack you right here and now?"

He smiled in turn. "I'll bet you've left a wide trail behind you of men taking cold showers," he said.

"Not really. You'll just have to take my word for it—I'm usually not quite this wanton or brazen," she said and laughed again. "The truth is, I've never behaved this way in my life. You do strange things to me, Rick Fleming." It was meant to sound lighthearted, but it struck so close to the truth that Karla tripped on the words and revealed how sincerely she felt them.

She saw a deeply troubled look cross his features before he quickly covered it with a smile. "It's called lust, my dear. And it's as old as mankind." There was a teasing twinkle in his eyes. "And it's a good thing, too. We might not be here without it."

Karla had to hide the quick stab of pain she felt at his words. Did he really believe that was all she felt for him?

Rick went back to start up the boat again, and within an hour they were winding their way deep into the recesses of his pristine cove. When finally they stopped and Rick had secured the anchor, Karla suddenly felt shy. She was unsure of what to do or what to say.

As if sensing her unease, Rick acted as though they had come to the cove for a picnic and a swim and nothing more. He went into the tiny galley and began to prepare lunch, while Karla went into the small bedroom to slip into her suit. Her hands trembled as she tied the strings of her bikini. When she was finished, she took a deep breath and stepped into the galley.

Rick put down the orange he was peeling and turned to watch her enter. He grinned mischievously. "I don't think I got around to mentioning it the last time you wore that suit, but you look breathtaking. Your body does wonderful things with tiny scraps of material."

Karla flushed furiously. "Thank you," she breathed. She looked down at the small patches of material covering her breasts and was even more embarrassed to discover her nipples pushing invitingly and obviously against the surface. What had happened to the aggressive woman she'd been when she had dreamed of this moment?

Rick wiped his hands on the towel hanging over the sink, reached out, grasped her by the waist and pulled her to him. As their mouths met in a deliciously hungry yet restrained kiss, his hands moved up her sides until they were even with her breasts. Slowly his thumbs began to make caressing, demanding circles around her hard thrusting nipples, until they captured the rosy flesh and pressed into it possessively.

When his hands moved back to her waist, Karla felt like crying out at the loss. She had been a steadily burning fuse since their first kiss over a week ago. And then there had been that frustrating episode by her aunt's pool. She now felt that if she had to wait any longer for Rick to make love to her, she would die of the pain and longing.

When he pulled away and went back to making the fruit salad, she felt like screaming in disappointment. How did he maintain such control, while she herself was unable to concentrate on anything but him?

Could it be possible that he didn't want her as much as she wanted him? She thought about their times together and knew that wasn't true. He simply must have learned the art of self-control, must have honed it to a fine edge. She stared at his back. *Well, Mr. Fleming,* she vowed, *we'll just see how long you can maintain that self-control today. We'll just see.*

Her new resolve gave Karla the strength to get through lunch without reaching out to touch Rick, who sat across from her looking as perfectly formed as Michelangelo's *David*. He had changed into the same suit he'd worn the day they met—a brief unencumbering piece of nylon that rested low and easily on his narrow hips. He looked as gorgeous now as he had then. She forced herself to stop staring, knowing her thoughts would soon destroy her resolve to maintain a controlled demeanor.

She looked up into the sky. The sun had peaked during their lunch and was beginning its journey to the horizon, bringing with it the hottest part of the day. Karla leaned back and futilely fanned herself with her napkin.

"Hot?" Rick asked, sitting comfortably under the shade of the awning he'd pulled out earlier.

"Nearing the boiling point." She smiled lazily at him. A thin sheen of moisture covered her body, making her by now almost bronze skin shimmer in the sun. Tiny drops had begun to gather together in the valley between her breasts.

She sighed and sat up. "I think I'd better move into the shade with you. I'm beginning to see dancing dots before my eyes."

Rick moved his feet off the chair next to him and turned it around. But instead of letting Karla sit there, he reached out and pulled her onto his lap, nestling his face between her breasts.

"Mmm, you smell good," he murmured.

"If you like the smell of sweaty bodies," she breathed. She felt him gently bite the rounded flesh of her breasts, leaving a tingling trail around the confining material of her top and starting a shiver that raised goose bumps on her arms.

"If the body happens to be yours, the smell is not only pleasant, it's an aromatic love potion."

Karla murmured her pleasure at the thrill his

words instilled in her. She ran her hands through his hair, then down the broad expanse of his back. Her fingers splayed across the taut muscles of his arms. She gloried in the feel of him under her wandering touch.

Rick's mouth came up and captured hers, and she tasted the saltiness of her own body. She felt his hands move to the tie of her top and she started to help him. As he adroitly untied the knot she realized with a pleased shudder that her help wasn't needed. With his quick, sure movement, her breasts were wonderfully free—free to be captured again by Rick's claiming hands. His mouth left hers, and with his tongue he lingeringly and tantalizingly traced a line down her neck and over the firm mound of her breast. Karla caught her breath when finally he took the rosy-tipped nipple into his mouth and massaged the thrusting flesh with his tongue, while gently holding the prize with his teeth.

She thought she would faint from the sweet agony of his touch as his hand began to explore her sensitive inner thigh. "Rick!" She gasped his name, arching her back in a movement of timeless, unconscious seduction. Shyly she added, "Rick, I want you."

She felt as well as heard his response; a deep rumbling moan of reciprocated desire vibrated in his chest. His arms trembled as he pulled her closer still. Karla smiled triumphantly. She felt heady with power, knowing she had dented the armor of his incredible control. Her heart soared with the knowledge that he wanted her, truly wanted her.

But not enough!

Forcefully Karla roused herself from the lethargy of passion. She unwrapped herself from Rick's arms and, trembling with desire, stood before him. More than the fulfillment of the moment, she passionately wanted Rick to remember this day. It must be more to him than just another afternoon with a woman, the memory of which would fade with the ensuing years. She wanted him to know and feel a hunger for her that was similar to the all-consuming need she felt for him. She wanted him to remember her with at least a shadow of the memory she would hold forever.

Slowly she untied and stepped from her bikini bottoms. As she stood in front of him, she was surprised to find that her nakedness brought her no embarrassment. Instead, she gloried in the pleasure she saw in Rick's eyes, and for the first time in her life she felt she might be beautiful.

Rick reached out and wrapped his hands around the backs of her knees. Slowly his hands moved up until they gently grasped her buttocks. He pulled her to him and began to brush quick hungry kisses along the tender, flat plane of her stomach. She gasped aloud with shock and pleasure as he moved lower and began tracing a line with his tongue where her tanned flesh met untanned skin. Her resolve to prolong their lovemaking for as long as she could nearly dissolved.

"Rick," she choked, "let me go."

He slid his hands back down to her knees and looked up at her questioningly.

Inanely she stammered, "I. . .uh, I just thought we could go for a swim—" her voice dropped to a whisper "—*before* we make love." She couldn't believe how stupid her words sounded even to herself.

A slow smile spread across his face. "I thought perhaps you were having a change of heart. But I can see that I was wrong." His voice was low and husky with passion and was like a spoken caress. He stood up and drew her into his embrace, thoroughly, deeply kissing her as if unwilling to ever let her go. She felt the evidence of his arousal pressing into the flatness of her stomach, and she finally, completely, willingly forgot her resolve. He bent over and picked her up in his arms. She felt his heart beating in excitement against her ribs. Suddenly the idea of swimming, no matter what the motivation, seemed like the silliest thing in the world. She was immensely pleased that he had chosen to ignore her suggestion.

And then she abruptly felt herself floating through the air. Before she realized what had happened she was surrounded by a blanket of cool water. She came up sputtering. Rick was leaning over the edge of the boat looking at her, his familiar lopsided grin on his face, a knowing twinkle in his dark brown eyes.

"How's the water?" he called down laconically.

Karla smiled, then dipped her head back to wash the hair from her eyes. "Just fine," she laughed. "Aren't you coming in?"

"In a minute," he said and disappeared.

Karla lay back in the water, letting the small waves wash over her. She closed her eyes and floated motionlessly, her highly sensitized skin acutely aware of the heat of the day and the coolness of the water. She had never felt so alive. With a quickening of her heart she told herself it was probably because she had never been in love before. Today had to be very special, she thought again. Special enough to fill a reservoir of memories. Special enough to last her a lifetime.

Silently Rick swam up beside her, curling his arm familiarly around her waist and drawing her to him. Instantly, at his mere touch, the flame inside her was reignited. She found she wanted him more than before, more than she thought possible. She wondered how people in love ever accomplished anything else, how they ever sacrificed time together for anything so mundane as the routine of daily living.

Rick leaned back and drew her along with him so that she floated lightly against his long torso. With a start she realized that he too had removed his suit. She smiled her pleasure at the discovery and ran her hand down his side and across the flat expanse of his stomach, seeking to touch him as he had touched her.

Rick playfully bit her shoulder and pulled away. "I thought you said you wanted to swim."

She picked up the undercurrents in his voice. He had known all along what she was trying to do. Some seductress she had turned out to be!

In answer she challenged him to a race and was immediately accepted. They swam out a distance they judged to be about fifty yards. On the count of three, they headed back to the boat. Rick proved to be a powerful swimmer, without a great deal of technique, but still able to beat Karla by several yards.

When she arrived at the side of the boat, he reached out and pulled her the final distance to the ladder. She braced her feet next to his on the last rung and hooked her arm around the railing the way he had hooked his. When at last she caught her breath, she loudly proclaimed herself the victor.

"Hold on, lady." Rick tried to make his voice sound stern as he looked at her through hooded eyes. "It seems to me that I arrived at this ladder slightly ahead of you."

"Oh, I'll grant you that much," she said, ruefully shaking her head, "but I hope you don't call what you were doing *swimming*. And the deal was to swim back here."

"So you think I lack style, huh?" he snorted.

Suddenly serious, she reached out and ran her hand along his cheek. "Only when it comes to swimming, Rick...."

She caught her breath. She found herself drowning in her burgeoning love for this man. Quickly she closed the distance between them and put her arms around his neck, pressing the length of her body into his.

Their mouths sought and devoured each other's in a kiss that seared Karla's soul. She felt his need for her shudder through him, and it built her own fire of yearning to a deafening roar.

Hungrily his mouth traveled down her neck. Karla reached up to pull herself higher out of the water, to give Rick's seeking mouth access to the throbbing need of her breasts. Instinctively she moved against him until she had her legs wrapped around his waist.

Rick's free hand reached out and grasped her chin. "Look at me, Karla," he demanded.

She opened her eyes, saw the need in his face and gloried in it.

"Are you sure?" he asked

"I've never been more sure of anything in my life," she answered him evenly.

His hand moved to the back of her head. Slowly he pulled her to him, then reached up to meet her lips with his own. With a single thrusting movement he was inside her. She accepted the pain and rejoiced in the finality of it. At last she was a woman in body as well as mind.

She waited for Rick to seek the pleasure she wanted to give him. When he didn't, she looked into his eyes. "Is something wrong?"

"Yes. It would never be good for you here." Gently he withdrew from her and guided her up the ladder.

Once on board he reached for a towel and caressingly began to wipe the water from her quivering flesh. When he was finished, she took the towel from him and lingeringly followed the long sinewy muscles of his body in whisper-soft swipes of the fluffy cloth. She dried his back first. Slowly, purposefully, she moved to his chest and down his hard narrow stomach. Rick caught his breath. He moaned his pleasure when she let her hands continue their searching journey until she had intimately touched him. With an urgent tenderness, he picked her up in his arms and silently carried her into the cabin.

Rick set Karla on the downy spread and covered her body with his. He reached up to brush the wet tendrils from her face. He looked hauntingly, unfathomably into her eyes. She knew she saw his need, but she thought for a moment there was something else. Slowly he bent his head to hers until their lips met in a kiss that wrenched her heart from her chest and made it soar.

"Karla...Karla." She listened to him call her

name, and the sound was sweeter than any she had ever heard. His mouth murmured her name again and again as his lips moved over her body in a claiming, demanding explosion of passion, tearing from her all reserve, all modesty.

She cried out for him to possess her, to give her the final culminating joy he had denied her until now. But still he waited, stroking, touching, kissing her until she felt she would die from the pleasure.

"You're so beautiful," he said as he raised himself above her and looked into her eyes. "You're perfection, Karla...all of you...."

Instinct ruled her, and she moved against him with an urgency born of need. She felt Rick's thighs slip between hers, and once again she welcomed him into her being.

He carried her to the pinnacle of ecstasy with expert gentleness, waiting patiently yet hungrily for her to cry out her surprise at the hurricane force that swept her away before he joined her in passionate release.

Afterward they lay wrapped in each other's arms, listening to the echoes of their heartbeats, each unwilling to break the perfection of the silence with mere words. The afternoon slipped away with painful ease, though Karla would have captured it and held it for eternity.

By midnight they were back at the airport. This time it was Rick who was leaving. He was to join his crew in Europe for an upcoming race.

A thousand thoughts and words stuck in Karla's throat as she walked him to the plane. There were no promises exchanged or false hopes given in their goodbyes—simply a lingering kiss, heartbreaking in its finality.

Karla watched the plane until the last of its flashing lights disappeared in the twinkling desert sky. Slowly she headed back to her aunt's sprawling, empty house.

She had been a fool to think she could have a whirlwind love affair with Rick and walk away unscathed. She felt an emptiness deeper than she could have imagined possible. Now she understood that a broken heart wasn't merely a poetic description of loss. It was an actual physical pain—a pain so severe that every breath, every movement, every memory hurt.

The house seemed to mock her in its silence, dispassionately pointing out that she was more alone now than she had ever been before. She changed into her robe and wandered through the cavernous rooms, finally lying down on the bed where Rick had slept, breathing in his scent in a futile attempt to be near him a little longer. After what seemed like hours, she fitfully dozed.

The sharp ring of the telephone woke her. She glanced at the digital clock beside the bed and knew a moment of panic when she realized it was still early morning. She lifted the receiver and hesitantly said, "Hello."

Rick's deep voice answered her. Without introduction or preamble, he said, "Marry me, Karla...please marry me."

There was a long pause while his poignant request and its far-reaching ramifications became reality to Karla's foggy mind.

"Are you sure?" she finally whispered, afraid if she spoke any louder she would break the magical spell and find that she was only dreaming.

Her earlier words to him, when he had asked her if she indeed wanted to give herself to him, now echoed in her ear. They brought her a joy as complete as her earlier pain.

With precise meaning, he said, "I have never been so sure of anything in my life."

CHAPTER FOUR

"KARLA FLEMING, this is Mary Davies." Steve Mc-
Donald handled the awkward introduction
smoothly, as if he believed the two women were
eager to meet.

Karla crossed the hospital room, her easy manner belying her inner turmoil. So this was the
woman Steve had told her about last week. The
woman Rick had dated. The woman Steve had
said helped to ease Rick's lonely hours. She was
no more than twenty-four or twenty-five years
old, and she was beautiful. Long dark brown hair
tumbled freely over her shoulders to lie like a
glistening cape against her full breasts. Tall and
willowy, she must be only a few inches less than
six feet, Karla guessed.

As Mary reached out to take Karla's hand, she
moved with the grace and assurance of someone
who relishes her height.

"I'm sorry, Mrs. Fleming," she said in a low
whisper, "I didn't mean to add to the pain you've
already gone through by being here when you arrived this morning. I was just about to leave." She

released Karla's hand and reached down to the chair beside Rick's bed to gather her belongings. "I hope you understand why I came. I had to see for myself that Rick really was all right."

Karla could see what the long hours of waiting and the hurt of not knowing had cost Mary Davies. Lines of fatigue and worry creased her forehead and accentuated the puffiness around her eyes. Karla's heart thudded heavily against her chest. Rick had not been a casual affair for this woman. She had loved him. *She still loved him.*

Karla glanced at the bed. Rick slept peacefully, oblivious to the tense scene being played around him. She looked back at Mary. "Did you have a chance to talk to him?"

"No." Wearily, softly, she smiled. "He's been sleeping like a baby since I arrived."

"Perhaps if you came back this afternoon...."

Mary stared at Karla. Her eyes sparkled with sudden unshed tears. "Thank you," she silently mouthed before she hurried out of the room.

Karla turned and stared out the window, mindlessly watching the steam rise from the laundry stacks. Steve came up behind her and slipped his arm around her shoulders. "You're a special lady, Karla. It's easy to see why Rick is so crazy about you."

Karla brushed a wisp of hair from her forehead. "Who is she, Steve?"

"I don't think I understand what you mean."

"How did Rick meet her? Where is she from? What does she do?" As she slowly asked her questions, Karla traced random patterns on the window with her fingertip. A cube, a circle, then a heart with a jagged line down the middle. "I feel I need to know as much as I can about her."

"Mary Davies isn't a threat to you, Karla," Steve tried to reassure her. "Rick has a blind spot when it comes to women. He can only see one, and you're it."

"I want to know about her." Karla turned from the window to face him. "Is there some reason I shouldn't?"

"That's just plain silly, and you know it." Steve rubbed his hand along his chin, then through his mop of rust-colored curls. "I can't see any good's going to come from dwelling on something that's over."

"Maybe it's over for Rick, but it's obviously not over for Mary. Her role may have changed, but her feelings haven't. I know that look, Steve." She swallowed. "I've seen it in the mirror."

Steve flinched. He shoved his hands into his back pockets and started to pace the room. Slowly, reluctantly, he began to talk. "Mary's been around racing all her life. Her dad used to drive, then he quit, bought a couple of cars and hired people to drive for him. When Rick first got started racing, he drove for old man Davies for a few years. As a matter of fact, that's where we met." Steve's voice softened. "Mary was only ten or eleven at the time. She used to follow Rick around like a puppy."

Karla blanched. Mary's love for Rick went back a long way. "Why did Rick leave?"

"Oh, the usual reasons. Some disagreements, Rick's restlessness to try something new, things like that. I stayed on with Davies for a few more years until Rick was established enough to ask for and get his own mechanic." He had walked back across the room and now stood in front of the window again, absently staring into the distance.

"I didn't see too much of Mary for a while after that. I heard later that she went away to some fancy women's college." He paused for several seconds, as if reluctant to go on. "But she would always find her way to several of the races each summer. She got married right after you and Rick did, but it didn't last long. Less than six months, someone said. I heard she never got tied up real tight with anyone after that."

"It couldn't be for lack of suitors," Karla commented. "Mary's a beautiful woman."

"Smart, too," he said defensively. "And one hell of a fine person. Funny thing about all this is, I know you two would have been real good friends under any other circumstances."

Karla leaned against the windowsill. "I guess it is funny in a way, but I think so, too," she murmured. "I wish I could hate her, but I can't. Now that I've met her I actually feel sorry for her."

The ensuing silence hung between them like a filmy gauze curtain, lending its own hazy distortion to the thought-provoking morning. Finally Steve glanced at his watch. "It's almost eight-thirty. I'd better leave for the airport now, or I'm going to be late." He crossed the room to the door, hesitated, then turned back. "One more time, now," he said, forcing a lightness into his voice. "I'm supposed to look for this super-tall lady with snow-white hair and a man about two inches shorter with black hair and gray temples."

Karla smiled. "Maureen will be wearing a blue dress with a white carnation and Roger will be in his standard uniform—three-piece suit with pinstripes."

"Gotcha." The door closed behind Steve with pneumatic efficiency.

Karla moved from the window and reached down to scoot the overstuffed vinyl chair closer to Rick's bed. As she moved the chair she discovered a silk scarf with a complex geometrical design lying underneath. Karla picked up the scarf and slowly, mechanically, folded it. It would have been so much easier if Mary Davies had been one of the typical driver groupies who hung around every racetrack. Karla could have dismissed her as one of dozens, each capable of taking the other's place. But Mary was decidedly different. Her memory wouldn't fade easily.

Karla looked down at Rick. Each day since the accident had brought wondrous improvement. And then last night he had been moved from intensive care into this private room, a room where he would be allowed visitors. As long as they didn't stay too long, or upset him.... *Or bring back too vivid memories of the past,* Karla felt like screaming, a new fear clutching her heart.

Mary had been willing to stay beside Rick, to go with him wherever he traveled. She had obviously been able to accept him for what he was and never let clouds of fear control her actions—something Karla had tried so hard to do, and she'd failed so miserably....

As she stood there lost in thought, Rick reached out and gently grasped her hand. He looked up into her eyes, searching them for several moments before saying, "Do you want to talk about it?"

Karla felt a sudden flush of defensive anger. "How long have you been listening?" She tried to pull her hand away, but Rick held it with surprising strength. She glared at him, realizing as she did so that she was using her anger to cover her pain. She knew she was being unfair, but her emotions refused to be ruled by reason.

"You woke me when you first came in," he answered softly. He still held on to her hand, as if by letting her go he would lose her.

"How could you?" she cried. Karla hadn't wanted him to know how deeply she had been hurt, and she knew that, although she had managed to hide her feelings from Mary and Steve, Rick would not have been fooled. "How could you just lie there and listen?" She fought a catch in her throat.

"Karla, I'm sorry," he whispered, not responding to her anger. "Not for listening to what happened between you and Mary and Steve, but for the pain I've caused you. I would do anything to erase it. I love you. More than my very life, I love you." His words tore at her heart, and she stopped trying to pull away from him. When he continued, it was in a carefully controlled monotone, as though he could only say what he wanted to if the flatness of his voice hid the feeling.

"In the explosive seconds of the wreck, when the car was collapsing around me, I felt this incredible flood of relief to know my life was almost over. While the flames grew until I could no longer see the crowd or the other cars, I actually experienced a moment of blinding joy. I thought the pain of losing you would soon be over, and I would be free at last. Then they pried me loose and brought me here. Only one thing mattered after that. I had to see you. I knew I couldn't go on without you. You see, my love...." He brought her hand to his lips and gently kissed the palm. When he continued, his voice was husky with emotion. "You see, you really are life itself to me."

Karla closed her eyes against the torment she felt and sank into the chair. Rick's hand went to her cheek, where he wiped her tears away with the backs of his fingers before he gently pulled her into his embrace. Her head rested lightly on his chest, her hair tucked beneath his chin. His breath became a warm caress as she listened to him.

"I tried so hard not to fall in love with you, Karla. But I think I knew, even as I fought it, that I wanted to lose." She felt a deep laugh vibrate through his chest. "Did you know that I left your aunt's house the second night you were there and drove all the way to the airport? That I had every intention of taking the first available plane out of town?"

She'd only known that he had disappeared for several hours that night. "Did you ever wish you had?" She held her breath.

"No, my love." His hand gently stroked her arm. "Never. You brought a joy to my life that made every day special. Before we met my world was gray. You gave my existence color."

She felt a tear slide across the bridge of her nose. "What color is the pain I've brought you, Rick?" she whispered.

"No darker than that I've given you," he said. He drew her nearer, holding her almost achingly close. She listened to his heartbeat and would have denied his words, denied her own nightmare to save him further pain, but he went on.

"After a while even loneliness became so familiar I forgot what it felt like to be without it. Then Mary came into my life and shattered my complacency. With only a word, or a simple mannerism that reminded me of you, she would throw me into a tailspin. The memory of you again became a palpable thing that haunted each step I took, every movement I made. During the day I would find myself unconsciously searching a crowd for you, or I would sit in a restaurant and wait for you to walk through the door.

"At night...." He sighed. The simple exhaled breath was the loneliest sound Karla had ever heard. "At night I would lie awake imagining you were beside me, that I only had to reach out or roll over, and you would be there. In the darkness I would think of funny things that had happened that day and imagine I could hear your laughter when I shared them with you. The ache grew, until one day I blindly reached out. Mary was there."

Karla lifted her head from Rick's chest and looked at him. She gasped when she saw his eyes. The torment he had suffered and the terrible, naked need that had nearly torn him apart were exposed to her like wounds. "I didn't know..." she sobbed. A crushing pain made it almost impossible for her to breathe. "I didn't know." She

What made Marge burn the toast and miss her favorite soap opera?

A Contemporary Love Story

LOVE BEYOND DESIRE

RACHEL PALMER

...At his touch, her body felt a familiar wild stirring, but she struggled to resist it. This is not love, she thought bitterly.

PRIDE AND
WHAT

A SUPERROMANCE™
the great new romantic novel she never wanted to end.
And it can be yours
FREE!

She never wanted it to end. And neither will you. From the moment you begin... *Love Beyond Desire,* your **FREE** introduction to the newest series of bestseller romance novels, SUPERROMANCES

You'll be enthralled by this powerful love story... from the moment Robin meets the dark, handsome Carlos and finds herself involved in the jealousies, bitterness and secret passions of the Lopez family. Where her own forbidden love threatens to shatter her life.

Your FREE *Love Beyond Desire* is only the beginning. A subscription to SUPERROMANCES lets you look forward to a long love affair. Month after month, you'll receive four love stories of heroic dimension. Novels that will involve you in spellbinding intrigue, forbidden love and fiery passions.

You'll begin this series of sensuous, exciting contemporary novels... written by some of the top romance novelists of the day... with four each month.

And this big value... each novel, almost 400 pages of compelling reading... is yours for only $2.50 a book. Hours of entertainment for so little. Far less than a first-run movie or Pay-TV. Newly published novels, with beautifully illustrated covers, filled with page after page of delicious escape into a world of romantic love... delivered right to your home.

A compelling love story of mystery and intrigue... conflicts and jealousies... and a forbidden love that threatens to shatter the lives of all involved with the aristocratic Lopez family.

↞Mail this card today for your FREE gifts.

TAKE THIS BOOK
AND TOTE BAG FREE!

Mail to: SUPERROMANCE
649 Ontario Street, Stratford Ontario N5A 6W2

YES, please send me FREE and without any obligation, my SUPERROMANCE novel, *Love Beyond Desire.* If you do not hear from me after I have examined my FREE book, please send me the 4 new SUPERROMANCE books every month as soon as they come off the press. I understand that I will be billed only $2.50 per book (total $10.00). There are no shipping and handling or any other hidden charges. There is no minimum number of books that I have to purchase. In fact, I may cancel this arrangement at any time. *Love Beyond Desire* and the tote bag are mine to keep as FREE gifts even if I do not buy any additional books.

334-CIS-YKB9

Name	(Please Print)	
Address		Apt. No.
City		
Province		Postal Code
Signature	(If under 18, parent or guardian must sign.)	

This offer is limited to one order per household and not valid to present subscribers. We reserve the right to exercise discretion in granting membership. If price changes are necessary you will be notified. Offer expires April 30, 1984.

PRINTED IN U.S.A.   SUPERROMANCE

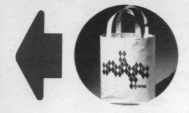

EXTRA BONUS
MAIL YOUR ORDER
TODAY AND GET A
FREE TOTE BAG
FROM SUPERROMANCE.

↙ Mail this card today for your FREE gifts.

Business
Reply Card
No Postage Stamp
Necessary if Mailed
in Canada
Postage will be paid by

SUPERROMANCE
649 Ontario Street
Stratford, Ontario N5A 9Z9

Canada Post
Postes
Canada
021

reached out to touch him, but Rick caught her wrist and stopped her.

"I have to finish, Karla. Then it will all be out in the open, and we can begin to put it behind us."

She swallowed and nodded. He would tell, and she would hear the end, no matter how painful. They would suffer their penitence together, each in his or her own way giving remuneration for the sin of loving too deeply.

"I knew immediately that I had made a mistake with Mary. I used her to try to fill a part of the day, to try to create a time when I would be free from you, but it didn't work. She would look at me with love, and I would only know it wasn't you. By letting her think there was a chance we might stay together, I was slowly, surely destroying another life. I couldn't do that to her. She's really a very special person—someone who didn't deserve to be hurt but wound up terribly hurt, anyway. I broke it off about a year ago, but not soon enough...."

They looked at each other, the pain they had both suffered a raw, bleeding thing between them. They were no longer children of innocence, able to blithely promise that everything would work out if only their love was strong enough. They had learned that love was not always benign. Their own had also been a fearful, damaging thing, a power strong enough to nearly destroy them both.

They were weak from the battle, leery, hesitant to try again.

Karla broke the silence. "What do we do now?" she asked, her eyes dark.

Rick cupped her chin with his hand and traced its outline with his thumb, then he slowly pulled her back into his embrace. He buried his face in the softness of her hair. "Do we really have any choice?" he replied, his voice full of emotion, of wanting her.

The weight disappeared from Karla's chest. She could breathe again and the air was sweet—the sweetest she had known in a long, long time. She was no longer fragmented, she was whole. Instead of being a mere existence, her life had meaning again. "Where?" she asked, not really caring.

Rick stroked her arm, a gentle touch conveying his need to be near her. "I've heard Puget Sound has an island where people who love each other might go to heal old wounds."

When at last she could answer, she said, "I love you so very much." But the words seemed so inadequate, so common. She wanted him to know how her heart swelled at the sound of his voice, how his pain made her bleed.

Rick's hand moved to her chin to lift her head so that she could look into his eyes. She saw his need, his hunger for her, and it was a force that needed no words. She felt an ache to hold him, to feel the length of her flesh pressed into his. It was

an ache that denied all reason. Her breasts, her
thighs, her lips responded to his need with a driving passion of their own. It had been so long, so
very, very long since she had known his touch,
since they had lain together in passion, in satiation.

"Karla, Karla..." he whispered hoarsely, her
name becoming a cry wrenched from his soul.
"My God, Karla, if only I could tell you how
desperately I've missed you." His hand touched
her hair, her temple, her throat, as if seeking confirmation that she was indeed real, that she was
not just another image he had summoned in his
longing. His finger traced the hollow at the base of
her neck, the soft curve of her shoulder before he
slowly, purposely, moved to her breast. His hand
trembled as he cupped the firm flesh. His thumb
hesitatingly sought, then stroked the swollen,
thrusting nipple.

Karla gasped. She felt herself slipping beyond
reason, beyond caring. "Rick...please, Rick,"
she begged. "You mustn't do this to me...I
can't—" His fingers pressed against her lips.

"Shh," he whispered and drew her to him.
Their lips met in a tender, fleeting kiss, a promise
of the years to come. "I love you, Karla," he murmured.

She could hear exhaustion in his voice despite
his attempts to hide it from her. Forcefully she
pulled away from him and nestled her head in the

curve of his shoulder. She stayed there until his breath slipped into the steady rhythm of sleep, then she carefully unwrapped herself from his embrace, leaned back in the chair and let her happiness settle over her like a golden gossamer veil.

SHE WAS STILL CURLED UP in the chair an hour later when Steve McDonald tapped on the door. Karla motioned for him to come in and take her place beside Rick, while she went into the hallway to greet her aunt and uncle. She was immediately encompassed in Roger's enthusiastic embrace.

"It's so good to see you," Karla said, her words muffled in the folds of her uncle's jacket. She heard him catch his breath as he squeezed her even tighter. When finally he released her, Karla saw a stream of tears dripping unabashedly from his eyes. Impulsively she reached up and kissed his cheek. "He's all right now, Uncle Roger," she reassured him. "The doctor tells me he'll be as good as new as soon as his leg mends."

He eyed her critically. "And you?"

Maureen possessively laid her arm on Karla's shoulder. "Now, Roger, you know she's going to lie to you and tell you she's feeling fine. You might as well not even bother asking. Why don't you get us all a cup of coffee while we wait for old sleepyhead in there to wake up?"

Roger smiled at Karla. "She still thinks she has people fooled with that gruff exterior. As if you didn't know she's been bawling like a baby all week.'' He kissed Karla on the forehead before disappearing down the hall.

Maureen stood Karla in front of her. ''All right now. How are you really?'' she demanded. Instead of waiting for an answer, she went on, ''I don't know why you insisted that we stay home until now. Roger and I could have been here to help out a week ago.''

Karla laughed. It was a delicious feeling, a physical expression of her newfound happiness as well as her delight in seeing her beloved aunt and uncle again. ''As I told you on the phone,'' she chided cheerfully, ''no one could get in to see Rick except Steve and myself, and I never came out of his room. You would have sat out in the hall all by yourself. Besides, I'm fine. No, I'm better than fine, I'm perfect. Rick and I—''

''You're back together!'' Maureen exclaimed, pulling her niece into her arms. ''Oh, Karla,'' she crooned, rocking her back and forth in her embrace, ''You should never have been apart. If ever two people loved each other, it was you and Rick. Come,'' she said, leading Karla to a row of chairs, ''tell me all about it. Where will you live?''

''For now, we'll live on the island. Later, I don't know. We'll just have to wait and see.''

''And Rick's racing?''

Karla froze for a moment. As usual, her aunt had immediately gone right to the heart of a subject. "Surely you don't think Rick is planning to go back to racing after what's happened, do you?" she said. It was as much a plea for Maureen to confirm her supposition as it was a question.

Maureen took Karla's hand in hers. Quietly she asked, "You haven't discussed this with Rick, have you?"

"No," she admitted.

"Don't you think you should?" she asked gently.

"Our peace with each other is so fragile right now." Her words were tortured. "I love him so much...I can't take a chance that....."

"Hush now." Maureen's expression was troubled. "You just forget I asked. To hell with tomorrow, live for today. Grab hold of every second of happiness you can get, and don't question any of it. God knows, you deserve it." They slipped into a thoughtful silence while they waited for Roger to return.

The morning passed faster than any of them would have liked. It seemed that only minutes had gone by when Karla walked down the hall to get a drink of water and on her way back glanced at the institutional-style clock over the nurses' station. She realized with a start that she would have to leave soon to make it through the crush of midday traffic. She had hoped that Rick would wake up before she had to leave.

Now that he was out of intensive care she could

no longer justify postponing a trip back to Washington. Since she had taken over the operation, the nearly bankrupt Artists' Co-Op had become so successful that the artists had started counting on the income. Without the money they made during the tourist season, many could not get through the winter.

She had left the care of the store with Maggie and Jeff Bimson, her neighbors and closest friends on the island. They were the artists who had first brought her into the shop almost two and a half years ago, by telling her about the abysmal mismanagement that was about to drive them all out of business.

Although they assured her in her frequent phone calls to the gallery that everything was running smoothly, Karla had to suppress a twinge of guilt every time she thought about them. She knew that every hour they spent in the shop was an hour away from their own work.

She walked back to her aunt and uncle. "I have to leave in a few minutes, but before I go I want to tell you how special you are to me. I deeply appreciate your coming all this way just for my peace of mind." She smiled sheepishly. "Rick doesn't know I asked you to come just to stay with him. I hope you don't mind, but I told him that Roger had a convention in Anaheim."

Maureen laughed. "And you think he believed you?"

"Why wouldn't he?" Karla asked.

"I think what Maureen is trying to tell you, Karla," Roger said, a sage smile curling the ends of his mustache, "is that Rick knows how much I loathe conventions. We have spent several rousing evenings recently debating their worth. I seriously doubt he believes I've changed so drastically in only a month."

Karla rolled her eyes in disgust. "No wonder he gave me such a funny look."

"Were you ever able to track down his parents?" Maureen asked, changing the subject.

"By the time we finally located them, in Perth, Australia, of all places, Rick was past the critical stage. They decided it would be anticlimactic to return. To be honest, I'm just as glad. Rick's parents didn't spend enough time with Rick and his sister when they were growing up to even get to know them. They're like strangers who appear in his life every once in a while demanding to be called mom and dad." The hurt Karla felt over Rick's parents' callous behavior made her want to strike out at them. Although he had denied it, she had seen the pain in Rick's eyes when he'd learned of their decision not to return. She would never forgive them for that pain. It had been so unnecessary.

Karla noticed a movement down the hall. Steve was strolling toward them. "It's about that time," he said as he approached.

"Is Rick awake?" Karla asked.

"No, but I think he'd be real unhappy if you left without waking him up and saying goodbye." He winked at Roger and Maureen.

Karla kissed her aunt and uncle and told them she would be back from Washington as quickly as possible. Then she walked toward Rick's room.

"Mrs. Fleming," a voice called.

Karla stopped and turned around. A nurse was coming down the hall carrying a huge basket of mail. "I thought you might like to go through these with Mr. Fleming," she said. "They don't seem to be slowing down any." She handed the basket to Karla.

"Oh, and please tell Mr. Fleming how much the children appreciate the flowers," she went on. "No one ever thinks to send children flowers when they're in the hospital, and they just love them. I've tucked all the cards that came with them in there," she said, indicating several smaller cards at the side of the basket.

"I'll be sure to tell him." She smiled at the young woman. "Perhaps, if there are no rules against it, he can visit the children's ward before he leaves."

"Oh, they would love that."

Karla smiled at the nurse's enthusiasm. Even after spending three years "on the road" with Rick, she was still taken aback when she saw people react to him with such awe. She had never seen him do anything to encourage or perpetuate such feeling. Nothing, that is, except drive a race car more successfully than any other living driver. *Living driver.* The words made her flinch. She felt a thin, cool sheen of perspiration coat her skin. Rick had come within a breath of becoming a legend. His name had almost been listed with all the great drivers of the past who had died in their prime. Clark, Reventlow, Revson, Villeneuve... and Fleming. Men of such promise....

Karla shook her head, forcefully pushing the depressing thoughts, which seemed to hover within an instant's reach, back into her subconscious. She smiled at the nurse and thanked her for the cards, then she turned and went into Rick's room.

Glancing through the basket as she laid it on the night stand, Karla noticed a card from her old boss at IBM. An image of his smiling face, crowned by an impossible leonine mane of white hair, sprang to her mind. He had been more than a boss, he had been a friend. Without his cooperation and understanding she would never have been able to hang on to her job as long as she had.

When she remembered those three years of mixing work with a new marriage and races that had her flying all over the world, it seemed now as if she had been a study in perpetual motion, a top spinning crazily across a gigantic table. But at the time it had been incredibly exciting. It had been a life filled with stimulation and challenge and glamour. But most of all it had been filled with the heady nectar of love, which grew more precious each day.

Until. . . Bobby.

Dear, beautiful Bobby, her special kid brother—the brother she had been closest to in a family of five boys and one lone girl. The one who'd gone along with every wild scheme she ever concocted and who suffered every punishment from the ones that went awry without so much as a disparaging glance in her direction.

The seven-year-old who had been the ugliest kid on the block, with red hair and freckles and missing front teeth that seemed to have taken two years to come in. The growing boy who only a few years later had become Lincoln High School's star athlete, voted most handsome and most likely to succeed. The eager young man who had finished college on a fully paid scholarship with a 4.0 grade point average; who gave up a contract to play professional baseball to learn to drive a race car. . . .

"Karla? Are you all right?" Rick was staring at her, concern in his eyes.

"What?" She jerked her head up.

"Is something wrong?"

"No," she lied, forcing a smile. "I was. . . just thinking of the hours you're going to spend writing thank-you notes. It looks like everyone in the country is taking time to wish you a speedy recovery."

He reached up, grasped her hand and pulled her down beside him. "And what do you wish me?" he bantered, honoring her obvious decision to leave sad thoughts behind them for now.

A mischievous smile crinkled the corners of her eyes. "I must admit that I'd like to see you out of *this* bed. But not out of bed entirely."

"Wicked woman." Rick's hand moved to the nape of her neck and he drew her to him. Their lips touched.

It was as if he were the explosive and she the lighted fuse. The years of longing, the ache, the wanting tore through them without the least subtlety. It ravished their senses and left them breathless with desire. There was no halfway point, no spot where they could pull back and be left unshaken. Their defenses were gone.

"Rick!" Karla cried. His name became a plea for him to help her, to be strong enough for both of them.

He stopped kissing her and held her face away from him, cradled between his hands, his thumbs gently caressing her flushed cheeks. "Nothing has ever been so hard for me to do. I want you more completely than I've ever wanted anything in my life. Every part of me aches for you. After all the time I've been without you, of sometimes wanting you so badly that I would drink my way into oblivion just to be free from you for a few hours—after all that time... my God, Karla, you can't imagine how hard it is for me to let you go.''

Slowly he lowered her mouth to his. Their lips touched with the gentlest of pressure, the fleeting caress of a flower petal that had fallen for an instant and then was blown away.

"Hurry back to me," he whispered before he tenderly kissed her again.

CHAPTER FIVE

KARLA ARRIVED IN ANACORTES in time to catch the commuter ferry to the islands. As she wandered around the deck with her cup of tea, she wondered how many of the dozens of nattily dressed men and women would live longer because of their daily journeys into the city by Puget Sound's one-speed ferry. No matter how rushed or frantic the pace on shore, the hour-long ferry ride home somehow always managed to bring everything back into perspective. If snaking through the magnificent fjordlike channels between verdant fir-covered islands didn't soothe frazzled nerves, a frolicking killer whale would at least bring a smile. The islanders liked to brag that there was no known immunity to the charm of the region. Even the air carried a heady scent, a mixture of sea and land as intoxicating as a fine wine.

When Karla had come here three years ago, her wounded spirit had responded to Puget Sound and Quiller Island as an injured wild animal responds to a dim, quiet cave. The people, the serenity, the incredible beauty had wrapped a healing cloak around her shoulders. No one had asked why she'd come, only how long she could stay.

Leaning against the railing, Karla impulsively reached up and pulled her scarf off to let her shoulder-length hair blow freely in the wind. She absently ran her fingers through the thick mass, and the salt-tinged air whipped the fine gold strands around her head like a halo. As the scarf fluttered in her fingers like a miniature sail, the designer name printed on it billowed toward her and she realized it was the same name that had marked Mary's scarf. Mary Davies. . . . How long would she feel Rick's loss? A few years? A lifetime?

Karla stared at the phalanx of sailboats that lined the shallows of the island they were passing. She watched the gulls as they dipped and swooped among the myriad colored canvases. Would Rick be happy here, she wondered. A sudden fear made her shiver, raising goose bumps on her arms. She knew he couldn't help but be enchanted but did that necessarily mean happy? Contented? How long would it take before restlessness began to dim the sparkling colors? Before the song of the gull became a screech?

Karla angrily turned from the railing. She hated it when she let herself slip so easily into morose thoughts. She hadn't done it in such a long time that it particularly galled her now. Dammit! She would not allow her newfound joy of living to be so fragile. She would hold this happiness to her, she vowed. She would embrace it with all the fervor and delight of a person who had just come back from the brink of death. She, too, had been given a second chance, and she would relish it, would cherish it instead of destroying it with questions.

She turned back to the rail to watch as the ferry maneuvered through Davenport Channel. When they passed the last promontory, Quiller Island came into view. By standing on tiptoe she managed to get a quick glimpse of her house, tucked back in its rocky cove, before they moved on and prepared to land.

As always, the sight of the town brought a smile of pleasure to Karla's lips. She loved this place. It had charm and warmth—and stubborn zoning laws that kept it that way. Several years earlier the farsighted shopkeepers had realized that the way to keep tourists coming back each season was to offer something most towns couldn't—a carefully preserved bit of history without a hint of slick commercialism. Instead of maintaining a section of the city called "old town," or one or two streets dedicated to nostalgia buffs, Marten's Cove had kept its business district and the houses surrounding it just as they had been for at least fifty years. Anything newer had been torn down or refurbished to blend in with its neighbors.

The result was a tourist attraction beyond anyone's imagination. During the summer season the town's population grew a thousandfold. Space in the harbor became a coveted prize. Lucrative summer jobs gave college students the money for another year at school and their employers the funds to see them through another quiet winter.

Perhaps the best thing about Marten's Cove, though, was the type of person who was drawn by its undeniable lure. Tourists who took the trouble to find and return to Quiller Island seemed to be special people. While impossible to categorize by wealth or social status, they all seemed to come with or adopt their own unique charm when they vacationed here. Crime or even simple rowdiness were almost nonexistent. Thank-you notes to the city council or to shop and innkeepers were commonplace. Karla kept all of hers. She had originally posted them on a bulletin board, but soon discovered she needed a file. Two years ago she had started sending Christmas cards to the people who had written to her. The cards announced the artists who would be selling through the shop in the coming year and how they might be reached for off-season commissions.

As the ferry drew nearer to the dock, Karla could see the Artists' Co-Op Gallery sitting in solitary Victorian splendor on its own tiny knoll. She moved toward the exit stairs, suddenly anxious to

be off the ferry and back into the familiar surroundings of the shop.

As she walked the few short blocks through
town to the gallery and her pickup truck, which
was parked at the rear, Karla mentally went over
the list of things she wanted to accomplish before
leaving again to be with Rick.

Rick.

Just thinking his name made her heart swell. It
was a pinch-me-to-see if-I'm-dreaming kind of
feeling that made her grin like a schoolgirl on her
first date.

She was still smiling when she walked through
the front door of the store and nearly bumped into
Maggie Bimson, who was coming to lock it.

"You look like the proverbial cat in the
cream," Maggie observed happily. She hesitated a
moment to stare approvingly at her best friend
before she threw her arms around her in a bone-
crushing hug. "You positively glow," she said.

The two women were a living testimony to the
adage that opposites attract. From their first meeting they had been drawn to each other like drops of
water on a pane of glass. Physically, Maggie was
dark whereas Karla was fair; her hair, her eyes,
even her skin with its Mediterranean tone were
darker than Karla's. Emotionally, Maggie was
volatile, whereas Karla was calm. But they had
discovered almost immediately that they fitted into
and understood each other's moods as uncannily as
twins. Maggie was the sister Karla had never had.

"Wait until you meet him, Maggie," she told her friend, "you'll understand, perfectly."

Maggie released her. "Let me close up, then we'll go to the back, and you can tell me all about this Rick Fleming of yours."

Karla walked across the shop and glanced out the rear window. "I don't see your car. Jeff coming to pick you up?"

Maggie nodded as she turned the shop sign to Closed and twisted the hands on the paper clock to ten and twelve, indicating what hour the shop would open in the morning.

"Why don't you phone him and tell him that I'll bring you home?"

"Good idea. I'll see if he's left yet."

Maggie's call reached Jeff just as he was preparing to leave. He expressed his delight in Karla's homecoming and invited her to share the stew he had prepared for dinner.

Karla gratefully accepted. She helped Maggie finish up, counting the receipts and posting the sales to the main ledger before adding them to each artist's individual record of sales. As she glanced through the books, Karla was pleased to see that while she'd been in Los Angeles Maggie had sold another watercolor. And Jeff's commission for a sounding whale cast in bronze, which the Whaler's Restaurant had ordered the previous fall, had finally picked up and paid for. Both checks would be welcome after a leaner-than-usual winter, she knew.

"Ready?" Maggie asked, coming down from the storeroom with her sweater and purse.

Karla closed the oak rolltop desk, tucking in the edge of a ledger so it would shut tightly. "Yes, I'm ready," she answered.

As they walked to the truck, they agreed to postpone talking about Rick until they had joined Jeff. He would want to hear all the news, and whatever Karla told Maggie now she would have to repeat in fine detail to Jeff later.

Karla drove the three miles home with a happy, bone-jarring disregard for her passenger or for the fifteen-year-old pickup.

"If I were this...this *thing*, I would refuse to start for you in the mornings." Maggie hollered over the noise, bracing herself against the dashboard.

"This truck loves me," Karla grinned. "We have an understanding. I don't poke and prod around under the hood where I'm not wanted, and it just keeps purring along like a kitten."

"Kitten!" Maggie screeched, grabbing for the seat as they bounced through a pothole. "This isn't a kitten, it's a mangy, grumpy old lion that's about to gasp its last breath."

"Bite your tongue. This truck is a fine example of Detroit's dedication to making vehicles that last." They laughed, a happy punctuation to the pops, clangs and groans of the loudly protesting truck.

Karla stopped by her house to wash the day's grime from her face and hands and to change from her awning-striped skirt and burgundy blouse into a pair of jeans and a sweater. While she waited, Maggie searched through the kitchen cupboards for a bottle of wine Karla was sure she remembered having put in there sometime last Thanksgiving.

"I give up, Karla," Maggie said after a few minutes, leaning against the bedroom door. "You either hid that bottle so well that it will be there forever, or you drank it and can't remember."

Karla flipped out the light and went into the kitchen, going directly to a cupboard over the refrigerator that Maggie had searched three times. Unerringly she reached in and withdrew a bottle of Chenin Blanc from the inside of an empty Shredded Wheat box.

Maggie shook her head. "I'm not even going to ask," she mumbled, following Karla out the back door.

Karla tucked the bottle of wine and a huge flashlight under her arm as she stepped over the porch railing and started to climb the hill behind her house. In the three years they had been visiting back and forth, she and the Bimsons had worn a path across the side of the hill that separated them. Although the houses were only half a mile apart the terrain between them was so rocky and irregular that the island's founding fathers had decided to forgo the expense of building a connecting road. For Karla to travel the short distance to the Bimsons by car required that she take either the unpaved meandering inner island roads or the more direct but slightly longer route back through town. At times the unpaved half mile between them was frustratingly inconvenient, but never so much so that any one of them would have traded their highly prized isolation for a connecting ribbon of asphalt.

The path meandered through a forest of Douglas fir and madrone trees carpeted with a thick underbrush of ferns. The stately firs parted now and then to reveal a spectacular view of sparkling salt water, the neighboring Davenport Island, and the rugged Olympic Mountains. Watching the sometimes golden, sometimes ocher, sometimes impossibly purple sunsets from the crest of the trail had become a nightly ritual for Karla when she'd first come to the island. It was here where she had met Jeff and Maggie.

But tonight Karla and Maggie ignored the pink sky as they passed, lost in animated conversation and anxious to share their news with Jeff. They were on the down side of the hill when Karla suddenly stopped, throwing her arm out to halt her friend. Somewhere in the underbrush she could hear an animal stalking them.

Karla motioned for Maggie to be quiet as they slowly resumed walking. The sound came again,

only louder this time, as if the animal was purposely thrashing around in the carpet of fallen
madrone leaves as it followed them. Karla moved
faster. The noise grew louder, closer. They were
within fifty yards of the Bimsons' single-story
clapboard house when a timber wolf burst
through the brush and ran toward Karla. She
screamed, turned and ran. Before she had traveled
ten feet the wolf was directly behind her, ready to
pounce. Karla swung around and prepared for the
attack. As he lunged toward her she threw her
arms around the wolf's neck. Both knocked off
balance by her action, they began to tumble in a
bed of fern. Before Karla could stop the squirming
animal, her face was covered with a series of
quick, moist slurps.

Maggie ruefully walked up to them, shaking her
head. "This is undoubtedly the most stupid trick I
have ever seen anyone teach an animal. Don't you
ever get tired of rolling around on the ground with
him?" She bent over to pick up the discarded wine
and flashlight.

"I didn't teach him anything," Karla laughed,
"It just kind of evolved."

"Well, thank heavens he doesn't do it to anyone
else. I can just imagine what Mrs. Pahlberg would
do if he tried this little number with her." They
both laughed. Mrs. Pahlberg was the Bimsons'
most vocal critic about someone on the island
keeping a tame wolf for a pet. That Sir Galahad

was taken to visit dozens of classrooms each year in Jeff and Maggie's personal crusade to change the wolf's image mattered not at all. Mrs. Pahlberg was convinced the day would come when Sir Galahad would turn wild, and that when that day came, no one on the island would be safe.

The back door of the house swung open and Jeff Bimson was momentarily silhouetted against the light from the kitchen, drying his hands on a towel. He tossed the towel across the back of a chair and ambled out the door, looking like a huge Swedish lumberjack in his bright red-and-black plaid shirt.

"Galahad let me know you were coming ten minutes ago. What took you so long to get here?" His deep voice sounded wonderfully welcoming. Karla brushed herself off, pulling bits of fern from her jeans as Galahad pranced around her, his tail taking care of everything below her knees.

Before Karla or Maggie could answer, Jeff had an arm around each of them and was guiding them into the house. "Stew's ready," he announced.

"It smells heavenly," Karla groaned, suddenly ravenous.

They started the meal immediately, feasting on spicy stew and homemade bread until one by one they pushed away from the table, unable to eat another bite.

"Let's take the rest of the wine out on the porch," Maggie suggested. "We can do the dishes later."

Once settled into the hand-hewn chairs, with Sir Galahad contentedly curled at their feet, Jeff raised his glass and proposed a toast. His massive hand held the fragile glass aloft with an easy elegance as he said, "To Karla, our dear friend. May the happiness that has brought such color to her cheeks and made her eyes sparkle like diamonds be hers forever." He looked at Maggie and smiled softly. "And may I always be able to give you whatever it is that makes your face light up like Karla's when you look at me."

Maggie blew him a kiss before they all took a drink of their wine.

"Now," Jeff said, looking back to Karla, "tell us about this man of yours."

Karla twirled the thin stem between her finger and thumb, watching the pale liquid cling briefly to the sides of the glass. How should she begin? Where?

"I assume you both know who Rick Fleming is?" she said at least.

An understanding smile lighted Jeff's eyes. "Rick's fame transcends racing circles, Karla. His name is known by people who have no real idea what he does, only that he's the best at whatever it is."

"How long have you known? That he and I . . . ."

"Were married?"

Karla nodded.

"Almost since the beginning. You mentioned Rick's name once, actually. And when you came, there was a pale circle of skin on your finger where a ring used to be. That was a dead giveaway. It wasn't hard for us to put two and two together."

"But you've never mentioned anything."

"It was obvious you didn't want to talk about it," Maggie said gently.

Karla stared from one of them to the other. Jeff, with his shock of almost platinum blond hair and his massive build, who with huge, clumsy-looking hands was capable of sculpting a hummingbird so delicate and lifelike that it seemed to be arrested in flight.

And Maggie, a five-foot-five-inch bundle of energy with black hair cropped in a no-nonsense cut. She could transform a forest scene or a storm-tossed sea into an emotion-laden watercolor that people would buy not because it was pretty, but because it spoke to their souls.

These two special people were her friends in the deepest sense of the word. They had waited patiently for three years to hear the reason she'd needed them so desperately when she had first arrived on the island. It was time to tell them. It was time to finally say aloud all the things she had kept inside for so very long.

"When I met Rick *I* had no idea who he was," she began. "Of course, that was almost seven years ago. His fame has grown astonishingly since then.'' She smiled. "But I didn't even know enough to be impressed when I did find out. I had never been around racing, had never paid the slightest bit of attention to it. When Rick and I were married a whole new world opened up for me. It was like stepping into fantasy at times—at other times it was all too real.

"In the beginning, Rick was just a 'normal' person to me," Karla continued, trying to explain. "The first time I went to a racetrack with him was quite a shock. The adulation, the deferential treatment he received was incredible. I had witnessed some celebrity type of attention with Rick before, of course, but it was nothing compared to this. I'm sure I must have spent the day with my mouth agape. I kept watching him to see if he changed somehow, if all of the attention lavished on him made any difference in his behavior. It didn't. After I saw him race for the first time, I began to understand.'' A bittersweet smile curved Karla's mouth. She paused to sip her wine.

"I can't adequately describe the feelings that came over me that day. More than the excitement of the prerace activities, I remember the race beginning. The sound of thirty cars lined up together, going around a track in tight formation, each tensely waiting for a green flag to drop—well, it's breathtaking. Even to someone like me who had never witnessed it before, who had no idea of what was happening, it was an awesome thing to see.

"My seat was in the pit area at ground level, where I could see the cars pass directly in front of me. They were nothing but blurs of color and sound. I couldn't comprehend how fast they were going, couldn't understand how anyone could react fast enough to steer a vehicle going that speed. Yet they were. They did. I saw films later, and there were several times during the race when only instantaneous reactions prevented accidents.

"When the race was over, Rick's car was taken to the victory circle." Her voice softened, faded, until Jeff and Maggie had to strain to hear. "He refused to accept the trophy or any champagne until I was with him. We were both covered in champagne...it ruined my silk dress. I didn't care, but Rick insisted on replacing it with a dress exactly like it." Karla sat up in her chair and sighed. Her voice became crisp and sure again.

"That was my introduction into Rick's world."

Jeff refilled their glasses. "It sounds like one hell of an introduction."

"It was. I had never known, never even *imagined* such excitement. As if that weren't enough, at the same time I was learning to share my life with my new husband. And, at his insistence, maintaining my executive status at IBM."

"IBM?" Maggie interjected. "We've speculated about where you gathered your business acumen, but never even considered IBM."

"I was recruited right out of college. As a matter of fact, I was on a circuitous route to the job when Rick and I met. He was so impressed with the amount of work I had put into getting my degree and the entry-level job I had been offered, that he was adamant I go ahead with my career plans.'' Karla laughed mirthlessly at the irony of her next statement. ''He was afraid that if I didn't, it would someday cause problems between us.

''Every once in a while I would grumble about jet lag—we were chasing all over the world to races—but he wouldn't relent. Finally I overheard a conversation between two of Rick's racing friends that made me realize how much *Rick* sacrificed, flying to Los Angeles to be with me while I was working. That's when I learned to keep my mouth shut.''

''It sounds as though you and Rick had something very precious going for you,'' Maggie said softly.

''Yes...we did.'' Karla set her empty glass on the table beside her, pulled her knees up and wrapped her arms around them. She stared at the black outline of Davenport Island across the channel. ''Everything was perfect. Probably too perfect, if you happen to believe in fate.

''About two years after we were married, my younger brother, Bobby, graduated from college. Almost from the day he had met him, Bobby had developed a severe case of hero worship for Rick.

Whenever he could, he hung around the track. It wasn't until later that I found out he had been after Rick from the very beginning to let him learn to drive. Rick had refused to even discuss it until he finished school. Then, when Bobby did exactly as he was asked, Rick was stuck. He had no choice, really...."

"Karla," Jeff interrupted quietly, "was Bobby's last name Thompson?"

She nodded, her eyes moist with tears.

"You don't have to tell me what happened. I know. It must have been terribly painful for you."

Slowly, hesitantly, she said, "For someone who had never known death or been faced with the finality of it, it was an almost insurmountable blow. I realize now that I must have subconsciously blamed Rick, but I couldn't see it then. To be truthful, I can't really see it now, but it seems a reasonable assumption.

"When I think back to those months, they all seem to blur together. I've lost touch with them—with the person I was. Nothing seems real anymore...nothing but the pain. It has remained." She forced the words past her constricting throat. "I left Rick...."

Maggie stopped her. "Karla, you don't have to tell us this."

"I know," she said. She looked first at Maggie, then at Jeff. She could see their love, their concern. "I want to tell you... I wish I *could* tell you. Maybe it would help me. But I don't understand it myself anymore—how I could leave Rick, loving him as much as I did—as I do." She glanced out at the running lights of a passing sailboat. "Oh, I remember the words I used at the time to convince myself, but I can't *feel* them anymore.

"I do remember being angry because Rick continued to race. I thought he should quit after what had happened. For a while I even tried to convince myself that if he really loved me he would see how much I suffered each time he did, and that it should be enough to make him stop." She laughed dryly. "I guess I expected him to be clairvoyant, because I never said anything.

"I've never admitted that to anyone." She looked directly at Jeff, then at Maggie. "I've only recently admitted it to myself."

Jeff reached for her hand. "Karla, perhaps I can help you understand a little of this. There are so few 'bests' at anything. There are many, many 'very goods,' but there can only be one best...."

Maggie put her hand on Jeff's arm and stopped him. "I don't think tonight is the right time for this, darling. It's late and Karla's exhausted."

Jeff smiled. "As usual, she's right. Another time."

Sir Galahad and Jeff walked Karla to the crest of the hill. When she insisted they go no farther, they stood and watched until she was safely in her cabin and had flicked the porch light twice to signal that everything was all right.

Home. She slowly wandered through her small house, looking at it as Rick might see it. While comfortable, it had nothing of the luxury he was accustomed to. She walked back through the rooms, turning out the lights, and a secret smile lighted her face. He would love it. Ostentation had always made him uncomfortable; he would fit into this house as easily as he would fit into her life.

Suddenly the house she had lived alone in for so long seemed terribly empty. Without the distraction of her friends, Karla acutely felt the loneliness that had hovered like a cloud since she'd left Rick.

She caught her breath. Was it real? Were they indeed going to be together again? Until now she hadn't dared to trust that possibility, knowing it would only prolong the agony of their parting.

She washed, put on her nightgown and crawled under the lemon yellow goosedown comforter on her bed. Once there she thought of all of the times she had lain on this same bed, unable to sleep—tossing, aching, calling for Rick until she saw the sky turn the purple of early morning. On some nights she had left her bedroom and wandered out to the porch to stare at the stars, wondering if somewhere in the world Rick was staring at the same section of sky. She had clung to that fragile thread of possibility as if it were a lifeline.

They had so much behind them, so many things to overcome.

She tried again to remember her feelings of three years ago, to understand what she had done, but it all seemed so insignificant compared to the pain that had resulted. Not only the agony she had caused herself, but the hell she had condemned Rick to go through....

Karla squeezed her eyes together and buried her face in the pillow, seeking to escape from Rick's haunting words, "I felt this incredible flood of relief to know my life was almost over...I would be free at last...."

How could she have been so blind, not realizing what losing her would do to him? She had never doubted his love. Could she *really* have been trying to punish him because of Bobby? *Oh, God, no,* her mind screamed, *please don't let that be the reason.* She wasn't sure she could live with that on her conscience.

It was several fitful, soul-searching hours before Karla finally dozed.

SHE AWOKE THE NEXT MORNING with a headache and an overwhelming desire to hear Rick's voice. Pulling on a robe and running her fingers through her hair, she went into the kitchen, dug through her purse for the hospital's phone number, and dialed. While she waited to be put through to Rick's room, she dumped the contents of her purse out on the table and searched for some aspirin.

When Rick finally came on the line she was at the sink getting a glass of water. The sound of his voice made her forget everything—her headache, the aspirin, the water.

"How are you?" she breathed, sinking into the nearest chair.

"Terribly lonely...and you?"

"Lost in a familiar land."

Rick laughed happily. "How wonderfully romantic that sounds."

"Just wait. I have a lifetime of romantic things to tell you. You'll soon get bored hearing them."

"You could recite the phone book and I would be in heaven from the sound of your voice."

"Not bad," she teased, "but I think mine was better."

His voice grew serious. "How long...?" He left the question dangling.

"I'll be on a plane tomorrow evening."

"I love you, Karla."

"And I, you, Rick," she whispered.

The rest of the day disappeared in a flurry of activity. Using every resource she could muster, she managed to make arrangements for someone reliable to watch the gallery during the day, arrangements that would relieve Jeff and Maggie of all duties except closing. She also talked her way into an early-morning appointment for the next day with the gallery's tax accountant, to be sure he had everything he needed for the upcoming audit.

The afternoon was taken up with pressing correspondence and the unwrapping and cataloging of new shipments of artwork. When she noticed how late it was getting, Karla left everything and went across the street to the antique shop, where she purchased a chest of drawers for Rick's clothes. That turned into the most satisfying part of the day.

The chest was delivered the next morning just as she was leaving. It cramped the small bedroom, but the tall, seven-drawer cherrywood bureau looked magnificent. As she ran her hands over the richly carved wood she imagined that Rick's clothes were already inside, then grinned at her uncharacteristic behavior. She hadn't felt this domestic even when she was a new bride.

Nor when she was a new bride had she had to fight the terrible, almost overwhelming yearnings that swept through her at every conceivable and inconceivable moment of the day and night. She was so hungry—hungry for Rick's touch, the look and feel of him. Hungry to be with him, to try to make up for the years they had been apart. Hungry to bring him pleasure, to hear him gasp with desire for her, to feel him shudder beneath her exploring hands. To lie beside him in the throes of passion, in the peace of satiation.

Had he changed? Had she? Did he still drink his

coffee with cream and sugar to "kill the taste"? His eggs with ketchup when he thought no one would see? Was the flat of his stomach still as sensitive to her touch? Would he still call out her name when they made love? With the same yearning? The same wonder?

Karla wiped a trace of dust from the top of the chest with her hand. She had a lot to do today, a lot to look forward to tonight. She smiled. She couldn't remember the last time she had looked forward to anything.

CHAPTER SIX

THE FOLLOWING WEEKS were like a rollercoaster ride for Karla. What sometimes seemed like an endless wait for Rick's release was interspersed with nearly frantic activity to get everything done in preparation for that day. She made two more trips to Quiller Island to help get the gallery ready for the rapidly approaching influx of tourists, went to Phoenix with Steve to close Rick's apartment and, while at the hospital, ruthlessly monitored a never-ending stream of well-meaning visitors.

After Rick had left intensive care, his and Karla's opportunity to be alone to discuss their future or simply share a quiet moment almost disappeared. The frustration finally became so keen that Rick convinced his doctors to release him early, with the promise he would "take it easy" for several weeks.

Karla had gone to the hospital pharmacy to pick up a pain prescription she knew Rick wouldn't take but that the doctor had insisted he have anyway. On her way back to the room she noticed

Rick in the administration office, signing his final release papers. As she approached him she saw the bouffant-coiffed woman behind the desk hand him a large manila envelope with the hospital's logo stamped on it.

Rick opened the clasp and poured the contents on the desk. These were the things he had been wearing when they had brought him to the hospital, Karla realized. She immediately recognized the watch that tumbled out; it was the one she had given him their first Christmas together. But it was the chain that was coiled around the watch that made her catch her breath. Her hand flew to her mouth to stifle a cry of surprise when she realized the chain held her wedding ring. The beautiful plain gold band with "forever" inscribed inside, which three years ago she had told Rick she no longer wanted to wear. As she quietly backed out the door to wait in the hall, she saw him slip the chain around his neck and tuck it into his shirt.

When everything was finally signed and the goodbyes had all been said, Steve drove them to the airport. Although he seemed anxious to leave them alone, Karla refused to let him go until she had elicited a promise that he would come to visit them soon. He told her that he would, saying he knew there were sockeye salmon swimming in Puget Sound with his name on them and that he figured it was about time he went after them.

After a plane trip to Seattle, then a ninety-minute

drive by rented car to Anacortes, Rick and Karla were finally alone, in a crowd of strangers aboard the early-evening ferry to the islands. They were made even more isolated, and therefore ignored, by the large number of tourists aboard, all of them attracted by the magnificent scenery surrounding them. Standing by the rail, Karla leaned lightly against Rick's chest and gloried in the pleasure he was taking in his unfamiliar surroundings.

"I don't think I've ever seen anything so peaceful," he said, wrapping his arms around her waist. "I can understand why you came here."

She nestled deeper into his embrace, resting the back of her head against his shoulder. "It can change overnight. See the clouds over there?" She pointed to the west. "We could be in the middle of a downpour in a few hours."

"Doesn't the unpredictability of the weather ever dampen the tourist crowd?"

"*Dampen* the tourist crowd?" she laughed. "I'd almost forgotten your unparalleled flair with words."

"I'm glad to see the years haven't dulled your wit." Rick brushed a kiss against the top of her head. "Or your tongue. Two of the things I love most about you."

"And some of the others?"

"Mmm, let me think." There was a long pause.

She laughed again when she realized what he was doing. "Touché," she said.

He relented. "I'm saving the others for later," he whispered into her hair, nuzzling her ear. "I plan to spend hours and hours telling you of my love for you."

Contented, Karla watched the smooth wake the broad-beamed ferry left in the water. As she let her gaze drift back to the distant outline of Anacortes, she laid her arms on top of Rick's and covered his hands with her own. They remained that way for the rest of the trip, occasionally exchanging a word or two, but mostly finishing the journey to Marten's Cove in an easy, trouble-free silence.

By the time they had docked and walked to the gallery, the sky was a dark gray, the usual showy sunset hidden behind a ceiling of fast-moving clouds. Karla had her hand in her purse to withdraw the keys and give Rick a quick tour of the gallery when she noticed with a start how tired he looked. Suddenly concerned, she tried to talk him into waiting for her while she went behind the shop to get the truck, but he insisted on accompanying her.

The truck wasn't there. In its place was the Bimsons' much newer station wagon with a note under the windshield wiper. Karla unfolded the square of paper, which had her name on it.

We figured your "mangy old lion" might be more than Rick's fresh stitches could take, so we traded vehicles. Keys are in the shop, usual place. We'll trade back again tomorrow—if Jeff and I live through the experience.

Love, Maggie

Karla smiled and handed the note to Rick. "Meet your wonderful new neighbors."

When they were on the road Rick asked, "Are Jeff and Maggie always this thoughtful?"

Concentrating on her driving, Karla stared straight ahead as she answered, "Anything I might say about them would sound too good to be true. You'll have to meet them and see for yourself how special they are."

Rick closed his eyes and leaned against the headrest. "I'm looking forward to it. I have a lot to thank them for." His hand sought hers. "They did for you what I couldn't."

Karla's heart pushed painfully against her chest. "Rick, I . . . ." But she knew it was the wrong time.

"I know, Karla. We have so much to say to each other. Some of it is bound to bring pain . . . but at least now there will be time, and the knowledge that we'll work it out, whatever it is."

He was asleep by the time Karla pulled into the driveway. She leaned across the seat and tenderly kissed him awake, her lips brushing the sensitive indentation at his temple. He stirred, then his hand touched her cheek. When he looked into her eyes, she saw his need as plain as if he had spoken to her. Slowly their lips met. Gently, hesitantly, his tongue explored the soft recesses of her mouth. His hand moved to the back of her head and pulled her nearer as his kiss grew to an urgent craving.

Karla responded with her heart, her soul, her mind. She kissed him back, her tongue meeting his with a message of its own. She wanted him; her body cried out for him. Her breasts ached for his touch.

"Karla," he moaned, drawing her nearer, crushing her to him. He raised his head and looked into her eyes. "Are you really here?" he whispered. "Are you really a part of my life again?"

She pressed her fingers to his lips. "For now, and for always, I will be a part of you, Rick, as you are a part of me. You're my joy, my happiness. I discovered I could exist without you, but my existence was hollow. My days all became twenty-four hours that I somehow managed to get through." Her gaze fell from his eyes to his mouth as she sought to hide the sorrow she knew he would be able to see reflected there.

Rick brushed the hair from her face and pressed his lips to her forehead. "Karla, I need you. I need your smile, I need the sound of your voice, I need you beside me sharing each day." She leaned her head on his chest, tucking her head beneath his chin.

His voice was soft as he went on, "When you left I thought the worst part would be finding a way to fill the hours. But it wasn't the hours that hurt so badly, it was the empty moments. In the morning I would look up from shaving and expect to see you beside me, brushing your hair, but I would see only emptiness. It was as if...as if the whole thing was happening again, only condensed to a few seconds. The enormity, the pain of losing you would hit me all at once, and I would—"

Karla finished, "I would cling to the basin, to the walls, to anything near that would support me.... I would cover my eyes with my hands, pressing my palms against them to hold back the tears."

The hushed moment between them grew into a thoughtful silence. Rick's hand gently caressed Karla's cheek. She lifted her chin to look into his eyes. At last she murmured, "Let's go inside."

Rick smiled softly and kissed the tip of her nose. She could see the weariness in his face, in the way he moved, despite his attempts to hide it from her.

Large quarter-size drops of rain started to fall as they left the car and climbed the porch stairs. By the time they were inside they were both in need of a towel. Karla made Rick sit in a chair while she dried his hair, easily escaping his fatigue-weakened attempts to pull her onto his lap when she had finished.

She found a loaf of homemade beer bread on the kitchen counter, with a note saying there was a crock of minestrone and some fresh sweet butter in the refrigerator. Beside the soup and butter was a bottle of vintage wine.

Rick came up behind her as she looked into the refrigerator. "The Bimsons?"

"Who else?" Karla smiled and reached for the soup. "Sit down while I warm this. It'll only take a minute." She took two bowls from the cupboard, poured a generous amount of soup into each and put them into the microwave.

Rick smiled, shaking his head in wonder. "Here we are in a rustic log cabin, nestled deep in the woods, and you warm our meal in a microwave oven. What modern man hath wrought."

"Modern man had absolutely nothing to do with this. It was modern woman. I had to go all the way into Seattle to find this little gem." The hum of the microwave ended with a loud ding. Karla stirred the soup and turned the oven on for another minute. "Shall I open the wine?" she asked, turning back to Rick.

"Why don't we save it? I'm intoxicated enough just looking at you."

Karla grinned. "I love the way you lie, Richard Allen Fleming. Don't ever stop. I thrive on it. With a little more practice you might even get as good as Aunt Maureen." She maneuvered past his outstretched arms, knowing that if she slipped into his embrace the meal would be forgotten in their hunger for each other.

Unconsciously she bit her lower lip as she sliced the aromatic bread. She was worried about the paleness she had noticed around Rick's eyes and his slow, almost lethargic movements. Should she have insisted that he stay at the hospital, no matter how strongly he would have protested?

It had been foolish of them to make the long journey to Marten's Cove in one day. They could have, should have, spent the night in Seattle. Hindsight! Damn, how she hated hindsight, the most futile form of knowledge.

Karla put the bread on a plate and tucked placemats, napkins, spoons and knives under her arms as she returned to the table. Rick finished his soup, the remainder of hers and half of the loaf of bread. When he leaned back in his chair Karla noticed his color was almost normal again. He took the dishes to the sink, then turned around and looked at her.

When he spoke his voice was low and full of meaning. "Shall we go to bed?"

Karla caught her breath. She wanted him so desperately. Yet....

Besides Rick's need for her, she could see his exhaustion, the fatigue that made him lean against the sink rather than stand in front of it. Although her body screamed its protest, its frustration at what she was about to do, she crossed the small room and affectionately kissed Rick on the cheek.

"What would you say if I told you I didn't want you to make love to me tonight? That I only wanted you to hold me, to lie beside me?"

He held her from him, his hands on her shoulders, and searched her eyes for a moment, looking for an explanation to her request. When he finally understood, he said, "I'd say that you tell a pretty mean lie yourself and that I love you for it." Pulling her to him, he laid his arm across her back and let her guide him to the bedroom.

When he had finished using the bathroom, Karla went in. Slowly she undressed, waiting to hear him getting into bed. She had to fight an almost overwhelming urge to go to him, to lie in his arms as she had said she wanted to do. But if she did, if she went to him now and their bodies were to meet. . . .

When at last she was sure exhaustion would have claimed him, Karla left the bathroom and eased into bed. She was wearing her primmest pair of flannel pajamas, a compromise she had reached with her conscience when reason dictated she sleep on the couch.

She maneuvered as close as possible, wanting to feel as much of his warmth as she could without touching or waking him. She breathed in his scent, and suddenly, overpoweringly, her mouth remembered the taste of him—the taste of his skin in winter after skiing, when his flesh was taut from the cold; in summer on a hot night when perspiration made it slightly salty. As her eyes adjusted to the darkness she studied his face, counting the nearly invisible lines at the corners of his eyes. Laugh lines. Lines that had already been there when they had first met and Rick was only twenty-eight. Lines of happiness, of smiling, of embracing life with loving abandon. Lines that had grown no deeper in her absence.

Without conscious thought, she reached out to touch the curve of his cheek. Rick turned and captured the exploring fingertip with his mouth, touching it, caressing it with his tongue. Karla held her breath when he reached up and moved her hand until her palm met his lips. Slowly his tongue drew a small circle on the sensitive flesh.

"Did you really think I wouldn't wait for you? That I would fall asleep so easily?"

Karla smiled. She had remembered everything about him so clearly, how could she have forgotten his determination and strength of mind? "I was afraid. . . ."

"That we would lose ourselves to lust?" He gently smiled at her. "As much as I want you right now, Karla, I want the time to be right even more. I want our first night of love to be a gift—a gift of myself that will express everything I'm too inept to say with words."

Karla nestled closer, lifting her head to make room for his arm. She fitted her body into his, carefully avoiding the still-sensitive scars on his abdomen and thigh. Her hand rested on the soft hair of his chest.

Rick brushed a kiss on the top of her head. "Karla?" he murmured.

"Mmm." She let her lips press into his skin.

"Do these pajamas come with a key?"

She lightly bit where her mouth pressed against him. "I'll show you how it works...tomorrow."

They slept, each with a smile.

KARLA AWOKE THE NEXT MORNING without the aid of her alarm. Slipping out of bed, she tiptoed around the room getting ready for work, trying not to waken Rick. On her way out her arm bumped the new cherrywood dresser and Rick's shaving kit fell to the floor with a monstrous crash. Karla groaned and reached down to retrieve the contents.

She was amazed when, instead of waking up, he simply rolled away from the noise. The sheet fell from his waist and Karla stopped to stare, absorbing the beauty of his unclad body. Even after weeks of being in a hospital bed his muscles were still tautly stretched over his lean frame, without any indication of atrophy. She supposed a chart on the human male would say that he was in his prime, but she couldn't imagine Rick's ever being less than he was now. He would become the seventy-year-old man who ran and won marathons, the gray-haired yachtsman who sailed around the world.

She continued to stare at his still-tanned back. Karla had never been able to decide whether Rick's shoulders were especially wide or his waist narrower than normal. She only knew for sure that she was just the right height to walk beneath his arm and that his waist perfectly fitted her reciprocal embrace. She smiled. It was all she *needed* to know.

She wanted to touch him—not so much in desire, but in the wonder and delight of being able to again. She wanted to run her hands over the powerful muscles in his thighs, feeling them tense and respond to her touch; over the delineated muscles of his back as he held her to him. She wanted to. . . .

Forcefully, Karla shook herself out of her daydream. Tonight. . . they would have tonight.

THE DAY SEEMED TO DRAG until lunchtime, when Karla had hoped to close the shop and drive home to have a quick meal with Rick. But when the eleven-thirty ferry disgorged its load of tourists they all seemed to head for the gallery. While pleased with the subsequent business, Karla was disappointed that she was unable to leave.

By afternoon business slackened, but not enough to allow Karla more than a quick phone call to Rick to tell him how much she missed him

and why she hadn't been able to get away for
lunch. Never a clock-watcher before, she found
her gaze drawn to the antique wall timepiece opposite her desk like a dieter's gaze was drawn to
the dessert table at a buffet. Finally the chimes
told her what she already knew, and she gently
shooed the remaining customers out of the gallery,
telling them when the shop would reopen the next
day.

The ride home was a delicious, anticipatory torture. Despite her resolve to concentrate on the
road, her imagination took over and carried her to
the point that her heart raced and her skin glowed.
She blushed more than once at the lack of timor-
ousness in her thoughts, and laughed out loud
when she pictured herself trying to explain to
someone why her complexion had suddenly taken
on the qualities of a flashing neon sign.

Because she still had the Bimsons' station
wagon, the ride took more time than usual. Karla
carefully avoided the chuckholes she would have
gleefully challenged in the truck. At last she
rounded the final rocky promontory. Somehow
the cabin looked different—more welcoming,
more hospitable. Karla smiled fancifully. The
cabin looked more *loving* since Rick's arrival.

Rick opened the front door so quickly when she
pulled into the driveway that Karla wondered if he
had been watching for her. She jumped out of the
wagon and bounded up the stairs and into his

arms, the only true home her heart had ever known. Their kiss was deep and filled with their need. It continued until they were both breathless.

"How was your day?" Rick asked, slipping his arm around her waist as they walked together into the living room.

"Impossibly long. I called the time operator twice to see if something was wrong with the clock at the gallery. I couldn't believe how long an hour could drag on...and on...and on."

Rick laughed happily and pulled her closer. "I've got you just where I want you, panting to get at me."

Karla's eyebrow rose in mock surprise. "Is that right?" she said. "I suppose you're going to tell me you spent your day totally absorbed in whatever you did, without pausing to give a moment's thought to me."

"Let me see...." He scowled, his forehead wrinkled in thought. "Perhaps, along about noon, when I couldn't find anything for lunch, I did spend a moment or two wondering when you would do some shopping."

Karla looked at him through hooded eyes. "Oh, is that right?" she drawled again. Slowly, with precise, deliberate movements, she pulled his shirt from his jeans. When the shirt was free, she slipped her hands inside and moved them over the bared flesh, exploring with eager, bold fingers the softly curling black hair that covered his chest.

With teasing strokes she moved nearer his nipples, feeling as well as hearing his quick intake of breath at her action. When at last she stroked the sensitive flesh, he moaned softly and reached up to cover her hands with his, pressing them harder against the rigid mounds.

His mouth sought hers, but she coyly turned her head. Slipping her hands from beneath his, she aggressively followed the narrowing trail of hair from his chest to his waist, then to the restricting belt on his jeans.

"Witch!" he growled. He again captured her hands, bringing them to his mouth, where he kissed one, then the other. He looked at her with dark, passion-filled eyes. "I missed you with every breath I took today," he admitted.

She had lost control of the game she had so easily started, but she didn't care. She responded to the message in his eyes with one of her own. She wanted him.

Still holding her hands, Rick slipped his arms around Karla's waist, crushing her to him. His mouth covered hers in a kiss that made it clear his earlier easy manner had been as much a facade as her own. His lips moved to the hollow of her throat, to her ear, to her temple. She moaned her pleasure as his mouth again sought hers. Her hands escaped from his and reached up to cup the sides of his face. "Make love to me," she whispered. "Please make love to me."

They turned toward the bedroom, but in her fog of desire, Karla absently saw that Rick had started dinner. The table was set. . . .

"Rick!" she cried out, suddenly, terribly afraid of the answer to the question she was about to ask. "Why is the table set for four people?"

"Damn," he swore, a world of frustration expressed in that single word. He leaned against the bedroom doorframe. "I've asked Jeff and Maggie to dinner."

"You've what?" Karla choked.

Rick looked at his watch. "As a matter of fact," he groaned miserably, "they should be here any time now."

"How?" she asked. "Why?" Her eyes were wide with disbelief.

Rick let out a deep, pent-up sigh. "Maggie came over this morning—" he glanced at Karla accusingly "—at your request, I take it?"

Karla swallowed. She had forgotten about asking Maggie to check on Rick.

"Anyway, we got to talking, and she wondered whether or not there was anything to eat in the house. We checked, there were four steaks in the freezer. . . ." He shrugged meaningfully.

Karla felt like screaming in frustration, but instead she started to laugh. She put her arms around Rick's waist and hugged him, burying her face in his shirt when another paroxysm of laughter struck. Catching her breath at last she laid her head against his chest. She could hear his heavily thudding heart echoing in her ear, and she passionately wished she were listening to it while lying on the bed only a few feet away. How wonderful it would be to finally be together without barriers, without watches...without the shirt button that now pressed so uncomfortably into her cheek. Karla lifted her head to see why the button felt so huge. Rick's shirt had only standard small black buttons, she noticed. It was then she realized he was still wearing her ring around his neck.

She looked up into his eyes. He returned her gaze, either not understanding or not wishing to answer the question she had mutely asked. Instead he kissed her lightly on the forehead. "Shall we try to suppress some of this passion with a short walk? I think Maggie and Jeff might feel a little ill at ease if they found us like this."

"You're right," she sighed and moved away from him. "Give me a minute to change clothes, and we can start the exercise-and-cold-shower regime."

Rick started to follow her farther into the bedroom, so she stopped and glanced seductively over her shoulder. "Are you going to watch me?"

"Just try to stop me," he growled. "It's one pleasure I have no intention of denying myself any longer—no matter what."

Timid at first, Karla soon lost the reserve that guided her early movements. She tried to imagine which actions Rick would find most pleasing, and prolonged them with a teasing smile. He leaned against the pillows he had propped up against the headboard and watched her through hooded, non-committal eyes. When she had finally pulled her jeans over her filmy nylon bikini pants and was about to don her sweater, he came over to stand beside her. Karla's head popped through the top of the light clingy sweater and Rick reached out to run his hands up the nape of her neck, gently tugging at her hair until it lay loose and full against the sea-green wool.

"Besides being terribly sexy, watching you dress gives me a feeling of triumph. It's a simple thing, but with such profound implications, a personal, intimate sharing that most people either ignore or take for granted. To me it's one more bit of proof that all this is indeed real."

Karla felt herself swaying toward him. He grinned and caught her by her shoulders. "The walk?" he said, and kissed her lightly on the nose.

"When did you develop this penchant for walks?" A trace of irritability seeped into her words.

Rick laughed. "When I started insisting people come to dinner."

Karla picked up her heels and put them in the closet. "I imagine you had to talk like a trooper to get Maggie to agree to come over tonight." Her voice betrayed her amazement that he had even made the offer.

"I think the expression is *swear* like a trooper, and I had to do everything but that." Rick laughed again and started back across the living room, pulling Karla with him. "I still can't believe I did something so dumb, but she was so adamant about not coming that it became a challenge to see if I could get her to change her mind."

Abruptly he turned to face Karla. His entire posture was altered, his face now serious, his voice husky with yearning. "Dammit, Karla, I want you so badly my stomach is tied up in knots. My legs are so twisted with aching they can hardly carry me."

"Good," Karla answered impishly. "Maybe you've learned your lesson."

He stopped and stared at her. His eyes narrowed ominously before he pulled her to him, trapping her head with his hands. He covered her mouth with his, ravishing the inner softness with a sureness and hunger that elicited an immediate unbidden moan of reciprocal longing from Karla. One of his hands moved from her face to her breast, cupping and stroking the firm flesh with barely restrained force. The other hand moved to her buttocks and pulled her closer to him, letting her feel his need against the flatness of her belly. Suddenly he released her, as if only then realizing how volatile the fuel was that he was threatening to ignite. Karla's breath came in short gasps as she said, "Rick . . . I give up."

He answered her with a groan. "If we don't work off some of this tension, we're going to explode. Come on." He took her hand, and they went out on the back porch. Looking around while he tucked in his shirt, he asked, "Where shall we go?"

Trying to get control of her racing mind and heart, Karla thought for a minute before she said, "Why don't we walk up the hill to meet Maggie and Jeff?"

They climbed over the railing. Rick swore as he stopped to pull a splinter from his pants before joining Karla. "Did you ever think about putting in a gate?" he asked sarcastically.

"*Moi?*" Karla asked, surprised. "Have you forgotten how inept I am with tools?"

"I've forgotten nothing about you, Karla," he said softly. "Not even your penchant for eating Granny Smith apples with salt."

Karla smiled. Her salt consumption had been a favorite thing that Rick had harped on. He would frequently tell her to lay off, saying he wanted her healthy in their old age, that he had a lot of things to do in life, and he didn't want to do them alone. "Not anymore," she said smugly. "I don't even own a salt shaker."

Rick glanced at her, a disbelieving but pleased look in his eyes. "How did this miracle occur?"

"You'll see," she promised mysteriously.

After they had crested the hill and started down the other side, Karla became so deeply absorbed in their lighthearted banter and in the pleasure of being with Rick that she hardly noticed the noisy stirrings in the underbrush nearby. She saw a peculiar puzzled expression on Rick's face but dismissed it as a reaction to something she had said and continued down the path. Before following her, Rick bent over and picked up a thick branch, pulling off and discarding the limbs as they walked. They had traveled several more yards when Rick suddenly stopped, grabbed Karla and shoved her behind him.

Stunned by his strange behavior, she barely managed to spit out, "Rick, what's wrong?" before she became frantically aware of what was happening. A loud thrashing sound reached her ears, and Sir Galahad came bounding out of the woods, his teeth bared in mock menace. Rick raised the branch, ready to strike the charging animal, and Karla screamed. Sir Galahad stopped in his tracks, leaving four skidding indentations in the soft earth. Man and beast eyed each other warily as Karla charged between them.

Recognizing his friend, the hapless wolf let out a guttural sound and took up his charge again. Karla's cries of explanation were lost in the melee that followed. Trying to intercept the wolf before it could reach Karla, Rick met Sir Galahad and

Karla in a crashing encounter that left all three rolling around on the ground gasping for breath. Rick recovered first and made a lunge for the wolf's neck, trying to wrap his hands around the huge animal's throat. Galahad responded by swiping his tongue across Rick's face, the time-honored greeting of pack mates in the wild.

"What the hell?" Rick stammered, staring up into the animal's friendly face.

Assured now that Rick was no danger to Sir Galahad, Karla leaned back on her haunches and smiled in relief at the sight they presented. "That's his way of telling you that you've been officially accepted into the pack."

Maggie's voice prevented any further explanation. "Dear heavens, I don't believe it. Would you look at this, Jeff?"

Jeff came up behind her. "I see you've met Galahad," he said. "I know you've met Maggie." He strode over to Rick, squatted down next to him and extended his hand. "I guess it's my turn. Hi, I'm Jeff Bimson."

During supper Rick leaned that Karla had forsaken salt because of the frequent meals she shared with the Bimsons, who neither cooked with it nor sprinkled it on their food afterward. "After a while," Karla explained, "I not only lost my taste for salt, I found I couldn't eat certain commercially prepared foods without gagging."

Rick inclined his head toward Maggie and Jeff.

"It appears the list of things I have to thank you for just keeps growing. Karla has told me in bits and pieces how incredible you both were to her when she came here and what good friends you've been since then."

"It goes two ways," Maggie said. "We wouldn't be able to live as we do—spending the year round on our painting and sculpting—if Karla hadn't taken over the shop and turned it around like she did."

"That wasn't anything special," Karla interjected. "Anyone who had some business skills could have done the same thing."

"That's not true and you know it," Maggie insisted.

Jeff nodded in agreement. "Karla not only straightened out the books to everyone's satisfaction, she managed to get the ten feuding artists who were the co-op part of the store to cooperate with one another, which was a brilliant feat in itself."

Maggie added, "And she has come up with fantastic ways to publicize the shop, to personalize the—"

"Hold it," Karla loudly protested, scooting her chair back from the table. "Enough is enough. If you lay it on too thick, Rick will suspect that I've hired you to be my press agents." She waved her arms like a hen gathering its chicks. "Let's go into the other room and light a fire. It's almost cool enough for one.'' When she heard Maggie's groan of protest, Karla said, ''If we get too hot we can open the windows.''

Rick started to clear the table, but Karla came up behind him, put her arms around his waist and stopped him. ''We'll do it later,'' she said.

''Actually, I was gathering the bones for old what's-his-name over there,'' he said, indicating a forlorn-looking Sir Galahad curled up by the door. ''I assume it's all right for him to have them?''

Karla laughed. ''I think Galahad has another convert, to his credit.''

They settled around the fireplace to the accompaniment of contented crunching on the back porch. Karla struck a match to start the kindling, then joined Rick. Half reclining on the sofa, he separated his legs and drew her against him so that her back was supported by his chest and his arm rested comfortably and possessively just above her breasts. The room soon took on a warm glow as the daylight faded and the orange flames created a cocoon of light around them.

The conversation was relaxed and comfortable despite Rick's recent entry into the group. When at last there was a pause, Jeff, who had been quieter than normal throughout the entire evening, spoke up.

''Karla, I've been watching you since we arrived and trying to figure out what it is that's different about you tonight. I think I've finally done it...." He looked at her thoughtfully.

"Well?" Karla coaxed.

An uncharacteristic flush colored Jeff's face, deepening his already dark tan. "I've always thought you were one of the most attractive women I've ever met, but since Rick's arrival you've taken on a glow that makes you positively beautiful."

Now it was Karla's turn to blush. She stammered a denial, telling him that he was looking at her through the fog of friendship, but Maggie interrupted her before she could go any further.

"No, Karla, he's right. I can see it, too."

"You're in a losing battle," Rick said. "I've been telling her for years how beautiful she is but she's never believed me, either."

Acutely embarrassed, Karla tried once more to modify the effusive compliments. "It must have something to do with the bride syndrome." When no one seemed to recognize her analogy, she said, "You know, the old saying that all brides are beautiful. I feel like a bride again, so I probably look like one."

A dignified "yip" came from outside and rescued Karla. She opened the door and Sir Galahad elegantly entered, as though he were the long-awaited guest of honor. He padded straight to Rick and laid his muzzle on his jeans-clad leg. Tentatively at first Rick ran his hand over the dense fur, finally digging past the guard layer and into the thick underhair to scratch around Galahad's neck. Large, liquid eyes stared up in submissive pleasure, capturing Rick's heart with astonishing ease.

"If someone had told me yesterday that today I would be petting a wolf as nonchalantly as I would a family dog, I'd have doubted his sanity."

"Galahad's a project of Maggie's and mine," Jeff said. "He's special, but he's not unique. We acquired him in Canada when he was barely old enough to have his eyes open. A backpacker found him trying to nurse on his dead mother's teat. He brought him into town and left him with us. The pup was the sole survivor of a small pack and a five-pup litter. The rest had all been shot.

"With the help of a friend, who also happened to be a vet, we brought him through, planning to eventually return him to the wild." Jeff laughed. "It didn't take us long to realize how wrong we were about that. Can you imagine Galahad as leader of a pack? He stalks Karla with all the finesse of a charging bull moose."

"We started reading everything we could find about timber wolves and were appalled by what we discovered," Maggie went on. "It gave us a banner we've been waving ever since. We joined the Brice Williams Foundation, and they helped us get Galahad into the United States as a spokesman for wolves. That's how we spend our winters now, going to schools and legislative meetings and political rallies—anywhere we think we can win a few converts to the wolf's side."

"That's quite a chore you've given yourself," Rick said. "Little Red Riding Hood has been around a long time."

"And she's just about won," Maggie said sadly. "There are only a couple of hundred timber wolves left in the entire lower United States, and they're hunted and killed with a vengeance Red Riding Hood's grandmother couldn't imagine."

"They aren't protected at all?" Rick's face showed stunned disbelief.

With less volatility than Maggie would have shown, Jeff explained, "Wolves are found only in three states. They are fully protected in two—one has a population of fewer than two dozen and the other has only infrequent sightings. The third state, which has a small fluctuating population because of its shared border with Canada, allows wolves to be hunted. The government responds to reports of killed livestock and deer by thinning the wolf population." He snorted. "The wolf has the misfortune of competing with man for the same kind of food. It doesn't seem to matter that the area we now allow the wolf to hunt is only three percent of his former range or that it is minuscule compared to the areas where cattle can be raised."

"Or that deer frequently become so overpopulated that hunters are forced to go in and *humane-*

ly thin the herds to keep them from starving,'' Maggie added.

''When we became actively involved in trying to protect the remaining wolves, we decided that the only way to be truly effective was at a grass-roots level. We came to realize that apathy was as deadly a weapon as a gun,'' Jeff said.

Rick rested his chin on the top of Karla's head. ''And have you been able to see any results?''

''Some,'' Jeff replied. ''But then it's a little early yet. We've only been going into the schools for a couple of years. It took twice that long to wade through the red tape to get permission.'' He walked over to the fireplace, stirred the logs and added another. ''The kids are our real hope. It's hard to change an adult's mind after a lifetime of prejudice.''

''But I should think the government would be the major, most important place to effect change,'' Rick said.

''Oh, we need the laws, but they don't mean a damn if there isn't public sentiment to push for their enforcement,'' Jeff said.

Maggie leaned forward. ''As an example, in 1974 four timber wolves were released in upper Michigan. It was a well-planned release, and there was great hope for their successful acclimatization to the area. All four died at the hands of humans. It's a sad fact that the wolf cannot live in close proximity to man. Each pack of about eight ani-

mals needs about one hundred twenty square, wild
miles. Put him any closer to man, and all domes-
ticated animals become fair game. And there goes
the wolf. No rancher, no matter how sympathetic,
is going to watch his profits disappear year after
year. To him the wolf is no better than any other
sneak thief.

"With the farmer it's understandable, but it
was only about ten years ago that the Department
of Defense ordered *two hundred seventy-seven
thousand* parka hoods trimmed with wolf fur—
even though the timber wolf and the red wolf were
on the endangered species list." Her words were
edged with rage and frustration and then a terrible
sadness when she said, "Since then the red wolf
has all but disappeared."

Jeff walked over and tousled her hair. "Take it
easy, Maggie. He's on our side."

Embarrassed by her outburst, she looked at
Rick and Karla and said, "Sorry, I didn't realize
I'd brought my soapbox."

"That's okay, Maggie," Karla said as she ran
her hand over Rick's arm. "If I know Rick,
you've managed to get him right up there with
you." She tilted her head back to glance at him.
"I'm right, aren't I?"

Rick grinned. "I do think it was a little insen-
sitive of the Defense Department to order all of
those parkas."

"Luckily several environmental groups found

out in time, and the order was rescinded," Jeff said. "Otherwise, there might not have been any wolves left at all."

"What happened to the red wolf?" Rick asked. "You said they've all but disappeared?"

"Over the years they were hunted so enthusiastically that it became difficult for the remaining wolves to find mates," Jeff answered. "They began to interbreed with coyotes, creating a hybridization that has taken over to the point that the only remaining pure red wolves, it is now believed, are in captivity."

"Are there plans to reintroduce them to the wild?"

"Periodic attempts are made, but for one reason or another they're not very successful."

"It would be a real tragedy if the same thing happened to the timber wolf, and we stood by and did nothing," Maggie said. "A tragedy I would have a hard time forgiving myself for."

Rick reached down to run his hand through the lounging wolf's fur. "Do you have much trouble with people when you take him away from home?"

Jeff laughed. "That's a whole other story. I'll save those charming anecdotes for a winter's fire."

"Anyone for coffee?" Karla asked. They all agreed it was a terrific idea, so Maggie and Karla went into the kitchen to start a pot brewing.

As Karla spooned the freshly ground beans into the percolator, she heard Jeff ask Rick about a race he had participated in the previous year, one that had been clouded with controversy. Rick's answer was lost, though, in the clatter of Maggie's clearing the table. By the time Karla had four steaming mugs on a tray—three coffees, one tea—and was headed back into the living room, she was once again aware of Rick's and Jeff's voices. As she started to enter the room, she overheard a broken snatch of their conversation.

"Does Karla know?" Jeff asked.

"That I'm going to continue racing?"

Karla felt as though he had hit her in the stomach. She stood gasping for breath as the tray slid from her hands and crashed to the floor. Hot liquid splashed against her jeans, quickly soaking the heavy material. They clung to her like a sheet of flame, but with Rick's words filling her consciousness, she barely noticed the pain.

"My God, Karla, your legs," Maggie screamed.

Rick's reaction was instantaneous. He leaped over the sofa and stripped off Karla's pants and shoes, then lifted her in his arms and headed for the bathroom. He sat her on the edge of the tub and began to fill it with cool water. When he started to put her into the water she inanely protested, "But my sweater...."

After Rick pulled the sweater over her head she swung around to ease herself into the cool water.

She began to shiver almost immediately. Rick grabbed a towel from the wall rack and wrapped it around her shoulders before he carefully examined her legs. Both of her upper thighs had turned a bright red. Her lower legs, where the denim had been loose, seemed to have escaped the scalding liquid.

"Does it still hurt?" he asked, adjusting the towel tighter around her shoulders.

"No, the water has stopped the pain," she answered woodenly.

Rick squeezed her hand. "I'll be right back."

When he returned, Karla asked, "Did Maggie and Jeff go home?"

"Yes. They said to tell you that they would take care of the shop tomorrow."

There was silence after that. The silence grew until it became an awkward thing between them. Finally Rick said, "Karla, we have to talk about this."

"Not now." The words sounded as though they had been dragged from her. She turned away from Rick to stare at the cream-colored tile that covered the wall.

"Then when?" Frustration was evident in his voice.

"I just don't want to talk about it now," she whispered, holding back tears.

"Dammit, Karla," he exploded, "if we don't get it out and over with it will hang over our heads like a guillotine. We won't know a moment without my racing coming between us.''

Several seconds passed before she said, ''I thought you were through. I thought that after almost dying you would stop racing.''

Rick breathed a deep sigh. ''Is it really what you thought, Karla, or what you hoped?'' he said slowly.

''Both.'' She answered so quietly it was little more than an exhaled breath.

Gently he said, ''I gave you no reason to believe I was going to quit. I said nothing to—''

''I know,'' she murmured. ''I know.'' She buried her face in her hands. Her happiness had dissolved like cotton candy in the rain. Such a short happiness, so fragile, after all. Not even a full day on her beautiful, beloved island, where she had been so sure they could live in such splendid isolation. A place where they would be away from the forces that had driven them apart once before.

''Karla, what would you have me do?'' His question was a plea.

She didn't, couldn't answer.

Rick knelt beside the tub and pulled her hands from her face. ''What would you have me do?'' It was as though the words had been wrenched from his soul.

She realized then, more than before, that the fantasy world she had imagined they would live in was just that—a fantasy. She had failed to remember how great a part of Rick belonged to the life he had led. How impossible it would be for him to completely retreat from that existence to live the quiet life she had found for herself on Quiller Island. Her fantasy had turned into an obscenity—one that mocked her and hurled its foolishness before her as though she were a female Don Quixote battling with windmills.

The tears broke through to drip from her eyelids and slide down her face, twin rivers of sorrow for what might have been. "I would have had you live here with me...I would have had you love me as before...I would have had you find happiness away from the grasping tentacles of racing."

Rick stood up and paced in agitation. "And greet you each day when you came home from work, as I did today? Did you plan to have me live only for your pleasure, Karla?" Bitterness edged his words. "What about me? Did you give any thought to my needs? Did you think it would be so easy for me to become a househusband, your pampered pet?" His voice softened in wonder. "Do you really know me so little?"

Silent sobs racked Karla's shoulders. She slumped against the cold tile, drawing her legs up until she had curled herself into a tight ball. Did she really know him so little, or had she lied to herself so completely? Could she possibly have forgotten how Rick thrived on the excitement of a race, how skilled he was at what he had chosen to do? Had she become such a consummate liar that she had been able to create arguments and reasoning that effectively denied the obvious?

Karla's heart felt as though it had been torn in two. It was over for her and Rick, over before it had even begun.

CHAPTER SEVEN

RICK REACHED FOR HER, and she came into his arms, clinging to him with a desperate fear. She held him to her and buried her face in the curve of his neck.

"My God, Karla," he cried into her hair, "what are we doing to each other?"

She sobbed into his shoulder, "Don't leave me, Rick. I don't think I could—" Her words were cut off when Rick's mouth sought hers in a kiss filled with his hurt, his need, his love.

Their reserves were gone. Their sensibilities were destroyed by the unbridled hunger expressed in that kiss. Only one thing guided them, only one compulsion controlled their actions—their need for each other.

Rick put his arm under Karla's legs and lifted her from the bathtub. He carried her the few steps to the bedroom and tenderly set her on the bed. His hands trembled as he unclasped her bra and slid the straps from her shoulders. She arched to meet him as he took the hard flesh of her nipple into his mouth. A moan of pleasure escaped her lips when she felt his teeth possessively close and his tongue circle the throbbing flesh.

She panted her need, calling his name over and over again, begging him to take her, to make her his. His mouth left her breast, and the sudden loss was a sharp pain in her abdomen. His hand stroked her cheek and he held her close. When she looked into his eyes she saw concern in their depths. "Your legs. . ." he said.

She was confused. She couldn't understand what he was saying. Why had he stopped kissing her? "My legs?" she repeated dumbly.

"Are they all right? Do they hurt?"

Suddenly she understood. "No," she answered truthfully. In a whisper she added, "But my breasts hurt. They ache beyond reason for your touch." She took his hand and placed it over the pained flesh, pressing it to her with a craving, with an urgency.

Rick moaned. His mouth took hers, plundering, ravishing, coaxing in a greediness that recognized no bounds. She met his voracity with her own, her tongue touching, caressing first his teeth, then his lips. They moaned their longing, their yearning, their thirst for each other in gasping breaths.

Rick covered her face with kisses. His tongue traced the outline of her ear, gently biting the lobe before moving to the hollow below. He touched each plane of her face with his lips as if memorizing the subtlest curve, the gentlest outline. When he pulled away to unbutton his shirt, his hand lingered only a moment at the first closure before it was drawn back to her body as if by its own volition. Gently he stroked her face, looking deeply into her eyes.

"I love you, Karla," he said. His words were a painful cry, expressing his loneliness. His face, stripped of all defenses, revealed his dread of losing her again. His eyes glistened in the dim light.

"Somehow we'll work it out. We *have* to work it out." His voice was a husky whisper. "My life knows no pleasure without you. My triumphs are hollow." His hand moved from her face to the ridge of her shoulder. "If I must give up racing to have you beside me, then I'll never race again."

"Rick—"

"No, let me finish. I can't promise you it will be easy. Racing is as much a part of me as my two arms. I'll miss it more than I would miss all but one thing—you." His hand cupped her chin. "I can't go on without you, Karla."

She felt a sudden fear that the sacrifice he offered was too great. For a moment she almost denied her joy at hearing him promise that he would never race again and told him of her feelings. But an image of a flaming race car catapulting across an asphalt track stopped her. Perhaps the sense of loss he would feel would be temporary, gone so quickly the memory would fade like early morning mist. Perhaps. . . .

Karla's attention turned to other things, as gently, with unhurried movements, Rick began to stroke the smooth skin above her breasts with the tips of his fingers. He moved lower, crossing the firm mounds of flesh with the light touch of an artist's brush. His hand continued to her waist and her muscles contracted in a spasm of anticipation. Lower and lower he traveled, until he met the barrier of her still-damp, clinging bikini pants. He traced the outline with his fingers, then leaned over and let his mouth course the same path along the taut elastic, leaving a burning trail on her cool wet skin. In instant response Karla's hips began to move almost imperceptibely against the pressure of his mouth. Her hands clasped his head, holding him to her. She called his name.

Slowly he slipped the garment from her hips, following it with his lips. When he traversed the tender flesh of her thighs, his mouth moved more gently than a dandelion blowing in the wind. He stopped to let his tongue caress the sensitive skin behind her knees, then moved again until he kissed the rising arch of her foot.

"You're beautiful, Karla. Every inch, every part of you is the perfection I remembered, the pleasure I dreamed."

Silently she reached for him, deftly removing his shirt with sure, steady hands. When she had finished, she ran her splayed fingers over his chest, caressing him, luxuriating in the feel of him. Her hands moved lower until she encountered the barrier of his jeans and belt.

She breathed her protest against his claiming mouth and struggled to unclasp the brass buckle. When at last she succeeded, she unsnapped the waistband of his jeans and took the zipper tab between her thumb and finger. Slowly, with precise, maddening movements, she moved the zipper one grip at a time. As the teeth released, she heard Rick's sharp intake of breath, felt his hands tighten on her shoulders. When the short journey had ended, he pressed against her hand, and she touched him with an aching tenderness. "I love you, Rick..." she whispered. "I need you...I want you!"

He left her abruptly, swinging his feet over the side of the bed to remove his boots and jeans. Karla followed him and knelt behind him, reaching around his waist to pull him to her. Her breasts pressed into the taut muscles of his back, yielding to its firmness. Rick sat up straight and leaned against her, his head turning to meet her questing mouth. She moved her hands from his waist to his chest, finding and touching his hardened nipples. Her mouth went to the hollow behind his ear, then to the nape of his neck where her tongue traced a path below the softly curling hair. She moved to his shoulder and gently bit the muscular line that ran from there to his neck.

She could feel his need for her in the tenseness

of his posture, in the trembling of his arms. Finally, with a deep moan, Rick turned and pulled her into his embrace.

His kiss destroyed Karla's last reserve, and with an eagerness born of years of denial she moved against Rick in the ancient language of desire, a language that required no words, no sounds, only touch. She swung her leg over his to straddle him. His hands moved to her waist, his mouth paid homage to her breasts. He pulled her to him, and they were one.

"Yes, oh, yes," she gasped as the unbelievable pleasure of being a part of each other again washed over her.

They moved in unison, with remembered ecstasy and practiced familiarity bringing each other enjoyment. All the ways, so lovingly learned, heightened each other's pleasure, until it was a power so strong that it swept them both away in the resulting flood. Their lovemaking was an act of giving, where each received more than had been given. It was a sharing, where each tried to make sure the other had the larger half.

In their ravenous need for each other, in their unbridled fervor, they quickly climbed to the final summit of their passion. Afterward they clung together as if parting would let the outside intrude and destroy what had just happened between them. Still holding her, Rick swung around in bed so that they lay side by side.

As they lay entwined, Karla lightly licked the sheen of perspiration from his shoulder, absently drawing designs on his skin with the tip of her tongue. They lay together in silence while their breathing and their heartbeats returned to normal. When Rick broke the silence, his voice was a low caress.

"Somehow, probably because of my keen sense of self-preservation, I had forgotten how truly special it is to make love to you. If what happened tonight had remained too clearly in my memory, I don't think I would have made it as long as I did without you." He paused. "It's not only the pleasure you give me, it's the unbelievable enjoyment I get when I know I've pleased you. To hear you moan, or call my name, or sometimes just when you catch your breath in delight—all of it does incredible things to me, Karla. I feel as if...as if my soul could soar in happiness." He turned to look at her, a sheepish grin on his face. "Does that sound as corny to you as it does to me?"

In answer Karla touched his cheek. Her hand went to the back of his head, and she drew him to her. She kissed him with the hunger he had so easily rekindled with just his words, kissed him with a fierceness that surprised her. She wanted him again. No, it was more than wanting him, she needed him. She needed him as surely as she needed air. She would want him and need him forever.

Rick's kiss consumed her, plundering with an appetite their earlier lovemaking had barely assuaged. Three years had been a long time. Time lost forever.

His unleashed desire tempered his normal gentleness, and he took her breast into his mouth with a hunger that made her catch her breath. She responded to his need by pressing herself into him, glorying in the feel of his teeth against her tender flesh. She wanted him. With breathless abandon she urged him to take her.

His hand pressed into the flatness of her stomach and she moaned her need. He caressed her buttocks, and she pleaded for the release only he could give.

Finally, when she thought she could stand it no longer, Rick separated her thighs with his own. They joined, and at the end of their ragged climb she knew an exploding, pulsating pleasure unlike any she had experienced before. The feeling seemed to go on and on, until she thought she would die from the prolonged ecstasy.

Slowly Rick brought her back from their height of passion, kissing her tenderly on the eyes, on the nose, on the chin. She looked at him in stunned disbelief, and he grinned with pleasure as he pulled her close beside him.

She rested her head on his shoulder, knowing a joyful peace that made the problems of tomorrow cease to exist. She was still swirling in delicious fulfillment when she felt Rick lift his head and remove the chain from around his neck. Expecting him to lean over to drop it on the nightstand, she lay perfectly still, tensely anticipating his movement. Clouds had covered the moon, leaving the room in deep shadow and preventing her from seeing anything but his angular profile silhouetted against the open window.

When she first heard him say her name she wasn't sure whether he had spoken aloud, or she had only imagined it. "Karla," he repeated softly, and she concentrated her whole being on what he wanted to tell her.

"When you gave this ring back to me three years ago, you said you didn't ever want to wear it again, that it had become a band of misery that constricted your life and brought you nothing but unhappiness. . . ."

The words were as painful and as familiar as if she had said them yesterday. They had been spoken in the agony of parting and in the misguided belief that if she didn't make their break so devastatingly permanent, he would never be free of her.

At the time she had honestly believed she was doing what had to be done, that it was the only way she could make him forget her. She had reminded herself again and again how she had felt, with a gut-wrenching sureness, that if she'd remained, or if she'd left him in any other way, the

daily agony of their lives would have destroyed
Rick's ability to drive with undivided concentration. And that without that total concentration, he
would have become a two-hundred-mile-an-hour,
out-of-control missile. That belief had colored
every action she'd made. It had given her the
strength to leave. How could she explain that to
Rick? Would he accept her explanation?

"Now I can look back to that day and see both
of us as pawns in a tragic chess game," she murmured. "I can wish that it hadn't happened—"
she caught her breath to hold back the sob constricting her throat "—but I can't understand yet
how it might have been different, how I might
have changed the ending...."

She told him about everything—everything except the fears that had guided her actions and
forced her to say the brutal words at their parting.
The fears that had convinced her Rick would die if
she stayed with him. Those she kept buried in a
sheltered part of her heart, knowing that someone
who had never felt such fear would never be able
to understand it.

She told him of the loneliness that had haunted
her days, her nights. Of the phone calls to Maureen
and Roger, during which she would wait like a
starving prisoner for a casually dropped crumb of
information about him. Of the days when she
would almost feel her life had meaning again, and
then she would open a magazine or a newspaper

and see a photograph of him, and her veneer would peel away like sheets of plywood coming apart in the rain, sheets that left the core jagged and useless.

At last Rick put his fingers to her lips to stop the painful and futile memories. "How could our love be so destructive?" he asked in wonder, not really seeking an answer. "How could something so precious, so rare, be so damning?"

"Perhaps only those who love as we do can hurt so deeply," she said softly. "Maybe it's the price we're forced to pay for the treasure we've been given."

Rick drew her to him, crushing her with a passion that bespoke the loneliness he had known. They had lavishly consumed the treasure tonight. When would they again have to pay the price? He leaned back against the pillow and stared blankly at the dark ceiling. The hand that held the chain and her ring was curled into a fist that rested on his stomach.

Karla's mind screamed for him to give the ring back to her. At the same time she understood his reluctance, his fear to so completely entrust his heart to her again. She started to reach for his hand, to ask him if she could wear the ring again when she brushed the scar from his surgery, making him jump in surprise.

"Does it hurt?" she asked, suddenly concerned at the possible consequences of their violent lovemaking.

"It's just sensitive," he assured her. "And your legs? How are they?"

Their conversation drifted from the intensely personal to the comfortably ordinary, and they soon felt at ease enough to sleep. Karla's body nestled closer against Rick's as she sought his warmth. Rick clasped her to him, but his hand remained tightly closed around her ring, even in sleep.

THE NEXT MORNING Karla awoke to an empty bed. She stretched, then stared at the sunlight streaming through the window, listening for sounds of Rick moving around the house. Everything was still.

Unable to resist searching for him any longer, Karla got up, put on her robe and slippers and began to look through the house. She finally found him outside, wandering along the water's edge.

Unnoticed, she watched him moving over the rocks, and her heart ached with love for him. He moved with the effortless grace of a runner, someone who was supremely sure of his body's strength and agility. And no matter how familiar he became to her, she always found him incredibly handsome. His angular face and almost black eyes could still make her catch her breath in admiration. And his body! When he was dressed, his leanness was deceiving. Under his clothing he was hard and muscular, with the strength to be gentle. He was only a little more than six feet tall—perfect as far as Karla was concerned, because his body accommodated her own with a natural ease.

She watched him bend to examine some citizen of the sea he had found floundering among the rocks. He caught the squirming flash of silver and stepped to another rock, where he bent over again and released it. Karla stared in mute wonder. The contrasts, the facets of Rick's personality never failed to amaze her. That he took the time and thought to concern himself with what most people would consider an inconsequential sea creature didn't surprise her. What did, and always had, was the startling difference between the soft-hearted rescuer, and the steely, professional race-car driver.

On a track, behind the wheel of a Ferrari or a Lotus or a March-Cosworth, Rick became a different person. She could still vividly remember the first time she had witnessed the change—a short while after she had become aware enough of racing and its customs to really pay attention to what was happening. A driver had made a foolish mistake, one that took three other racers out of the day's competition. After the checkered flag had dropped, and Rick had left the victory circle, he'd looked for that driver with a vengeance, and Karla had accidentally overheard their confrontation. Rick had been ruthless. He had told the other driver that if he ever saw or heard of him driving in another race with less than total dedication and concentration, he would personally find a way to make sure the fellow never drove again.

As the head of the drivers' organization, Rick had verbally flailed rookie and veteran alike for minor infractions of safety rules. Throughout his career he had repeatedly refused to race at tracks where the operators were more concerned with profits than with driver or crowd safety. He'd even lost a championship one year because of such a refusal. About the same time she had witnessed Rick's fight with the driver who had caused the accident, Karla had finally been able to appreciate the consummate skill needed to pilot a car around a track, whether it was oval or a road-racing course or an endurance race. It was then she had been able to discern for herself just how cold and calculating Rick became when he was behind the wheel of a race car. She had looked for that side of his personality away from the track but had never been able to find it.

Now that she was in a position to look back, she could understand more easily why Rick had investigated Bobby's crash with a fanaticism that bordered on compulsion. He had watched films of the wreck over and over again, unable to accept the fact that a minor chassis bolt could have been the entire reason for Bobby's death. When he could find no other reason, he had locked himself away physically and mentally to mourn in his own intensely private way. Then he had begun his odyssey to forget, the odyssey that had taken him all over the world to be a participant in every race he could enter. The odyssey that had nearly destroyed Karla while it had healed him.

That had been so long ago, yet it still seemed like yesterday. But now, after last night, it was over forever. Racing would no longer be the controlling factor in their lives. They were free.

Karla ignored a sudden shiver of foreboding, pushing the premonition into her subconscious. Instead she left the porch and followed the path to the boulder-strewn shoreline. Slowly she made her way over the rocks to Rick. She was teetering precariously on a particularly slippery boulder when her thin slippers lost their grip, and she fell forward with a small cry. Rick looked up and grinned when he saw her standing ankle-deep in water, an expression of disgust on her face. She lifted her robe and gathered the hem in her hands, wringing out the salty water. The lovely crimson garment slapped wetly against her legs as she stepped from the pool and sloshed in her soaked slippers to meet him.

They came together on a broad, smooth stone where Karla frequently sunbathed. Rick clasped his hands around her waist and covered her upturned mouth with his own.

"Good morning," he said, and she knew with certainty that it was.

She smiled and replied, "Good morning, my love." As he kissed her again, his hands went to the sash of her robe and untied it with a gentle tug. His fingers moved to the deep V where the robe met on her chest. Lightly he traced a line down her flesh, a line that sensuously parted the silky material. He stared at her, a triumphant gleam in his eyes.

"I saw the way your body moved as you walked toward me, and I was sure you were naked underneath this beautiful robe. My imagination has been having a field day. Did you come here like this with intentions of seducing me?" he murmured against her throat. "Or perhaps you've forgotten how easily I'm aroused by the sight of you?"

"Neither," she answered. She caught her breath as his mouth moved to where his hands had been. "Both," she admitted and arched into him.

His hands moved to her shoulders and eased the material back so that her whole torso was exposed to his gaze. "Rick..." she started to protest.

"There's no one to see us. I've checked." He kissed the line of her collarbone and the hollow it formed. "You see, I wished you here. You had no choice but to come to me." He squatted before her and separated the robe at her hips. The light touch of his fingers passing over the sensitive skin of her stomach made her quiver. He pressed a fleeting kiss there before he carefully examined the irregularly shaped patches of red at the top of her thighs.

"Looks like you got off easily. There's no sign of blisters," he said.

"It doesn't even hurt this morning," Karla replied, her attention caught by her body's growing need for Rick's touch.

She let her robe slip down her arms and over her wrists so that it finally lay in a circle at her feet and she stood before him naked. Tentatively, almost reverently he reached out to her. She shivered at his touch, a shiver of building passion that was wondrous in its feeling of rightness. As he stood up again her arms went around his neck, and she pressed herself against him, meeting his mouth with her own. Their kiss was unhurried and filled with an aching sweetness, as if they now truly believed they would have more time together, time in which they could love unhurriedly, time to let their passions build slowly. It was a delicious moment that each of them savored.

When at last Karla moved her head to allow his eager mouth access to her throat, she noticed the tip of a sail over Rick's shoulder. Fiercely she clung to him. "I thought you said you checked," she cried out in alarm.

He glanced behind him. "Damn!" he swore. "Where did they come from?" He tried to hook her robe with his boot, but only succeeded in pushing it farther away. Karla started to giggle.

"You seem to be taking this rather well," Rick drawled.

She only laughed harder and snuggled against him, confident the passing sailboat couldn't see her. She was reluctant to tell Rick that the people on the boat were probably too busy maneuvering through the channel to even bother to look their way.

She started to unbutton his shirt, and when he protested, telling her to behave herself, she explained that she was cold and continued on to the next button. Pulling a corner of material out of his pants she slipped her hands beneath his shirt and wriggled her fingers under the waistband of his jeans. She felt his muscles quiver as her hands slowly returned to the front.

"Karla," he said slowly, in perfect tempo with her movements, "if you don't stop that *right now*, the people in that boat are going to be given a show they will never forget."

Her smile broke through, making her eyes sparkle mischievously. "Whatever do you mean, Mr. Fleming?" she asked, batting her eyelashes coyly.

"Only this. . . ." He plundered the depths of her mouth. "And this. . . ." His hands found her breasts.

"You rat—" Karla's breath was ragged "—someday I'll win. You just wait." She could feel a chuckle rumbling in his chest.

"I'm willing to let you try again. Anytime. Anyplace you want."

She nuzzled her face into the soft fur of his chest and her teeth gently nibbled the sensitive flesh. This time the rumbling she felt was a deep moan. His hands moved over her hips and down to her buttocks, where he held her and pulled her closer to him.

Suddenly serious, he said, "I can't believe how badly I want you. Will this craving never cease? Will it always be so heavily on my mind that I can hardly think of anything else?"

Karla looked at him. The truth of her response was plainly written in her eyes. "Why should you be any different than I am?"

"Will you make love to me?" he whispered. "Now?"

She smiled. "Here?"

Rick looked around, then gave a rakish grin. "I see several interesting possibilities, but I think that wide, wonderful bed in the cabin would be better suited for what I have in mind this morning." He checked the position of the boat, then picked up her robe and held it while she slipped her arms into the sleeves.

They spent the rest of the morning leisurely making love, exploring ranges of emotion and heights of pleasure. Afterward they slept, their bodies melded together in a natural embrace. Rick awoke first and curled tighter against Karla before whispering in her ear, "I'm starved."

She stretched and turned around to face him. "And to think you told me that my love was all you needed."

He took her wandering hand and brought it to

his mouth, tasting first one, then another of her fingers. "Nice, but not very filling."

"Can your stomach wait long enough for us to get dressed and go into town?" Karla asked. "I know a restaurant that serves fantastic omelets."

Rick smiled knowingly. "Still hate to cook, huh?"

She grinned back, "With a passion."

"Well, hurry up, then. I may not make it."

Karla hopped out of bed and started toward the bathroom. She stopped at the door and turned around to look at Rick. Her hair was disheveled from sleep and from their lovemaking, and her body was flushed to a rosy glow. Unconsciously she struck a pose that made Rick catch his breath. She looked beautiful and wanton and yet naive.

"Want to shower with me?" she asked, her eyes wide with innocence.

He threw a down-filled pillow at her and growled menacingly, "Get out of here, you shameless hussy."

She laughed. "Why, whatever do you mean?" She ducked into the bathroom just as another pillow came flying through the air.

CHAPTER EIGHT

THE OMELET HOUSE was everything Karla had promised. It was tucked unpretentiously between two large Victorian structures on an out-of-the-way alley. Rick expressed his surprise that it had survived at all, let alone prospered. Although they arrived well past noon and hours before dinner, there was still a long line of customers waiting on the sidewalk out front.

Rick expressed his dismay, saying even a hot dog would satisfy him as long as he could have it right away. Karla ignored his wails of hunger and took him around the back of the building, where they entered through a door marked Employees Only.

"Daniel Olsen, who happens to be the owner of this little bistro, and I have an agreement. I send him customers, and he feeds me without any waiting. Between him and the Bimsons I've managed to keep starvation at bay."

It was obvious that Karla was a favored customer by the greetings she received from everyone, including the latest addition to the staff, a sixteen-year-old busboy.

Daniel himself came out of the kitchen, balancing a tray of luscious-looking omelets on one hand and holding a Pyrex pot filled with coffee in the other. He was muscular, tall and blond and had sparkling blue eyes that came from his long line of Norse ancestors. Even to the casual observer, it soon became obvious that he had inherited more than the good looks of his Viking forefathers—he had inherited a large portion of their devilishness, too.

"Karla," he exclaimed happily. "Where have you been?" He maneuvered his load so that he could get close enough to give her a welcoming kiss. "Can't tell you how I've missed you. Maggie and Jeff refused to tell me where you'd gone.... I considered getting really mad about the whole thing, but what the hell, they're such terrific people I'd just have to find some way to apologize later." He kissed her again and was off before Karla had a chance to say anything. He had either not seen or had not cared to acknowledge Rick's presence.

"That was Daniel," Karla explained with a laugh. When Rick didn't answer, she turned around to look at him. To her amazement there was a glowering expression on his face. His eyes sparkled with fire, and his mouth was pinched in anger.

Karla was so stunned she merely stood there with her mouth open and her eyes wide with disbelief. She couldn't imagine what had made Rick so angry. Then the reason occurred to her, like a wisp of smoke from a far-off fire.

Rick was jealous!

She was stunned. Rick was *never* jealous. Their relationship had always been based on a mutual trust that precluded any reason for jealousy. Karla didn't know whether to laugh or to cry. Reaching for his arm, she guided him to the private back patio that Daniel reserved for the townspeople. When she saw the glass-enclosed room was empty, she stopped and stared at him accusingly.

"Would you like to explain what I saw back there?" She stood with her hands planted firmly on her hips.

He stepped around to pull out her chair. "Whatever do you mean?" he said sarcastically, mocking her with her earlier words.

"That ridiculous display of temper over a friend's simple greeting."

"Friend? Simple?" he snorted. "You may not realize it, but that Swedish gorilla is in love with you. And with you running around looking the way you do, I'm not surprised." He glanced down at her legs meaningfully. She had purposely worn a pair of brief clinging shorts to keep the heat of long pants or nylons off of her still-tender burns.

Karla was dumbfounded. Rick had expressed pleasure over her choice of clothing less than an hour earlier. And where had he ever come up with the idea that Daniel was in love with her? "We're just good friends," she stammered. "Besides, Daniel's Norwegian."

Rick let out an exasperated sigh and raked his hand through his hair. "What does that have to do with anything?"

"You seem to be having trouble getting your facts straight all the way around, that's all." She plopped down into the chair. Growing steadily aggravated the more she thought about Rick's unusual behavior, she said, "You only saw him for thirty seconds at the most. How can you possibly interpret Daniel's motivation in that period of time?"

Rick sat down opposite her, lazily leaning back in the padded wrought-iron chair. When he stretched his legs out to the side they took up most of the aisle. "Karla, I realize that you've always had a tough time understanding sexual signals...." His voice sounded far more reasonable than it had earlier, but his words rankled just as much.

A discussion they had had more than six years earlier sprang to her mind. He had accused her then of not responding to signals he'd claimed to have sent her. That had been during the first week they'd known each other; could she possibly still be that naive?

"But I had no idea you'd be so dense that you couldn't recognize those." His voice rose again.

"Mr. Olympus in there has done everything except wear a sign."

Karla's eyes narrowed. "All right," she gave in, knowing she didn't have a chance of changing his mind, "so what if he is? I'm not acknowledging that it's true, mind you—I'm only agreeing for the sake of argument. Why does it bother you so much when you know I have no reciprocal feelings?"

The fire and fury left Rick's face like an outgoing tide. "I'll be damned if I know," he whispered, his face reflecting his own stunned feelings. "I've never behaved this way before. I can't imagine what's happened to me."

Unable to think of anything to say in response, Karla stood up and went over to a wooden pocket on the back of the door, took out two menus and returned to the table. When she handed Rick one of the tall rectangular cards he absently thanked her and laid it in front of him. He stared out the window at some passing gulls, and when he spoke it was in a hushed voice. She wasn't sure if he was talking to her or simply thinking out loud. "I guess I'm jealous of anyone who had you with him when I didn't. You've built a successful and meaningful life without me, Karla. I don't know—perhaps...."

Karla put her hands over his folded ones. He looked into her eyes and finished what he had started to say. "Maybe I shouldn't have had Steve call you. I have a gut feeling that I'm not going to bring you the happiness you deserve.''

The words made Karla's spine grow rigid with fear. "I wouldn't trade what we've had this month for ten years of peace,'' she said softly. "Let's not talk about what tomorrow may or may not bring, let's live each new day as though it were a separate time, a new beginning.''

"I hope you never change your mind." His words were spoken just above a whisper.

A waitress poked her head through the door. "Ready?" she asked cheerfully.

Karla picked up the menu. "Give us a few more minutes, will you?"

"Sure. If you're having trouble making a decision, however, the fresh fruit and yogurt looked real good this morning," she said as she closed the door.

Rick looked up, the waitress's intrusion ignored. "I can only promise you to do everything in my power to make sure I never hurt you again...." He paused. Karla unconsciously held her breath as she waited for him to continue. "Someday, though, we're going to have to talk about it. We're going to have to dredge through all the old, painful memories to get what happened between us out in the open. I still don't understand what went wrong." His voice, his eyes were filled with remembered pain.

Karla wanted to scream at him to stop. The day

was so bright and shiny and perfect, and Rick's words were creating storm clouds that threatened to destroy it. "Can't it wait, Rick?" she pleaded. "Can't it wait just a little while longer?"

She could see the words forming, words that would deny her request, but then a resigned look filled his eyes. "You're right." He smiled. "This is a pretty poor choice of places to start something so private." He took her hand in his and turned it over so that he could see the palm. His nail traced the line that began between her index finger and thumb and went to her wrist. His lips were twisted into the lopsided grin that Karla remembered so well, the one that spoke of their carefree days of courtship, of greetings at so many of the world's airports. "It appears we have some time yet." He placed a kiss on her palm, a kiss that softly claimed her lifeline to be his own.

"I love you," Karla murmured.

When he looked up at her again, his eyes twinkled. "But will you still love me when I'm a ninety-five-pound emaciated weakling?"

Karla eagerly met his change in mood, almost desperate to leave the other behind them even though she knew it was but a temporary respite. "Probably not," she teased. "I like my men burly."

Rick's eyes narrowed menacingly. "And Swedish, I suppose?"

She laughed happily. "Norwegian's not bad.

But, if the truth be known, I would just as soon not go through all the trouble of breaking in someone new. I'd much prefer you ate a good lunch and kept up your strength. I have plans for later.''

"You're insatiable," he laughed.

Karla smiled. "And you love it."

He met her smile with a devastatingly wicked one of his own. "Oh, you'd better believe I do," he growled. He gazed at her a moment longer before he turned to the menu and began to read the list of over one hundred omelets. After only a few seconds he looked up at her again. "Sour cream and strawberries? In an omelet?"

"Read on. It gets better."

"I hope so," he grumbled.

Karla watched him over the top of her menu, having known before they arrived what her choice would be. All traces of his earlier anger were gone, but she could see that something still troubled him. He looked up and caught her staring.

"I'm sorry about the caveman display I put on earlier, Karla. It will never happen again."

"Oh, I don't know," she teased, trying to make light of the situation. "It's not every twenty-nine-year-old woman who can drive her husband into fits of jealousy. Maybe I should be flattered."

"God forbid!" he groaned. "You can't take as a compliment one of the most stupid things I've done recently."

"But compliments are so few and far between when you reach my age," she teased.

His eyebrows rose in disbelief. "Only if everyone around you has gone blind."

"What a gallant thing to say," she smiled innocently. "That one lovely sentiment is worth putting up with all of your dumb behavior."

"You never let go easily, do you?"

"Never!" It was a cry of victory.

With a wry grin Rick went back to perusing the menu. "I hate it when there's such a huge variety. I can never make up my mind with so much to choose from."

"Have what I'm having."

"Which is?"

"Artichoke hearts, bacon and cream cheese." She looked up to catch Rick's reaction, a grimace of disgust. "All right," she laughed, "try the ham and cheddar cheese. It's good, too."

This time it was Daniel who came in to take their order. He walked across the room jauntily, managing to look well dressed even in his chef's apron. "Who do we have here?" he said, indicating Rick.

Karla couldn't believe what happened next. Both men bristled visibly at the sight of the other. The air was charged with their instant mutual dislike. Rick started to get out of his chair, and Karla almost overturned her own in her rush to stand beside him. Feeling rather foolish, she hid her sigh of relief when she realized Rick had just stood to shake Daniel's hand. Before she could make the introductions, he said, "I'm Rick Fleming, Karla's husband."

As she sat down again Karla saw Daniel's ruddy complexion turn pasty white. "Daniel Olsen," he said with a great deal of aplomb, considering his agitated state, "proprietor, waiter, dishwasher, what-have-you, for this humble establishment." He took Rick's proffered hand, shook it and turned to Karla. "You didn't tell me you were planning to get married." His voice carried an accusatory ring. "How did you manage to hide your future husband from us island folk? Especially one so famous."

"We've been married for six years," Karla said.

"And separated for almost three," Rick added, explaining his absence.

Daniel glanced at Rick, then back to Karla again. "I see," he breathed. "Damn it all, anyway! Looks like I've lost out." He chuckled. "Looks more like I never had a chance. Well, congratulations," he said sincerely. "I hope everything works out for you this time."

Karla saw both men relax perceptibly. Daniel turned to Karla. "You know, of course, that my heart has just been broken." He said it lightly, but with enough meaning that she knew there was truth behind the frivolity of his manner. "I've had my eye on you since the first day Jeff and Maggie brought you here."

She was at a loss for words and the "I told you so" in Rick's eyes didn't help. "Oh, Daniel," she stammered apologetically. "I didn't know."

"Of course you didn't," he added softly. Looking at Rick he said, "I would tell you how special she is, but I'm sure you already know that. All I can add is, take care of her. If you don't, I will." This too was said lightly enough not to be offensive, but strongly enough to let Rick know that he was sincere.

Karla glanced at Rick to see what his reaction would be. Strangely enough, he seemed to accept Daniel's quiet threat without anger and without animosity.

With a gallant bow Daniel assumed the role of waiter and asked them for their order. When he'd finished, Rick watched him go before he looked at Karla. "Nice guy," he said.

Karla's mouth flew open. "That's the fastest about-face I've ever seen anyone make. Do you mind telling me what changed your mind?"

"You can't fault the guy for recognizing quality."

"Why do I suddenly feel like a piece of meat?"

Rick grimaced. "I think 'prize filly' might be a better choice of words."

Their lighthearted banter continued throughout the meal, touching nothing more serious than whether or not Karla could take another day off from work.

After they had eaten, they drove to the gallery to trade the station wagon for the truck and to give Rick the grand tour. Maggie greeted them and insisted on taking Karla outside to better examine the damage the spilled coffee had done to her legs. They all three filed out to the wide veranda, where Maggie remarked in amazement how lucky Karla was not to be covered with blisters. She related the story of another friend of hers who had had the same type of accident and had ended up in the burn unit of a hospital.

When Maggie was assured that Karla really was all right, they went back inside and began the tour. Rick was obviously surprised at the quality of work in the gallery. He told Maggie and Karla that he hadn't expected to find such excellence displayed in an area that catered exclusively to tourists.

Maggie stopped before a painting with a price tag in the five-figure range and explained, "Before Karla came, none of us put anything in the shop that was priced at more than a couple of hundred dollars. We sent all our higher-priced pieces to galleries in Seattle or San Francisco or Carmel. After she analyzed the tourists who come to Marten's Cove—"

Karla interrupted. "All I really did was look out at the harbor one sunny afternoon, at all the yachts worth half a million dollars. I figured if they could afford something like that to play in, they could afford quality pieces of art." Karla's enthusiasm gave her an animation that made her sparkle.

"Anyway," Maggie continued, "after she decided there was money coming into Marten's Cove that we weren't going after, she convinced all of us to show a few good pieces as a trial run. You can guess the rest." She walked over to a small bronze seal. "We still handle less expensive work, too. Karla insisted the gallery carry something that anyone who walks through the door could afford. She's even managed to get everyone to devote a portion of time to creating such pieces, much to the chagrin of a few of our members, I might add."

"A couple of artists thought that once they had established themselves enough that people were willing to pay thousands of dollars for their work, they would be demeaning themselves by doing anything that cost less," Karla said. "They felt they would be undercutting the price of their more expensive pieces."

"It took a lot of talking on Karla's part to convince them that they were not only building good will, they were gaining future clients for their higher-priced pieces," Maggie said.

"That must have taken some real work," Rick exclaimed, open admiration in his eyes. "I know how stubborn people can be about working for less, even if it means more profits in the long run. In racing it's hardly possible anymore to get someone to put in time for a percentage of the winnings.''

"Let's just say it never went so far that we had to offer to buy out anyone's interest in the shop,'' Karla said.

"She's being modest, Rick,'' Maggie said. "She hung in there with one old coot far longer than Jeff or I would have.''

Karla laughed. "I think he's winning, though. Look at this.'' She walked over to a shelf, took down a three-inch ball of glass and handed it to Rick.

"I hate to tell you what I think this looks like,'' he commented, turning the paperweight over in his hand and noting the one-hundred-dollar price tag.

"This one's the worst he's sent since our little head-to-head confrontation,'' Karla said, "but the others haven't been much better. Now look at this.'' She took another paperweight from a lighted display case.

Rick gazed into the clear glass. A miniature forest scene with a doe and a fawn grazing in a flower-speckled meadow was embedded in proportionate perfection in the center of the small sphere. Rick turned it over and whistled when he saw the price.

"And someone will come along and pay that," Karla said. "It's a fine work of art and worth every penny. But this...!" She grimaced as she indicated the first piece of glass.

Maggie laughed. "I've bet Karla a tea at the Empress Hotel in Victoria that someone will come along this summer and buy it."

"You'd better save your money, Maggie," Karla said, returning the paperweight to its case. "This is one bet you're going to have to pay. No one in the world has taste this bad."

Their conversation was interrupted by the sound of the back door opening. They all turned as Jeff came into the room. It was clear that he was trying to hide the fact that something was terribly wrong.

CHAPTER NINE

"WHAT'S THE MATTER?" Maggie asked, hurrying to meet him.

Jeff forced a smile. "Nothing. At least nothing worth putting a damper on a sunny afternoon."

She refused to be put off. "You might as well tell us what it is. Karla and Rick will hear about it sooner or later, anyway."

Jeff reached into the breast pocket of his shirt and pulled out a folded letter. He handed it to Maggie, then, unable to hide his dejected feelings any longer, he slumped down on the oak bench that lined the wall by the desk, resting his elbows on his knees and wearily burying his face in his hands.

Maggie's brow furrowed in puzzlement as she read the letter. At one point she glanced at Jeff, then went back to reading. "I don't understand," she murmured at last. "Does this mean that Sir Galahad can no longer visit Albert Einstein Elementary School?"

"I didn't understand, either," Jeff said. "So I phoned the Board of Education. It means we can no longer take him to *any* of the schools in the Seattle area. Or, if Jamie Longacher's mother can manage it, to any of the schools in the Tacoma area." His voice grew louder. "Or, if she gets her way, to any school in the entire state of Washington."

"But why?" Karla cried.

"Our dear Mrs. Longacher is convinced Galahad is a menace, a *dangerous* menace. And that the schools are recklessly endangering the lives of children by allowing this dangerous menace into the classrooms. According to the man I talked to at the district office, Mrs. Longacher has taken up the cause as a personal crusade." His words were heavy with sarcasm and bitterness. "It seems she has been so successful in this campaign that a groundswell of support has come forth to urge her to run for her district's school board in the upcoming elections."

"You're kidding!" Rick exclaimed. He shook his head in disbelief. "The people at the district office knew what she was doing, and they still allowed her to get away with it?"

"They had little choice, really," Jeff said. "She went around privately to the heads of all the PTAs she could locate and put pressure on them. She told them she had the backing of all the other PTAs and that if they didn't stand behind her, too, they could be held personally responsible for anything this vicious animal did. I understand she even mentioned possible lawsuits and misquoted a few liability laws.''

''Why didn't someone get in touch with us to let us know what was going on?'' Maggie raged.

Jeff's hands hung loosely between his knees. ''I guess no one took her seriously enough. She was very clever. She told everyone she contacted to delay any action until she was sure the districts weren't going to do something on their own. Of course the districts just considered her a lone disgruntled voice. They had no idea she was planning to run for office and needed an emotional issue to unseat one of the incumbents.''

Maggie sank down on the bench beside Jeff. ''Now what?'' she asked in a sad, disheartened voice.

''I'm going to Seattle tomorrow to see what I can do. I'll contact some of the people I know in different environmental groups and see what kind of support they can muster for us.'' He put his arm around his wife's shoulders and drew her to him.

''Is there anything Karla or I can do?'' Rick asked gently.

Jeff looked up, a small resigned grin playing at the corners of his mouth. ''Welcome to the fold, Rick. Don't think for a minute that I'll hesitate to call on you once I know the direction we have to take.''

They mechanically went through the motions of closing the gallery. After everything was secured, they stood in the back parking lot for a few minutes, trying to think of something cheerful to say before finally giving up and bidding one another good-night. Karla and Rick waved as the station wagon disappeared around the building.

Karla turned to Rick. "Want to drive?" she asked, holding out the keys.

Rick looked at her outstretched hand. He glanced at the truck. "Is it safe?" he joked dryly.

Karla covered her heart and gasped as though she had been wounded. "How can you say such a thing?" She looked lovingly at the truck. "Have you ever seen a vehicle more artistically designed? One more beautifully or originally molded? Look at these." She walked to the truck and ran her hand over several dents and dings. "How often have you seen this breathtaking patina so masterfully applied?" She ran her finger over a particularly thick coating of reddish orange rust and held it out for his inspection.

Rick took her finger and pressed it to the end of her nose. "Now that is what I call *masterfully applied*."

She vigorously wiped the back of her hand across her nose, turning it as red from the friction as it had been from the rust. Then she looked at Rick and grumbled, "I don't know about you types who can't appreciate true art."

He grinned and reached for her. "Come here, woman. I'll show you what I appreciate."

"Just as I suspected," she said, wrapping her arms around his waist. "You're only after my body, you care nothing for my fine mind."

He nibbled her neck. "Body first, mind later."

She sighed. "Don't start something you're not prepared to finish," she warned. "Once aroused, I'm uncontrollable."

"Promises, promises," he murmured between quick kisses.

A fleeting thought struck Karla, and she leaned her head heavily against Rick's chest.

"What's wrong?" Rick coaxed, sensing her change in mood.

"I feel a little guilty hoarding such happiness when Jeff and Maggie's world has been tilted off balance."

"It will all work out okay." She could feel Rick's chin press into the top of her head with each word.

"How can you be so sure?"

"They're the good guys." His voice was full of confidence.

Karla smiled. It was so like Rick to assume the side of right would win no matter what the obstacles. She had decided long ago that either he didn't know, or he had never accepted, the fact that there wasn't a knight in shining armor standing around every corner ready to come to the aid of good causes.

"Still a cockeyed optimist, huh?" she asked.

Rick pulled her tighter to him. "It hasn't failed me yet. Only been a little slower than I would have liked sometimes," he said meaningfully.

Karla looked up and saw his love for her radiating from his eyes. He dipped his head slightly and kissed her. She was filled with a need to tell him how much she loved him, but nowhere in her mind could she find words to express the depth of her feelings. They stood for a few more minutes, silently locked in each other's embrace, before Rick turned and led her toward the truck, his arm resting lightly across her shoulders.

"You drive," he said. "I have a feeling your charming vehicle's idiosyncrasies are beyond me this evening."

BUT TWO WEEKS LATER, when Rick had walked the three miles into town to accompany Karla home, he gratefully took the keys from her outstretched hand.

"It's not that I don't think you're a terrific driver, Karla," he said seriously. "It's just that my teeth have begun to work loose."

She playfully punched him in the arm. "I get you where you want to go, don't I?"

On the way home that evening they sailed over the rough road far more smoothly than Karla had ever made the journey. Rick effortlessly missed most of the pits and holes she had come to accept as inevitable. When they had pulled up in the driveway, Karla hopped out of the truck and glared back at it. "Don't get spoiled," she muttered threateningly.

While she waited for Rick to walk around and join her, she heard the phone ring. Her heart jumped, because she automatically thought of another time she had been greeted by a ringing telephone. Her gaze flew to Rick—he was here, he was safe. To cover the fear she knew he would be able to see, she smiled quickly and issued a challenge. "I'll race you!"

Rick smiled back. "You're on."

They bounded up the stairs, across the porch and to the front door in a dead heat. They made it to the phone before it had stopped ringing. Karla picked it up.

"Hello," she said breathlessly.

"Karla?"

It was Steve McDonald. "Yes, Steve. It's me."

"Is Rick around?" he asked tentatively.

Karla laughed. She could tell by Steve's tone of voice that his overactive imagination had assigned more complicated reasons for her breathlessness than simply racing up a flight of stairs. "He's right here." She handed the receiver to Rick.

While the men exchanged greetings, Karla went to the bedroom and changed. When she returned she mimed drinking a cup of coffee. Rick nodded, and she moved past him to start a pot brewing.

"That's great!" she heard Rick say, and then, "Where?"

"Hey, do me a favor, will you?" There was an infinitesimal pause while he confidently waited for an affirmative answer before going on. "Stop by Seattle and see if you can talk Michael Whittaker into coming up with you for a few days. Tell him I'll arrange for a boat and guarantee him the best company he's had since the night we all went with Paddington after the race at Nürburgring."

Rick laughed. "I didn't say as wild a time, only as good."

There was another pause during which the smile left Rick's face, and a sadness stole into his eyes. "How is she?" he said.

Karla's heart skipped a beat. She felt as though she was eavesdropping on something she shouldn't hear, something she didn't want to hear. She started to move into the other room, but as she passed Rick he reached out and drew her onto his lap.

"Let me know if there is something I can do. All right. See you later then." He gently, thoughtfully put the receiver back on its hook. Karla looked at him expectantly.

"Steve's coming for that visit you talked him into," Rick said.

Karla smiled. "I'm glad. I want him to think of our home as his." She waited, but it soon became obvious that Rick had no intention of offering any more information.

"Who is Michael Whittaker?" she softly prodded.

"An old friend. We go back over ten years."

Karla knew that any other information about the phone call was either going to have to be pried out a piece at a time, or left alone to drift out by itself in later conversations. She decided not to pry even though she desperately wanted to ask if it was Mary Davies whom Rick had asked about. She could imagine all too well how Mary was doing, how she was feeling. Karla didn't need anyone to freshen her memory. She needed nothing to recall how empty the days were without Rick.

She thought about the graceful, willowy woman who had so completely fallen in love with Rick. From what Steve had said, it seemed Mary had been in love with him for years, even before she herself had come along. Karla had destroyed Mary's dream. And when it appeared that Mary might have had a chance after all, it had led to a brief, disillusioning love affair.

As sorry as Karla felt for her, and as much as she could empathize with the pain that Mary must now be suffering, she still felt an intense, gnawing jealousy when she thought of Mary lying with Rick.

It was easy to rationalize on an intellectual plane why the affair had happened, and to feel sorrow for the tragic consequences Mary had had to pay. But on an irrational, emotional plane, thinking of them together and knowing how desperately Mary had loved Rick, how longingly Rick had sought comfort in her embrace, Karla hated Mary. She hated her with an unreasonable ferocity, for loving Rick enough to stay beside him when Karla herself had fled, abandoning the very love that Mary futilely sought.

With a small corner of her heart Karla hated Mary, even though she knew that on the whole it wasn't hate she felt but grudging admiration. She knew with painful certainty that, in her place, Mary would never have left Rick. She would never have put him through a three-year sentence in hell. Knowing all this made Karla doubt her worthiness to be loved by Rick. Would she *ever* understand what had driven her three years ago? Why she had chosen flight instead of finding some way, any way, to work things out?

She started to get up from Rick's lap, but he held her there. She could tell by the way he looked at her that he knew something was wrong.

"What is it, Karla?"

"I was just wondering where we're going to put Michael Whittaker and Steve," she lied. "Do you suppose they would mind sleeping together? We could clear out the back bedroom and put them in there. Or—"

"What's *really* troubling you?" he insisted.

"Nothing!" she said, louder than she had intended and far less convincingly.

Rick reached up to cup her face between his hands. He held her so that she had to look at him. "Why won't you tell me?" he asked softly. "Are we to have secrets from each other? Secrets that cause such torment?"

"They're foolish, petty thoughts that I would just as soon not share."

"About Mary?" He touched her cheek with the back of his fingers in a fleeting caress.

"How did you know?" Karla stared at her hands, which were tightly folded in her lap.

"It wasn't too hard to figure out." Softly he added, "Can we talk about her, Karla? Can we get what happened out in the open and then leave it behind us once and for all?"

"Do you know that she still loves you?" she finally asked.

"Yes," he answered simply.

"Did you ever love her?"

"No."

"...make love to her?"

Softly, "Yes."

Now she knew for a fact what she had only guessed before. It hurt far more than she had imagined it would. She closed her eyes against the pain. "Why didn't you love her?"

"I tried. But my heart was so filled with you that I found there was no room for anyone else."

"She's so beautiful...."

"Look at me, Karla," Rick demanded.

Their eyes met. She saw his soul in the look that he gave her. It spoke to her as no words could, telling her of a love as great, as all-consuming as her own. She knew that to Rick she was the beauty of his life.

"I love you," he said. "I cannot erase what happened between Mary and myself, and I can't keep telling you that I'm sorry it happened. We must find a way to ease your mind about it so that it never comes between us again. Do you understand?"

She nodded.

"What can I do to help you understand what happened, to help you to forget?"

"It isn't what you think, Rick," Karla began. "Oh, a part of me recoils when I close my eyes and picture you together, but that isn't what ties me in knots when I think about Mary. . . . It's knowing how I failed you, knowing how much more she deserves your love than I do." The tears she had managed to hold back until then spilled over her lashes, and she quickly reached up to wipe them away. She felt Rick stiffen. He rubbed his hand across his forehead.

"Why would you say something like that?" His voice was edged in anger. "Since when has our love needed a scorecard, to be dished out according to how deserving we are? You sound like you would willingly turn me over to Mary if it were possible." His gaze bored into her, his eyes cold.

"What would you do then, Karla? Wear a hair shirt as punishment? Come and watch Mary and me together so that you could punish yourself a little more? What in the hell has happened to your backbone?"

Karla tried to move away from him, but he caught her arms and held her in a viselike grip.

"What happened to the woman I once knew?" he demanded. "How did such a coward sneak in and take her place?"

Karla felt as though he had struck her. She drew away from him, stunned. "How can you say such a thing?" she cried, no longer fighting the tears that now coursed down her cheeks. "It took a lot more guts for me to stay away from you than it would have taken to come back."

"Oh, come on, Karla. There isn't another person alive who would consider running away to bury herself on an island an act of bravery. Cowards run away." His words were a scathing indictment.

He had only said what she'd already told herself a hundred times over, but she couldn't let him believe that of her. She had to defend herself against his attack.

"I left you because I thought it was the only way I could keep from killing you. I left you even though I loved you a thousand times more than I did on the day we were married. It tore me apart so badly that if I had not had someplace dark and private to crawl away to, I felt I would have died from the pain." She wrenched away from him. "How dare you call me a coward! Had I been less brave I would have stayed and chanced your life. I would have stayed and...." She choked on the words and was unable to continue.

When she saw Rick start toward her she tried to run for the door, but he caught her and held her against the wall. "Not again, Karla. Never again will you run away from me. I'm sorry I said what I did, but it was the only way I knew to get you to talk to me. I've tried everything else." His voice cracked as he spoke.

Karla wearily leaned her head against his shoulder, all of her fight gone. Rick's hands smoothed her hair as he asked, "Why did you think you would be responsible for my death?"

She didn't want to answer. She only wanted to lean against him and have him hold her until the pain eased and they were one again. "I became so afraid that something would happen to you, that you would get in a wreck like Bobby's, that I almost went out of my mind. You must remember how strangely I behaved back then—each hour a little worse as a new race day approached."

"I remember."

"I began to believe my fears would spread to you...that in the middle of a race your concentration would falter. That you would die because of it and I would be the one to blame."

Rick held her away from him, his forehead furrowed in puzzlement. His dark eyes were weary.
"How could you honestly believe that?" His voice
was filled with wonder. "You've always known
that when I race there's nothing else, that I completely close off the rest of the world. I would
never have gone as far as I have in racing if I
hadn't been able to isolate my thoughts and give
my full concentration to what I was doing. You've
always known that, Karla."

"Please, Rick...please understand." Her voice
was a whisper that begged him to listen as poignantly as though it were a shout. "I believed it and
it terrified me."

"Why didn't you tell me?" he asked, skepticism
cloaking the words and making them daggers.

"I couldn't." A sudden chill made her grasp her
arms. "I tried, but then I knew you would never
let me leave and that once you knew how I felt,
each race would be even more dangerous for you,
knowing how I suffered while you were on the
track."

He turned away from her and ran his hands
roughly through his hair, his face a mask of torment and confusion. His hand was on the back of
his neck when he turned back to look at her. "This
is why you left me?" His words were said in an in-
credulous staccato. "Why you told me you no
longer loved me...that life with me was hell for
you?"

"You *don't* understand," Karla sobbed.

He stared at her, his eyes full of anger and pain. "You're right, Karla. I don't." He yanked his jacket from the back of a chair, flung open the door and walked out into the rain.

It was an unexpected rain, a rain that had started to fall at the same time as Karla's tears. Karla ran to the closet and grabbed her poncho, but by the time she had arrived back at the door, Rick had disappeared. She stood on the porch and scanned the dense woods, finally catching sight of his bright red Pendelton jacket as he disappeared into the thick Douglas fir. Carelessly running after him, she slipped several times on the rain-slick soil, falling to her hands and knees, then quickly getting to her feet again.

He didn't understand! The words rang through her mind like a loudly clanging bell, incessantly repeating its terrifying message. She crested the first hill and looked through the trees for a sign of him or for an indication he had passed that way.

"Rick!" she shouted. His name became a plea for him to answer her. "Rick," she repeated, only less loudly this time. She said his name again and again until it was little more than a sob, then she leaned against the trunk of a madrone. Her salty tears mixed with rain and dripped down inside the collar on her apple-green poncho.

He didn't understand. Karla sank to the ground. She leaned against the ragged peeling bark on the trunk, oblivious to the increasing storm. Nothing mattered anymore; what she had feared had come true. And how could she change it? How could she make Rick understand something she no longer understood herself?

She had no idea how long she had been curled up between the two massive roots at the base of the madrone when she became aware of Rick standing over her. In the tension between them she became keenly aware of the sounds of the forest. Somewhere above her a bird shook itself violently, creating its own miniature storm. High in the trees tiny drops of water slid from one leaf to the next, gathering momentum on their downward journey until they splashed to the forest floor below, an incongruously happy sound.

"Get up, Karla. We're going home."

He made no effort to help her as she slowly rose from her cramped position. They walked down the hill in silence. The only sound that marked their passage was the soft swish of ferns slapping against their blue-jeaned calves. When they were inside the now cold living room, Karla turned to Rick. He tried to walk past her, but she reached out to stop him, her hand resting on his arm. The look of disappointment and anger he directed toward her made Karla catch her breath. But more painful still was the hurt she saw in his eyes. "Rick, I . . ." she stammered.

"Not now, Karla," he said tiredly and removed her hand. He started toward the bedroom.

"Damn you!" she sobbed.

He stopped and slowly turned to stare at her. She had never seen him so defeated, so lost.

"I told you I didn't want to talk about it," she said. "Why couldn't we have left it alone? Does what did or didn't happen three years ago have to destroy what we have now?"

His eyes grew cold and his stance rigid. In a precise, clipped voice, he asked, "And how am I to know that sometime in the future you won't decide again that you should leave me for my own good?"

Karla stood frozen, unable to breathe, unable to move. She began to sway, and she felt like the room was spinning around her. She was going to be sick. As she turned and made her way to the bathroom, she was only marginally aware that Rick had gone into the bedroom.

Their Camelot was mythical after all. Princes and princesses only lived happily ever after in fairy tales.

Karla sat on the edge of the bathtub staring unseeingly at the closed door until the room grew so dark she could no longer make out the fine-grained pattern on the wood. She roused herself and went to the sink to brush her teeth and wash her face. She splashed water on her puffy eyes. When she left the bathroom she discovered that the house was completely dark. Only the soft sounds of rain blowing against the window broke the silence. She easily made her way along the familiar path to her dresser, where she took out a nightgown before she went back to the living room, planning to sleep on the couch.

She wasn't aware of how purposely slow her movements were until she quietly closed the bedroom door. It was then she realized how much she had wanted Rick to say something that would have stopped her from leaving.

The fire was laid in the stone-and-brick fireplace and only needed a match to bring it crackling to life. Karla stared at the dancing flames for a long time before she finally went over to the old captain's chest under the window and took out a large comforter and a pillow. Rather than lie on the couch, she sat in the chair Jeff always claimed when he visited, and tucked her feet under her legs, draping the downy quilt around her. She knew she wouldn't sleep. Memories and "might have beens" would keep her awake until dawn brought its permission to start another day.

Only three months ago it had seemed an impossible dream to have Rick with her again. Now the dream had turned into a nightmare, one that was not going to disappear by so simple a thing as waking.

As she stared into the fire, Karla kept telling herself that she should do something, plan something—that if she didn't, this time it would be Rick who would leave. He would leave, and he would never come back. But she was too numb to think clearly, too deeply mired in the pain she had seen in Rick's eyes.

She didn't hear the bedroom door open, she only knew that one moment Rick was beside her, where he hadn't been before.

"Come to bed, Karla." He held out his hand to her.

She looked up into his eyes and knew nothing had changed. There was a wall between them where there had been open fields before. She started to refuse but didn't have the strength to argue, so instead she put her hand in his and let him impersonally lead her into the bedroom.

They lay side by side, neither sleeping, neither touching the other. Her bed had never felt more lonely. The barrier between them had grown so monstrous that she was actually afraid that she might accidentally brush against Rick when she turned onto her side. The realization made her heart ache.

They had lain together a few minutes—an eternity—when Rick asked, "How could you believe that, Karla? How could you believe my training would desert me, that I would suddenly become prey to wandering emotions while in the middle of a race?" His words betrayed more than his desire to know the answer; it told of his desperate need.

How could she answer him? She had already tried. She knew no other words to make him understand. Hoping to reach him with her love, she opened her hand to touch him. As her hand brushed his arm she felt him recoil from her, and she knew a despair that made her wish she were dead. Her hand flew to her mouth to stifle a cry of pain. Before it reached its goal, however, she found herself being enfolded in Rick's arms, being crushed in an embrace that pulled her hurt from her and made her weep tears of relief. She was in his arms again. She was home.

Rick whispered his love for her into the soft hair of her temple as he held her close and waited for her sobs to subside. When she was finally still, he said, "Forgive me, Karla. I had no right to question your reasons for leaving me. Whatever they were, I know that at the time you must have felt them so strongly you thought you had no choice. I cannot understand what you did, Karla, but—"

She stopped him with a kiss that turned the coin from hurt to healing.

Rick groaned and pulled her on top of him. His hands held the sides of her face, his fingers in her hair. "Karla, my beautiful, Karla." He brought her mouth to his and explored it with a fierce tenderness. "Love me, Karla," he poignantly begged. "Fill my life so completely that I will no longer be able to remember the pain."

She looked deeply into his eyes. Slowly she said,

"I will love you with every breath, with every thought and with every fiber of my being—for now and for always." She kissed him, trying to reiterate her words with the touch of her lips. Her mouth moved over his face, his neck, his chest, until his breathing became ragged with desire. She touched him until he knew the same incredible paths of ecstasy she had traveled because of his skill.

And then he made love to her—slowly, maddeningly, bringing her near fulfillment, then making her wait until the moment was perfect, and she was left deliciously spent. When their lovemaking slowed to the comfortable silence before sleep, Rick drew her to him once again. He held her tightly and they clung to each other in a need beyond passion. They remained locked together until dawn colored the room with golden promise.

CHAPTER TEN

MONDAY WAS KARLA'S DAY OFF WORK, and the day Steve and Michael Whittaker were to arrive. She and Rick had an unspoken agreement not to talk about their earlier argument, each obviously unwilling to take a chance that the new wound might grow larger instead of being healed. They shared their days as before, but no longer with the same fearless bliss. A crack had developed in the shield of their love. It was not an irreparable crack, but it was deep enough to make them wary.

They spent the morning taking the bunk beds in the spare room apart and putting fresh linen on them. Karla had been told by the real-estate agent that the room had once housed twin boys. She had been using it to store odds and ends and couldn't recall the last time she had even bothered to look inside.

When they were finished cleaning, she stood in the middle of the room and looked around, shaking her head. Three of the walls were covered with pictures of branding irons, horses, lassos, cowboys and Indians, all splashed garishly across a bright blue background. The beds, while neatly made, had mismatched blankets and sheets, and one was topped with a soft lavender spread, the other with a deep forest green one.

"Let's make sure they don't eat right before going to bed," Karla groaned.

"It looks fine," Rick assured her. "As a matter of fact, I kind of like the wallpaper."

She spun around to look at him. "You what?"

"Well, maybe it's not the paper so much as the idea behind it."

"Meaning?" She looked back at the mismatched conglomeration.

"A child." He walked up behind her and put his arms around her waist. "We've never seriously talked about having children. Maybe we should sometime." He nuzzled her back.

Karla shivered at his touch. Perhaps they had rarely discussed having a child, but she had thought about it often. When they were first married and both of their careers had made such heavy demands on their time, they had decided it would be unfair to start a family. Then when they were apart, and she had sincerely believed they would never be together again, she had wished with all her heart that they had had a child. Someone who was a part of both of them yet singularly different. A child she could watch with joy as it grew and discovered the magical world around it. Someone to love.

In answer Karla turned to face Rick, putting her arms around his neck and kissing him tenderly. "Boy or girl?" she murmured against his lips.

Rick smiled down at her. "Things must have changed without anyone telling me. I thought you just made love and took a happy gamble. Then nine months later you loudly proclaimed that the end result was exactly what you'd really wanted all along."

She looked at him through hooded eyes, fighting a smile. "I was merely asking your preference," she patiently explained, "not requesting a scientific discourse."

They stood with their hips pressed together and their arms comfortably locked around each other. Rick hesitated a minute before answering, his face mirroring the deep consideration he was giving her question.

"When I picture myself with our child I close my eyes and see the most beautiful little girl. She's walking beside me, her hand lost in mine. She looks up to me and says one word—'Daddy.' And when that happens, I feel as though I'd been covered in ice, and she has magically melted it.

"But then. . .sometimes I see a little boy with soft blond hair, just about your color." Rick picked up a lock of her hair and let it curl softly around his finger. "He's sitting on my lap and pointing to the sky and seriously telling me which is the moon and which is a star. When I finally get them right, he gives me a wonderfully wet kiss, and I hold him to me until he squirms away in protest.''

Karla wondered how many times Rick's hand had been held as a child. How often had he sat on someone's lap? She had a sad feeling that it hadn't been very often. He would make a wonderful father, loving and fair. And now that Rick's racing was behind them, he would have the time that being a parent needed.

With her fingertips Karla gently tugged on the hair at the base of Rick's throat. She put her mouth where her hand had been and made a slow circle with the tip of her tongue. ''Want to talk about that little boy or girl now?'' she queried softly.

Rick's hands slid down to her buttocks, where he cupped the rounded flesh. Pulling her closer to him, he made sure she could feel his answer as well as hear it. ''I'm yours to command, my love. Lead me and I will follow.''

LATER THAT EVENING, Karla was in the kitchen making out a shopping list when Rick came in and told her it was time to pick up Steve and Michael Whittaker. They drove into town, and when Karla pointed out how early they were, Rick insisted they stop by the gallery and invite Jeff and Maggie to dinner. Karla mentally added another course to the meal she'd planned, trying to stretch four steaks six ways. She didn't understand Rick's mysterious insistence on including the Bimsons this particular evening, but gamely followed him up the stairs.

Jeff and Maggie said they would love to meet Rick's friends, but countered his invitation by suggesting they all go over to the Whaler's Restaurant for dinner. Jeff glanced meaningfully at Karla. "Their check for the bronze whale has bounced twice, and I decided I'm going to get paid if I have to take it out in trade."

"You should have told me," Karla said. "It's my job to chase down bad checks."

He looked at her, glanced at Rick and then back at her again. He smiled. "You've been a little tied up lately."

Karla felt a flush rising up her neck and knew her cheeks would be red within seconds. She looked down at her nondescript slacks and cotton blouse and quickly changed the subject, "I can't go to the Whaler's looking like this," she said.

"You look fine," chorused Rick and Maggie.

"Something tells me that's hunger speaking, not admiration." Karla had just started to suggest that she run home to change while they waited for Steve and Michael, when a long whistle blast followed by two short ones stopped her. The ferry was early, already making its way into the harbor.

Rick and Karla went to meet the boat while Maggie and Jeff finished closing the shop. The giant, four-hundred-foot white-and-green vessel maneuvered into the V-shaped, creosote-soaked pilings as easily and adroitly as if it were a tiny cabin cruiser. Within minutes the passengers were hurrying down the wooden sidewalk and into town. From the bottom deck, cars quickly spewed out of the ferry's belly, each clinking in turn as it bumped over the ship's connecting tongue.

Karla was the first to spot Steve. Dressed in a sport coat and slacks instead of his usual casual attire, he looked strangely unfamiliar. The transformation was so complete that she had to remind herself not to stare. She lost her battle with decorum when he smiled and winked and called out to her. Running to meet him, she threw her arms around his neck and said, "You look fantastic! Wait until the women around here get an eyeful of you. I'll have to hire a guard."

Steve beamed his pleasure, almost ignoring Rick, who had followed her.

"Just remember you're spoken for, woman," Rick growled at Karla playfully before he reached for his friend and drew him into a bear hug. It wasn't until he released him that Rick noticed the man standing directly behind him. "Mike!" he shouted, grinning broadly.

The two men hugged each other in turn, laughing and exchanging greetings until Karla came over to them. "I hate to be a spoilsport," she whispered, "but there are several people behind you who would like to get off the ferry before it leaves for Sidney.''

Rick turned and apologized profusely to the crowd, which was bottlenecked behind them. He backed off the ramp and slipped his arm around Karla's shoulders, performing the delayed introductions as they walked.

"Michael Whittaker, this is my wife, Karla—" he glanced at her and brushed a kiss against her hair "—the love of my life."

Mike groaned. "Steve warned me about what I might find," he said, a grin lightening his words, "but I refused to believe that the hard-as-nails Rick Fleming I once knew could possibly be the same man he described."

"Believe it," Rick said, drawing Karla close. "I'm sure everything he told you is true."

Karla looked at Rick's friend, who was now walking beside her. He was shorter than Rick and leaner, almost gaunt. He wore steel-rimmed glasses that sat slightly below the bridge of his nose. They were low enough to allow him to glance over the top periodically, as though he sometimes doubted what he saw through them and needed a quick confirmation. Karla placed him somewhere in his forties. Men seemed to change so little in that decade that she could never tell whether they were at one end or the other. His rakish grin would have made her guess forty, but his eyes, which were world-weary and filled with wisdom, made her wonder.

As they walked to the gallery, Rick told the new arrivals of their dinner plans and of the boat he had hired for the next day's fishing. After another round of introductions when they joined the Bimsons, they all piled into the station wagon and headed for the restaurant.

The Whaler's Restaurant had been converted from a lumber-baron's mansion into one of the finest seafood-and-steak houses in the greater Puget Sound area. Because of the owners' careful planning, its Victorian charm had survived the transition beautifully.

The rooms had been left as close to the original as possible, with even their elegant wallpaper still intact. Each had become a cozy dining area, where part of a customer's fun was knowing that the person at the next table might be the state governor, a movie star or a close neighbor.

Although Marten's Cove was a resort town and casual in most respects, dining at the Whaler's was formal. Dressed as she was, Karla was positive she would not be allowed inside. When she tried once more to convince the others, Jeff stopped her by saying, "If they won't let you in, I'll simply demand that they empty the cash register as down payment against this bad check." He patted his shirt pocket.

Karla didn't doubt that he would do exactly as he threatened. He had been in a fractious mood since the infamous Mrs. Longacher had started her campaign against Sir Galahad.

When they arrived at the elegant white-and-blue building, which hugged the shoreline like a Goliath challenging the sea, Rick gave a long low whistle. He was obviously appreciative of the glorious structure that had been rescued almost intact from another time. "This is really something," he said as he helped Karla out of the station wagon.

"It could become a real moneymaker, too, if it had some decent management," Maggie said. "As it is, though, they pay all their bills at least a month in arrears and have to constantly juggle their accounts at the bank. The only one who gets paid on time is the chef, and that's because they're scared to death they'll lose him if they don't."

While he waited for the others, Jeff stopped a moment to run his hand affectionately over the snout of the bronze beluga whale he had sold to the restaurant. The sculpture looked spectacular beneath the restrained, hand-carved sign.

Rick came up and walked around the three-foot whale, which had been posed in a permanent dive. He sat on his haunches and looked at the underside. After running his hand reverently over the whale's back, he looked at Jeff and said simply, "It's beautiful."

Jeff flushed with pride. "Thank you," he said, obviously delighted.

They entered the restaurant, Rick first, with Karla his shadow, followed closely by the others. When he saw them the maitre d' cleared his throat, and Karla would have sworn he was about to tell them that the restaurant was reserved for the evening. When he looked up, however, his manner changed completely. In a beautifully modulated voice heavy with an aristocratic English accent, he said, "What can I do for you this evening, Mr. Fleming?"

Karla glanced over her shoulder in time to see Maggie's mouth fly open in surprise. The maitre d' at the Whaler's had a reputation of being almost inflexible, influenced by little less than a hundred-dollar bill. Surreptitiously Karla put her hand under Maggie's chin and pushed it lightly, so that her mouth closed. "I had forgotten about this," she whispered, motioning toward the fawning maitre d'. She shrugged. "You get used to it after a while."

They were soon being led to a prominent table. As they walked past some of the other diners, the fellow said very loudly, "Right this way, Mr. Fleming."

When it became obvious that he intended to seat them in the main dining room, where most of the other guests would be able to watch them eat, Rick put his hand on the man's shoulder and drew him close. "Do you suppose," he said in a low tone, "that we might be able to get a table with a little more privacy? My wife feels underdressed for the occasion and would like to draw as little attention as possible."

For the first time the maitre d' looked at the five people accompanying the celebrity. "Karla!" he exclaimed, "I didn't know you were, uh...." His accent disappeared as quickly as his cheeks crimsoned.

"Hi, Eugene," Karla said, her eyebrows lowered in irritation. She was beginning to feel exceedingly uncomfortable with the attention they were already attracting.

Immediately regaining his poise, Eugene took them to one of the small dining rooms. He exited in a rush after hastily saying, "Have a good meal, folks."

After they had been served their cocktails and had ordered, Mike leaned his elbows on the table and looked directly at Rick. He toyed with his drink, twisting his wrist so that the amber liquid came dangerously close to spilling out, yet never did. "I would love to be able to convince myself that I'm here because you were pining for my company, Rick, but I've known you for too long. You're as transparent as a pair of women's underwear ought to be."

Rick smiled and leaned back in his chair. "I can't tell you how I've missed your charming ways and subtle manner, Mike."

"Subtlety gets you put in the back of the line, a place I've never relished." Mike grinned. "And don't forget, my charming ways have gotten me four wives."

"And four divorces," Steve chimed in. Even Mike laughed at that.

It was obvious to Karla that Rick, Steve and Mike had known one another well and for a long time. She wondered how she could possibly have missed meeting him before now.

Rick tossed onto the table a small piece of paper from a matchbook cover that he had been absently folding. "I guess now is as good a time as any," he sighed. "Although I did have plans of filling you in on some background beforehand, Mike, there really isn't any reason we can't discuss it over dinner."

He looked from Maggie to Jeff. "Mike is a reporter for the *Seattle Times*." He waited a moment while they absorbed the information. "I thought that he might be able to give you a hand in getting Galahad back into the schools. Why don't you tell him the story...."

Rick glanced back at Mike, whose relaxed posture had changed to one of sharp awareness with the introduction of a possible story. "He's a fairly good reporter," he said with a smile.

Mike snorted. "Only about as good at reporting as you are at racing cars."

Rick laughed. "Well, show them your stuff."

Something clicked in Karla's brain. Snatches of long-ago conversations drifted back, conversations between Rick and Steve about a friend who had won a Pulitzer Prize for reporting. The man had uncovered a web of corruption in a religious cult that had used kids to panhandle and steal for them, she remembered. The leaders had been jailed or deported as a direct result of the series of articles, and hundreds of kids had gone home to frantic, grateful parents. At the time, Mike Whittaker had been a real hero to families everywhere whose children had joined fanatical religious cults.

Karla was immensely impressed. Rick had summoned some big guns to help Maggie and Jeff in their fight with Mrs. Longacher.

Maggie and Jeff took turns telling Mike about Galahad and answering his detailed questions. He took notes on a small leather-bound pad he had pulled out of his coat pocket and laid beside his plate. The conversation continued throughout dinner.

Watching Maggie and Jeff, Karla knew that their calm exteriors belied the excitement they were feeling inside. Their battle with Mrs. Longacher was not going well. She had done her work so meticulously that they had found many doors closed to them when they'd tried to get appointments with key officials. Karla had never seen her friends as depressed as they had been lately. . . .

She looked at Rick, who was avidly following the conversation. Leaning against him lightly, she put her hand on his leg and lovingly stroked his thigh. His hand covered hers, and he turned to look at her.

"Thank you," she silently mouthed.

He smiled. It was only a gentle curving of his mouth, not even large enough to show his teeth, but it was enough to make Karla feel as though she would drown in the depths of its meaning.

"It was nothing," he said softly, only to her. He took his napkin and dabbed at the corner of her mouth, wiping away a trace of melted butter from the scampi she'd eaten. He let his finger trail across the fullness of her lower lip, and she pressed her mouth to it in a fleeting kiss.

Suddenly Karla became aware that the conversation around them had ceased. She looked up to see not only everyone at their table staring at them, but the people at the next table, as well.

Mike shook his head. "I wouldn't have believed it if I hadn't seen it with my own eyes." In mock despair he added, "What have you let this woman do to you, Rick?"

Rick brought Karla's hand to his mouth and gently kissed the smooth skin on its back. He grinned at Mike. "Nothing I haven't wholeheartedly encouraged."

Karla looked at Maggie, silently pleading with her to help change the subject. The other woman looked radiant. Her face was alive with the hope Michael Whittaker had brought to them. She smiled understandingly, reached for her wineglass and suggested it was time for a refill. The waiter immediately appeared to do so, effectively distracting everyone's attention from Rick and Karla. He discreetly inquired how they had enjoyed their meal before fading again into the background.

"I hope you know how to cook one of these, Karla," Steve said, pointing to the remains of his salmon steak, "because I intend to catch a nice big one tomorrow."

"I can cook anything, Steve," Karla said brightly.

Maggie choked, Jeff's eyes grew wide and Rick chuckled, but Karla ignored them all. "I didn't say I could cook it well, mind you. Only that I could cook it."

"If you catch one, Steve, I'll cook it for you." Maggie promised.

Karla smiled to herself.

STEVE CAUGHT THE FISH he had claimed was waiting for him, and the next night they had a huge salmon-and-beef barbecue that at the end had them all complaining about their unbridled gluttony. Sir Galahad, at his charming best, had singled out Mike to work his magic on this evening. Wherever Mike went the wolf followed, staying a foot or so away until Mike offered to pet him, and then turning his soulful eyes up in supplication and pleasure as though honored by the mere touch of this masterful creature.

Finally Karla could take it no longer and went over to the wolf, which was now sitting at Mike's heels. She reached down and cupped his muzzle in her hand, lifting his nose until he was looking at her. "Have you no pride, Galahad? Where is your wolflike demeanor? Show us some bared teeth! Let us hear a lonely howl or two!"

In answer, he licked the tip of her nose.

Mike watched the exchange with a professional detachment. "Can you make him do that on command?" he asked Jeff.

"You mean what just happened with Karla?"

Mike nodded.

"It isn't a command type of thing. It's simply his way of greeting people he likes. Those, that is, who don't pass out when they see him open his mouth so close to their faces."

"Does he do it every time he sees Karla?" Mike had piqued their interest and they all waited for the answer.

"Yes, I think so," Jeff said.

"Do you think he would behave this way even in front of a photographer?"

Now it became evident what Mike had in mind. Jeff and Maggie looked at each other and smiled. Jeff put his arm around his wife's waist and drew her to him. It was a heady feeling to know they had the power of the press on their side.

"We don't know how to thank you," Maggie said. "To us Galahad and all that he stands for are important beyond words."

"It may not work, you know," Mike said slowly. "Not every good cause gets the backing it deserves or the support it needs." His voice betrayed a reporter's cynicism. "Now how about letting me finish the interview we began yesterday so that I can get going on this tomorrow."

"But you just came," Rick protested. "I have the boat for another week."

"And I'm still sick from the outing we went on today." Mike looked from Rick to Karla and then back to Rick again. "Now, if you would agree to letting me stay behind while you and Steve go out, I could probably rearrange my schedule. . . ."

"We're going to miss you, Mike," Rick said meaningfully. "Be sure to keep in touch."

Mike and Steve laughed uproariously at the uncharacteristically jealous behavior Rick exhibited.

Karla moved closer to her husband, hooking her hand over his belt and resting her arm along the back of his waist. Her eyes twinkled mischievously. "Don't let them get to you, honey," she teased. "I find Mike only moderately attractive. His incredible talent and brilliant mind hardly impress me at all. And as for that sexy lock of hair that tumbles so enticingly over his broad masculine forehead. . .well, all I can say is that with a little more than minimum effort I have been able to control myself and not reach out to brush it back. . . ." She let out a deep sigh.

Rick pulled Karla to him and gave her a lusty

kiss. "Be still, woman," he ordered gruffly. "Us he-men types don't put up with no messing around."

Karla joined the others in laughter. It had been a long time since she had felt such unequivocal happiness, such complete joy.

Jeff moved two more chairs to the front deck, and they all gathered there to watch the crimsoning sky. It had been a glorious day, filled with sunshine and laughter. A day spent with friends; a day of love and of slowly building trust for Karla and Rick. Their lives together became more real with each passing hour, as if getting through it meant the next would be stronger, surer.

Streaks of snow were still visible on the distant, rugged Cascades. With the sky darkening to ocher over their peaks, the snow looked like ermine tails outlining the bottom of a flaming cape. The flamboyant beauty of the sunset left the small group on the Bimsons' cedar porch speechless. They sat in silence until the mountains were faint black silhouettes against the rapidly darkening sky.

Mike broke the silence. "I've been meaning to tell you how remarkably healthy you look, Rick. After that gruesome accident, I wasn't sure what to expect."

Karla grew rigid, but in the faint moonlight no one seemed to notice her discomfort.

"I didn't come through totally unscathed, but

I'm really none the worse for it. A small scar on my leg and one on my side, but that's about all.''

Karla wanted to scream her protest at the easily uttered falsehoods. The scar on his leg was more than twelve inches long. The one on his side looked as though, in the urgency to save his life, he had been ripped open in the operating room. And *her* scars.... They weren't so obvious, but they were every bit as large and ran twice as deep.

The conversation drifted easily and naturally into past races, with spicy stories about famous drivers interspersed with anecdotes of hair-raising finishes. Jeff listened avidly, enjoying the behind-the-scenes stories. Only Maggie seemed aware of Karla's unease and glanced at her frequently throughout the evening.

After what to Karla felt like hours spent in torturous reminiscences, Mike casually dropped the question Karla had been lulled into believing would not be asked.

"How long before you rejoin the circuit, Rick? The boys in the sports department tell me you might still have a shot at the European championship."

The abruptness, the stunning swiftness of the attack left her numb. A pregnant silence hung in the air before Rick quietly, slowly said, "I won't be going back."

"You're not going to finish the season?" Mike asked incredulously.

"Not this one...or the next." His voice was wooden. "I'm giving up racing."

A silence hung over them like the blade of a guillotine. The edge slashed the quiet when Mike said, "You're kidding, aren't you?"

Rick shook his head.

"Why?"

Despite the dark, myriad emotions could be seen on Rick's face in the seconds it took for him to form the answer. Resignation was there when he said, "It's time."

"Bullshit!" Mike shouted. He jumped from his chair, nearly tipping it over. "Don't try to feed *me* that line! I know you too well to swallow that garbage. What's the real reason, Rick?" His reporter's instincts refused to let go even when a friend was involved.

Anger made Rick's eyes blaze. "That's the only reason you or anyone else is ever going to get."

Mike walked to the other end of the deck, running his hand through his hair as he mumbled thoughts aloud. When he reached the railing he swung around.

"You know what everyone is going to think, don't you? What they're going to say? How in the hell can you end one of the most brilliant careers racing has ever known on a note like this? Dammit, Rick, why are you *really* doing this?"

Karla felt sick. She wanted to tell Mike to back off, but she knew Rick would not welcome her interference. She had known this moment was coming, but she had not expected it to be the devastating end to a beautiful day. What right did Mike have to question Rick? What right did he have to make Rick doubt the decision he had so recently made? She felt as though she were fighting for her life, but that she was being forced to do so without uttering a word.

Rick stood and began to gather the glasses beside him. "It's over, Mike. Let it go," he said, his jaw clenched in anger.

Karla looked at Steve. He had remained quiet throughout the disclosure, but now she could see the expression of disbelief on his face, as though he was having trouble absorbing what he had just heard. So Rick hadn't told him, either.

The tension around them was so thick that Karla felt she would be able to touch it. Finally Mike crossed the deck to stand in front of Rick. "I'm sorry," he said. "The emotional outburst was inexcusable." Softly, stubbornly, he added, "but every word is valid."

He turned and graciously thanked Maggie and Jeff for their hospitality, promising to be in touch with them within the week. He glanced at Steve. "I'm heading back now. Do you want to come along?"

Steve nodded. He expressed his thanks to Maggie for cooking his salmon and headed down the steps in Mike's wake.

For the first time since she had known them, Karla was unable to think of anything to say to Maggie and Jeff. She stumbled over an apology that she knew was unnecessary and listened to Maggie say how sorry she was that such a happy evening had ended so badly. They wished each other good-night and Rick and Karla left.

On the way home Rick remained locked in his own thoughts, thoughts that Karla could only imagine—could only dread.

THE NEXT MORNING Karla awoke at her usual hour to discover she was alone in the house. A note in the kitchen explained everyone's absence.

Mike was anxious to start working on Gala-had's story, so Steve and I took him to the ferry. You looked so peaceful that I didn't want to wake you to say goodbye. See you this evening.

Love, Rick

Cryptic and to the point. A note she would have smiled at and forgotten under other circumstances. But today the words were as telling for what they didn't say as they were for the false tone of normalcy. Karla crumpled the piece of paper into a tiny ball and jammed it into the pocket of her robe.

Was Mike's reaction to Rick's announcement

going to be the way all his friends accepted the news, she wondered. Her certainty of the answer made her slam the kitchen door as she went back into the living room.

Dammit! They had no right to do that to him. Rick was not a piece of public property subject to a popular vote. He did not belong to his fans. Or to his friends, for that matter.

Echoing persistently in some far corner of her mind was the reminder that Rick did not belong to her, either. He was his own person. As desperately as she wanted to believe otherwise, she could not convince herself that Rick's decision to leave racing had been anything other than an outgrowth of his love for her. He had not quit because he truly felt "it was time," as he had told Mike. He had quit because of her.

Angry with the way her thoughts were going, Karla stomped out of the living room and onto the front porch. It didn't matter why he had quit, only that he had. Now he would live to have the children he had said he wanted. And the grandchildren. Perhaps even a great-grandchild or two. He didn't owe his public a thing. If anything, they owed him. He had given of his talent over and over again. Miraculous finishes where he had summoned that extra something to beat his equally matched opponents were the norm with Rick, not a once-in-a-lifetime incident that turned into an old man's anecdote. He had earned the right to retire alive.

Unshed tears of frustration made Karla's eyes glisten in the early-morning sun as she stood on the front porch and futilely looked at the empty berth on the wooden dock in front of the cabin. She scanned the water for a glimpse of the tan cruiser Rick had rented, but it was nowhere to be seen. In her heart a silent pleading voice called out to him, "Don't listen to them, Rick. Please don't listen to them."

CHAPTER ELEVEN

ANYONE WHO WORKED in Marten's Cove during the summer found the season anything but lazy and relaxing. For the permanent residents of Quiller Island, summer was a time of frantic activity. They worked like squirrels, diligently gathering the harvest of the season so that they could relax in the winter months.

The summer disappeared quickly for Karla and Rick, therefore, as each busy day worked into the next and then the next. Before long they were preparing for the big explosion of vacationers on Labor Day weekend, which would taper off to the stragglers of September.

Toward the end of June, Rick had grown bored with convalescing at home and had started going to the gallery in the afternoon to help Karla with mailings and sales. That freed her to get the books in order earlier, so that they could leave as soon as the shop closed. Word that the famous Rick Fleming was working at the Artists' Co-Op spread quickly and the shop had far more browsers than ever before. Sales climbed slightly, but not enough to pay another employee, so Rick's status remained as he had laughingly requested—visiting salesman.

Although it seemed he answered the same question about his career at least a dozen times a day, Karla flinched each time. Rick's answer was always the same curt, "It was time," whenever anyone insisted on pursuing the subject. He quickly developed a way of saying it that discouraged further inquiries.

Karla believed everything was working out for them—simply because there was no alternative. She refused to recognize Rick's restlessness or to see the pain or the faraway look that sometimes filled his eyes when he thought he was alone.

In the middle of July, Rick began to have trouble sleeping. He would rise in the deepest black of night and go for a walk along the water's edge or through the forest. The first time Karla woke up and found him missing, she knew a terrible panic. Afterward, whenever she discovered him gone, she felt a gnawing dread. She never questioned why he left or why he was unable to sleep. Instead she believed, because she so desperately needed to, that he couldn't sleep because he had not yet adjusted to such a radically different life-style.

Over the summer they became regular customers at the Whaler's Restaurant, after a while even becoming good friends with the chef. It was a surprise to everyone, tourist and local alike, when in early August a discreet For Sale sign appeared and the doors were locked against the usual huge Friday night crowd. Even Jeff, after his experience with their bouncing checks, had been surprised.

The summer had been particularly busy for Maggie, Jeff and Sir Galahad. When Michael Whittaker's brilliant series of articles about endangered species had ended with the plight of the wolf and with the Bimsons' efforts to help, all three had become local celebrities. Several television crews had come to the island to film the "ferocious beast" in his lair and to record the local people's reactions to having a wolf in their midst. One interview in particular provided several nights' worth of conversation for Karla, Rick and their friends. Mrs. Pahlberg, the neighbor who had sworn Galahad would one day revert and kill them all, had done a complete about-face when she went before the cameras. She had dramatically proclaimed her deep affection for the gentle animal that lived next door.

When one of the magazine-format shows filmed Jeff and Maggie's studios as well as Sir Galahad's haunts, commissions and inquiries about purchasing their artwork began to flow in. Had they ignored everything else, they could have increased their bank balances enormously. But they chose instead to attend every function that could possibly give the wolf's cause a boost.

As August was nearing its end, the initial commotion began to settle down a little, giving them all a brief breathing spell. Jeff and Maggie even started to make plans to get to their logjam of work—after their next excursion, this one to Olympia, where they would visit the governor's office.

While they were there, a clever photographer caught Galahad in a nose-to-nose confrontation with one of the swans that lived in the lake behind the Capitol. The showdown was over within seconds but had provided the photojournalist with a visual record of this particular wolf's temperament. The irate swan had definitely come out the winner, and the final picture in the series was of Galahad, peering out from around Jeff's legs at the glowering bird. The next day Quiller Island's lone wolf was front-page material not only in Seattle, but also in almost every newspaper throughout the nation.

Mrs. Longacher's already shaky campaign didn't stand a chance after that. Invitations to have Galahad visit came pouring in from schools all over Washington. Telegrams came from neighboring states, offering to pay all expenses if the Bimsons would bring their wolf. Several special-interest groups who had previously considered the wolf's cause a lost one suggested sending Galahad to Washington, D.C. as spokesman for all endangered species. And so, on a wonderfully optimistic note, the summer ended.

School had been in session three weeks and Galahad was on his fifth trip to the mainland—this time only with Jeff—when Rick decided to spend an afternoon with Daniel Olsen on his sailboat while Karla did some end-of-the-season work at the gallery. After their inauspicious first meeting, Daniel and Rick had become close friends, frequently spending Daniel's off hours together exploring the waters of Puget Sound. Rick had easily transferred his affection from powerboating to the quiet serenity of sail under Daniel's adept tutelage. Eventually, the Norwegian had even managed to get Rick to do something Karla had said was impossible—to sample some of the more exotic omelets on Daniel's huge menu. He even admitted he liked a few of them.

That day Karla finished at the shop earlier than she had anticipated, so she closed up and went home to prepare dinner. When she got there, however, she remembered that Rick had told her he and Daniel would probably grab a bite to eat in Friday Harbor.

Ill at ease with her own company and with the nameless fears that had recently begun to haunt her every waking moment, she decided to head over the hill to visit Maggie. The forest floor was littered with dry madrone leaves that rustled underfoot, as well as rusty-looking strips of bark. At one point Karla bent over and picked a long, graceful fern frond. Absently she began to pluck off the individual leaves one at a time, much as she had done to daisy petals when she was a child. In her mind a litany of "he loves me, he loves me not" began. Before she had reached the middle of the frond the words had changed to "he will stay, he will not stay." When Karla realized what she was saying, she threw the half-stripped fern away from her as though it had suddenly turned into writhing snake, ready to strike.

Not wanting to be alone any longer, she started to run. When she reached the Bimsons' house she was gasping for air. She knocked loudly against the white door, and when there was no answer, knocked again. After another minute the door swung open as though by itself.

"Maggie?" Karla said. She heard a noise behind the door. "Maggie, is that you?"

"Come in, Karla." Maggie's voice was little more than a choked whisper.

Karla stepped into the room and looked behind the door. "My God, Maggie! What's happened?" Her friend looked drained of all color. Although her eyes were dry, they were swollen and streaked with red. Her normally well-coiffed hair was disarranged, as though she'd been pulling at it.

Karla put her arms around Maggie and hugged her. She could feel rather than hear her sobs as she started to cry again.

When it became obvious that she couldn't speak without her voice being choked by tears, Karla led her through the living room into the kitchen. She sat her at the table and brought her a cold wet cloth, and while Maggie pressed the compress to her face, Karla put a kettle of water on the stove. Gently she began asking a series of mundane questions, starting with the location of the tea and ending with the strength Maggie preferred. It worked. Maggie stopped crying and laid the wet cloth on the table, folding the hot-pink washcloth into smaller and smaller squares as she finally managed to tell Karla what she was upset about.

"Someone has poisoned Galahad." She caught her breath before going on, her face reflecting the deep dismay that now gripped her. "The vet in Tacoma doesn't think he'll live through the night."

"Oh, Maggie." Karla set the teapot on the counter with a clunk and once again put her arms around her friend. "Who would do such a thing?" she murmured into her hair.

"Jeff said that he left Galahad in the station wagon while he checked in with the school officials this morning, and that when he returned, Galahad was acting a little strange. But nothing else seemed out of the ordinary. He thinks that someone must have slipped a piece of meat laced with poison through the window while he was gone." Maggie visibly fought for control before going on.

"Apparently Galahad didn't begin to act sick

until around noon. Jeff thought that . . . that maybe he was just tired so . . . so he put him back in the wagon and went to lunch with the principal and teachers.'' Maggie covered her eyes with her hands. ''Oh, Karla, he feels . . . he feels that Galahad is going to die and that it's partly his fault because he left him alone when there was still a chance to save him.''

It was several seconds before Maggie went on, ''When Jeff got back to the car, Galahad was in a coma.'' With a sob of anguish she finally whispered, ''He went through all that suffering alone, Karla.''

In a daze, Karla stood beside Maggie. She felt utterly helpless. She wanted to reach inside and take some of Maggie's pain, but she didn't know how. There were no words of comfort for such a senseless act, no platitudes to ease the sorrow.

''I hate them, Karla.'' The venom in Maggie's voice made her draw away in surprise.

''I hate them all! No one really cares—not the kids, no one. They were just riding with a popular wave, enjoying being part of Galahad's new-found notoriety. Where were they when Mrs. Longacher was spreading her own kind of poison?''

''You don't mean that, Maggie,'' Karla said softly.

''Don't I?'' she hissed.

''No, dammit, you don't. It's just that sometimes, when pain becomes unbearable, we use anger to help to diffuse it. That's what you're doing now—you're using your anger to cover your pain.''

Maggie reached for the washcloth and pressed it to her eyes. As she looked down at her, Karla desperately tried to think of a way to help. If only Jeff were here...Jeff! He needed Maggie right now every bit as much as she needed him, Karla was sure. Rushing into the living room, she quickly thumbed through the small island's phone directory. When she found the number she was looking for, she made a brief call and then returned to the kitchen.

"Get up, Maggie," she said, prodding her friend to her feet. "You're going to Tacoma."

Karla helped Maggie change her clothes and pack an overnight bag, then they walked back over the hill to get the truck. When they arrived at the dock in Marten's Cove, they found the water taxi waiting for them. Maggie hugged Karla and climbed into the small cockpit, and the bright red seaplane revved its engine and skimmed along the water like a bird of prey.

Although she knew the odds against Maggie's seeing her were huge, Karla waved at the rapidly climbing plane when it took off and headed for Tacoma. She blinked back tears and hugged herself, watching the seaplane until it disappeared.

Karla had no idea how long she had been standing on the dock lost in thought when she became aware of Daniel's sailboat making its way into the harbor. Even from that distance she had no trouble distinguishing Rick as he agilely moved around the front of the boat, doing last-minute chores before the vessel slipped into its mooring. Watching him made her heart swell with love. He would soon be beside her, and she would have someone to put her arms around. Someone with whom to share the tragic news, who would care as deeply as she did. And because of that caring, because of the sharing, her own pain would be less. It was strange, she mused, how pain diminished when it was shared, but happiness multiplied.

As the boat moved closer, Karla could see that the day's outing had not lessened the haunted look Rick had developed over the summer. She knew he had a pain that was growing each day, one that he held close and didn't share with her. A pain that was eating at him like a cancer. Fear of the reason for that pain, fear that bordered on panic, kept Karla from asking about it. Instead she watched for signs that his inner turmoil had been resolved. And she tried to fill his days with her love, hoping it would provide the needed salve for his wounds, hoping it would be enough.

When Rick spotted her and shouted a greeting, Karla waved and walked to the end of the dock to take the line he tossed her.

"I didn't expect you to meet me. Have you been waiting long?" he called.

"No, just a little while," she answered simply.

He jumped onto the rough wood planks, landing beside her and giving her a quick kiss before securing the line.

Daniel smiled and called out a greeting. "We had a glorious day. Just enough wind to fill the sails but not so much that we had to work too hard. You should have come with us. You know what they say about all work and no play."

"Next time," Karla promised.

"I've heard that story before," Daniel laughed. "By the time you get around to finding a free day, Rick will be an accomplished sailor with a boat of his own. I'll never get a chance to dazzle you with my skill unless I kidnap you one of these days and make you come along."

Karla smiled at Daniel's words, then crossed her heart. "Next time."

"I'm going to hold you to it," he vowed and went back to securing the boat.

When their work was finished, Rick slipped his arm around Karla's waist, called out his thanks to Daniel and started down the dock.

"Aren't we going to wait for him?" Karla asked.

Rick smiled. "Our friend Mr. Olsen has a hot date tonight—that's why we're back early. He's going to prepare a five-course candlelight dinner for some absolutely gorgeous woman he met at the restaurant last week. His head has been in the clouds all day. It seems she's going to be here all winter—as he puts it, 'all the long, lonely winter.' She's renting one of the summer people's houses...something about her getting away from it all to write a book, I think he said." Rick gave a low chuckle. "Actually, I should be able to give you minute details about her. I've spent the whole day hearing about little else."

When they arrived at the truck, Rick tossed his gear into the back and turned to face Karla. He took her by the shoulders and looked into her eyes. "Want to tell me about it now?" he asked.

"Am I such an open book?" Karla tried to smile.

"Only to me," he said softly as he drew her to him. With gentle strokes he pushed the hair away from her face as she nestled into the baby-soft flannel of his shirt.

"Jeff called Maggie from Tacoma," Karla began. She swallowed against the tightness gripping her throat. "Galahad has been poisoned. He isn't expected to live the night." She felt Rick's muscles tense before a deep, frustrated sigh warmed the top of her head.

"Why am I not more surprised?" he said aloud, although it was obvious he expected no answer to his rhetorical question.

"You can't mean that you expected this to happen?" Karla said, looking up at him.

"No...only that it doesn't surprise me that it did."

"Well, I don't understand it at all. How could someone do such a cruel thing? Galahad never hurt anyone. He was the gentlest animal I've ever known." She buried her face in Rick's shirt again. "I'm going to miss him terribly." Her muffled sobs were barely audible. "It's just...not... fair," she hiccupped.

Rick held her away from him. He lifted her chin so that she had to look in his eyes. Wiping away her tears with his thumb he said, "Few things in life are fair, Karla. After a while it's something you learn to accept."

Why did she suddenly feel that it wasn't only Galahad that Rick spoke of?

"I may have to face it, but I'll never be able to accept it," she said.

Rick started to reply, but stopped. He waited a minute before he said, "Why don't we go home and wait for their call? Maybe there will be a miracle and Galahad will pull through. Seems to me one little miracle could be spared. I haven't seen too many floating around lately."

THE MIRACLE Rick had asked for occurred. Galahad made a recovery that amazed even the veterinarians who treated him. By the next afternoon they could see no reason to keep him any longer, especially, Maggie told Rick and Karla later, when she almost got down on her knees and begged to take him home.

Karla and Rick met the trio at the ferry slip, laughing with commiseration and happiness when they spotted Galahad wobbling down the exit aisle. His tail made a feeble circle that turned into a pathetic wag when he saw Karla and Rick.

"I know it looks cruel to make him walk," Jeff said, "but after carrying him all day, it was either his legs or my back. I think two hundred pounds of potatoes would have been easier to tote than this big lug." His words were sharp, but his tone was filled with relief. "It would have been one heck of a lot easier if the police had been through fingerprinting the station wagon and we could have left him in it, but Maggie didn't want to wait around. She was anxious to get Galahad home."

"At least we'll never have to go through anything like this ever again," Maggie said. "Galahad has made his last trip off the island."

Both Karla's and Rick's eyes automatically went to Jeff, checking to see if he concurred with his wife's proclamation.

"She's adamant," he said. "I tried to get her to wait a while and think it over, but she refused. Even announced it to the reporters who met us at the vet's before we left."

Karla wanted to remind Maggie of the commitment she had made and of the determination she had expressed to help to change public opinion about wolves, but when she saw the rigid lines around Maggie's mouth and the cold gleam in her eyes, she decided to remain quiet for the moment. She buried her hands in Galahad's muff and scratched the spot where he always seemed to itch. "Glad to have you back, fella," she said. "Come on with me, I've made a special treat for you."

When they reached the truck, Maggie smiled in appreciation at the fluffy bed of old blankets Karla had prepared in the back for Galahad. The big animal tried to jump in when Rick dropped the tailgate, but he managed to lift his front paws only a few inches off the ground. Obviously he was too weak to climb into the back of the truck by himself, so Rick picked up the hundred pounds of feebly protesting wolf and gently eased him onto the truck bed. Before settling down, Galahad looked forlornly at Karla and nuzzled his nose into her cheek.

Karla sighed. "You too, huh? Boy, it seems like everybody's a critic. All right," she groaned, "I won't drive."

It was enough to break the tension and to give them all something to laugh about. After Galahad coaxingly licked Karla's nose, she insisted on riding in the back with him rather than squeezing all four of them into the cab. Before they were out of town Galahad had curled up, put his head on Karla's lap and fallen sound asleep.

TWO DAYS LATER when Karla came home from work she found a note from Rick on the back door.

"Dinner at Maggie and Jeff's. Come as soon as you can. Big surprise! Love, Rick."

She could just imagine the mischievous gleam in Rick's eyes when he had written the note. Patience over discovering "big surprises" had never been one of her strong points.

By the time she reached the back steps of the Bimsons' house, Karla had sorted through a score of possible retaliatory measures she could take against Rick, without finding one that would frustrate him nearly as much as she had been frustrated wondering about the mysterious surprise awaiting her.

Maggie met her at the door, once again with tears glistening on her cheeks. When she saw Karla's immediate look of concern, she wiped the tears away and said with supreme happiness in her voice, "I'm sorry. I didn't mean to scare you, but I've been doing this so much this afternoon that I've grown used to it. Come in. Something wonderful has happened."

Karla let herself be led by the hand into the living room, where with open mouth and eyes wide in disbelief, she stared at the cluttered mess she found. Covering every piece of furniture, and a large portion of the floor, were various sized pieces of paper, some in rainbow hues. Jeff and Rick sat in the middle, smiles making crescents of their mouths. Galahad, oblivious to what was happening around him, lounged lazily in a patch of sunshine.

"What's all this?" Karla asked, standing with her hands on her hips and slowly looking around.

Maggie cleared a place on the sofa for her to sit down. "I suppose it would sound sappy to say that—" she held out a stack of papers "—well, that it's an outpouring of love, but I'll be darned if I can think of any other way to put it. Here," she said, "look for yourself."

Karla glanced down as Maggie handed her a bundle of unopened envelopes. She looked at the writing on the first envelope. Sir Galahad's name was printed in a childish hand. Beneath his name appeared only the words Quiller Island. Nowhere on the envelope was there anything even resembling a zip code. And as for a return address, the neatly printed Sandy, on the upper right-hand corner where a stamp should have been, might have been any one of thousands of Sandys in the cancellation area of Seattle. So much for the hard-hearted image the post office had been using to impress the public with the need for exact addresses, Karla thought.

Karla looked up at Maggie. "I don't understand."

"Open it," Maggie beamed.

Karla glanced at Rick. He smiled and winked his encouragement.

She tried to pry open the well-glued flap but it had been sealed so enthusiastically that she finally gave up and tore the envelope open. Inside was a

get-well card with a handwritten message for Galahad and a school photograph of a freckle-faced little girl Karla guessed to be about six. She had
signed her name on the back in orange crayon.

Karla looked at the next letter. This one was ad-
dressed to Maggie and Jeff, and the handwriting
was decidedly adult. Inside was a letter written on
expensive parchment stationery expressing sorrow
over Galahad's poisoning and joy over his recovery. Also tucked inside was a check for a large
amount of money, which the writer asked be given
to whatever organization the Bimsons felt would
use it most effectively in continuing the fight
against ignorance about wolves.

"Now what?" Karla asked Maggie.

She shrugged. "Looks like I'm going to have to
rethink my statement that nobody cares," she said
sheepishly.

Karla stood up and hugged her. "Indeed it
does. Now what can I do to help?"

Maggie looked around. "I don't know. I can't
seem to get organized. I just keep wandering
around in a daze." She laughed. "And believe it
or not, it's going to get worse. The post office
called about an hour ago and told us there's
already twice this much mail for tomorrow's
delivery. Today, rather than make us go all the
way into town to pick it up, they sent the launch
directly to our house. I can't tell you what a shock
it was to see a postman walking up to the front

door with this huge bag flung over his shoulder. He looked like a blue Santa Claus.'' Her voice grew soft. ''He certainly brought us a fantastic present.'' Tears started to form again in her eyes.

''If you don't cut that out, Maggie, you're going to have a ferocious headache and be completely useless to everyone!'' Karla admonished.

''I know,'' Maggie sniffed. ''Isn't it wonderful?''

Jeff shifted several of the stacks of letters to a central location. ''I know something you can do, Karla,'' he said. ''We intend to answer every one of these letters, but it's going to take quite a while. In the meantime I don't want all this money just sitting around until we can get to it. Why don't you catalog the letters that have checks and cash in them so we can deposit them into a special account tomorrow.''

''You mean you've gotten more money than this?'' She looked at the check in her hand.

''Rick estimates we've hit five figures already,'' Jeff said. ''And we haven't opened half of the letters.''

''But why? You don't represent any particular group. Why are people sending money to you?''

Rick answered, ''I think it's a concrete way for people to express their sorrow and their outrage about what happened to Galahad. They trust Maggie and Jeff to see to it that the money is used wisely.''

Karla sat down cross-legged next to Rick in the spot Jeff had cleared. She grinned. "I forgive you for the note," she said magnanimously. "You'd have had a tough time trying to explain this."

Rick reached up and wrapped his hand around her neck, pulling her to him and giving her a quick kiss. "I could hear you fuming all the way over here," he laughed.

"And you loved every minute of it."

Rick kissed her again. "Now get to work, woman. There's still lots to do."

Karla began to write down the names, addresses and amounts of money that had been sent. Three hours later when they stopped for something to eat she was still at it. During dinner she listened contentedly as Jeff and Maggie discussed plans for taking Galahad back into the schools and the precautions they would take from then on.

It was almost midnight before they decided to call it quits. Karla and Rick left for home, promising they would return the next day.

It wasn't until a week later that the mail finally began to slow down. During that time Jeff and Maggie made several calls to their regular vet and after one examination it was determined that Galahad was at last strong enough for a return voyage to Tacoma.

Reporters and cameramen met the threesome at the school they had gone to visit, and Galahad was once again on the front page of several papers as well as a star attraction on the evening news. The end result of their first trip back was an ecstatic wolf and two humans with the flu.

Between sneezes, Jeff told Karla and Rick that going into a grammar school was like playing Russian roulette—if there was a germ or a bacteria or a virus anywhere, it would be found in a classroom full of kids. In the next breath he nonchalantly asked if Rick and Karla would mind accompanying Galahad into Seattle the next day, where a school full of children would be brokenhearted if he failed to appear.

The following morning, after listening to half an hour of last-minute instructions, Karla, Rick and Galahad set off for the ferry. Karla absently scratched Galahad's ear as she looked out the truck window at the numerous summer homes that were now empty and boarded up. "Jeff and Maggie are going to be worried the whole time we're gone," she commented.

"We'll call them before we head for home and let them know that everything worked out okay." Rick turned sharply to avoid a large hole in the road. He swore softly and grumbled about how much more sensible it would be to have a road-repair party instead of a Remainder Party.

Karla smiled as she listened to his by now familiar complaints about the disreputable roads. Perhaps a repair party would be more practical, she thought, but if the islanders ever decided to take up Rick's suggestion, she would miss the Remainder Party immensely.

The party was an annual affair, although no one quite remembered who had started it or when. Only the purpose was clear—to celebrate the end of the tourist season. For many years the restaurant owners had gathered together with their "remainders" of the season. They would bring a big pot and throw in whatever they had that wouldn't keep through the winter. The various conglomerations had made for some legendary feasts and not a few upset stomachs the next day. But with plenty of wine to wash it down every year, no one had seemed to care what it tasted like.

Now all the local people were invited, and while the feast was more predictable—a succulent seafood stew called chiapino—everyone still had the same good time. Driftwood was gathered and large bonfires were lighted on the beach. It wasn't uncommon for the party to still be in full swing when the sun came up the next day. It was a grand way for the year-round inhabitants to officially end the season, and it was something Karla had since early summer looked forward to sharing with Rick.

When Karla and Rick caught the ferry to Anacortes they stayed on the lower deck to be with Galahad, which made it seem almost as if they were alone on the huge ship. They walked Galahad around the nearly deserted deck a couple of times before going back to the truck, where they made him rest.

After the ferry docked they took the highway to Seattle. Normally the drive took ninety minutes, but today it seemed to pass in half the time. Rick was more animated than he had been in months, and Karla responded to his change of mood as though she had been drowning and he had thrown her a lifeline. Their conversation was lighthearted, filled with the same easy banter they had once shared so long ago. She took it to be a sign that Rick had finally come to grips with the problem he'd been wrestling with all summer.

Following Jeff's detailed map through Seattle's sprawling suburbs, they had no trouble finding Vancouver Junior High School. Rick pulled into a spot marked Visitor and went to find the principal's office while Karla stayed behind with Galahad. In an uninhibited moment of joy, Karla threw her arms around the wolf's neck and said, "It looks as though Rick and I have made it, Galahad. It finally seems that everything is going to work out for us after all."

She glanced up to see Rick coming toward the truck, with a man following close behind who looked as if he belonged in a movie studio. He was almost Rick's height and had the same athletic build and grace of movement. Karla had frequently heard the tired old joke men used when they saw a beautiful woman teacher, but it was the first thing that came to mind: if she'd had a teacher who looked like this man, she would have thought twice about graduating.

Rick came around to open her door. When she and Galahad were out of the truck, he introduced her to his companion. "Zack Miller, this is my wife, Karla Fleming."

The man's handshake was firm and warm, his smile aggressively friendly. "I can't tell you how much I appreciate the time and energy you've spent bringing Sir Galahad to our school. When Jeff called and said that he and Maggie were sick...." He smiled and shrugged helplessly. "Frankly, I was afraid to tell the kids. They would have been terribly disappointed."

"You do understand that we're novices at this?" Karla said. "And that there wasn't time enough to work up any kind of formal presentation."

"Oh, don't worry—the kids will take care of that for you. They'll have a hundred questions that Jeff assures me you'll be able to answer. Now if you're ready, I know they are." He turned and walked toward a set of double doors.

As Karla started to follow, Rick leaned over and whispered in her ear. "It's not nice to drool, Karla." He gave her a bold pinch that hurried her along and let her know that he was not terribly amused by her obvious appreciation of another man.

Karla smiled to herself. It would do him good to feel a little green-eyed. When they reached the door, she leaned against him and softly said, "But you told me I could look, as long as I don't touch." He started to reach for her again, but she scooted away, confusing the dignified Galahad with her sudden burst of speed.

They were led to the cafeteria, where several classes had been assembled in a semicircle around a portable stage. As soon as the children spotted Galahad, they broke into spontaneous applause. Karla was amazed at the wolf's reaction to the sudden noise. He seemed to grow in stature. His walk became springier, and he held his head regally high.

Why, he's a born ham, Karla thought. *His talents would have been wasted in the wild.*

Zack Miller went to the microphone and motioned for quiet. "Ladies and gentlemen," he said, "we have a double treat for you today. Not only is Sir Galahad, Washington State's own world-famous wolf, with us...."

Karla felt as if her heart had suddenly stopped beating. She glanced at Rick to see what his reaction would be to the words she knew the principal would utter next. His face was a mask, hiding the anger she knew he was feeling. Dammit, she swore vehemently to herself, why couldn't people leave them alone? They were here to help Jeff and Maggie, not to put a feather in Zack Miller's hat for arranging to have a celebrity come to his school. Their day had been a beautiful glass Christmas ornament, shiny and bright. And now it was about to be knocked from the tree to shatter into a thousand pieces.

"But accompanying him is Rick Fleming, the finest race-car driver America has ever produced."

Zack Miller led the applause. Turning around he glanced at Karla and obviously misunderstood her scowl. Hastily he grabbed for the microphone to add, "And his wife, Karla, is also joining us this morning."

The day went downhill from there. More than half the questions in the question-and-answer period were about racing, even though Rick valiantly fought against it, reminding his audience time after time that they were at the school to talk about wolves. With the boldness and brashness of youth old enough to be aware of the world around them, the students pointedly dug away at Rick's defenses, repeatedly asking thinly disguised variations of the question why he no longer raced. Karla had never seen the hands of a clock move more slowly.

When at last the fifty minutes neared its end, Zack Miller came over to stand beside Rick. He slipped his arm familiarly around Rick's shoulder as though they were long-time friends and asked the kids to show their appreciation for the time

Rick had given them out of his "busy" schedule. For the life of her Karla could no longer see what she had found attractive about Zack Miller. His fawning behavior and purposeful manipulation of the situation made her ill.

The applause that marked their departure was less enthusiastic than when they had entered, but Galahad obligingly wagged his tail in farewell as though they had brought down the house.

Karla started to reach for Rick's hand, but he passed her in a cloud of anger that prevented him from noticing the gesture. She saw the tensed muscles in his tightly clamped jaw and ached to put her hand there to draw away the frustration and hurt. As they neared the door they passed a group of boys who sat with their chairs tipped against the wall. In a stage whisper loud enough to be heard by everyone around him as well as by Rick, the largest of the boys said, "My dad says the real reason Rick Fleming ain't racing no more is because he's chicken."

Karla saw the telltale twitch at Rick's temple, indicating he had heard the cruel statement, but she was sure no one else had been able to detect whether or not the words had even reached his ears.

The journey home seemed endless. When they finally arrived, Karla volunteered to walk Galahad over to Maggie and Jeff's, and Rick readily accepted her offer.

She stayed long enough that they wouldn't suspect anything, assuring them that all had gone well and that the trip hadn't been an imposition. Maggie was faring better with the virus than Jeff was, but both were so ill that they were unaware of Karla's false attempts at good humor. After making sure they didn't need anything and fixing each of them a mug of warm cider, Karla bade them goodbye and left.

She came back to find the house empty. A scrap of paper with two rapidly scrawled words, "Gone Walking," lay in the middle of the floor, where a gust of wind had blown it when Karla opened the door. She slowly bent over to pick up the triangle-shaped paper, lifting it as though it were a message of doom.

For a long time she sat in a chair by the fireplace waiting for Rick to come home, until her head began to nod in fatigue. But when she took a blanket from the chest and curled up on the couch she felt wide awake again. She had no idea what time he finally did come home, only that somewhere in her consciousness she remembered the clock striking twice before she had drifted off to sleep.

Rick woke her with a kiss. She responded to his questing mouth with a hunger made even more intense by the dream she had been having. She'd been standing on the rock where Rick had removed her robe such a short time ago. This time she had been dressed in jeans and a sweater. Rick was kissing her and telling her how deeply he loved her when a fabulous yacht came into view. As the craft came closer, Karla recognized three of the people on board—Steve, Michael and Mary. They were laughing and joking with a crowd of faceless people, all beautifully dressed, all obviously having a wonderful time. Suddenly they turned and came to the side of the boat, where they began to shout for Rick to join them, telling him that if he didn't hurry he would be left behind. Steve told him that they were on their way to Monaco.

In the dream Karla could feel the battle raging inside Rick. Desperately she clung to him, while at the same time a story her grandmother had told her when she was a child echoed in her ears. "Remember, my child," her grandmother had said in the wonderfully gentle way that she had had, "people are a lot like baby chicks. Wrap your fingers too tightly around them, and they will fight to get away. But let them rest in your open hand, and they will snuggle against your palm."

Forcing her dream back into her subconscious, Karla wrapped her around Rick's neck and pressed her face into the hollow at the base of his throat. Not a word passed between them. She felt herself being lifted and carried into the bedroom. Gently, as though she were a sleeping child, he set her on the bed, then he lay down beside her and pulled her into his arms.

From the depths of his soul he said, "I'm sorry

I was gone when you came home. I know it looks as though I didn't want to be with you, but it wasn't you...it was myself I was trying to run away from...that I've been trying to run away from all summer." He held her face in his hands. Even in the near blackness she could see his eyes trying to communicate their painful message to her.

"Karla—" her name sounded like a sob wrenched from his soul "—I can't run anymore."

"I know, Rick," she whispered, at last accepting defeat. Her heart cried out against the knowledge, but her mind refused to hide any longer what she had known almost from the beginning. The chasm that separated them had not been bridged after all. Only their fingertips had touched in their desperate attempt to reach each other. Now it was time—time that they go their separate ways.

"Oh, my beautiful Karla!" His words were a cry filled with sorrow. "If only I could love you less."

Karla touched her fingers to his lips. "Love me now," she said. "Love me with every breath you take—for as long as we have...." There were no words to express the agony that would soon be theirs, so none were spoken. Instead the night became an offering to their doomed love.

Slowly, as if every movement must be savored because there would never be another time for them, they made love.

Rick opened the buttons of Karla's blouse and kissed the flesh beneath, his lips trembling with words left unsaid. Wherever clothing had covered her, his mouth pressed its warmth, enveloping her in a blanket of desire. "Come with me, Karla."

She could tell by the way he asked that he already knew what her answer would be. "I can't, Rick. Nothing has changed. Please don't make this any harder for me," she pleaded.

Karla reached for him with desperation. She wanted to hold him to her until the essence of him became a part of her. To melt the impression of her own heart and soul into him so that he would know forever, beyond any doubt, how completely she had loved him.

With a tenderness that made her catch her breath, Rick kissed her face. He pressed his lips to her eyes and down the bridge of her nose until, at last, he captured her mouth. She could taste herself on his lips. She licked away the lingering traces so that it was only Rick who filled her senses. She breathed in the scent of him and held it until she felt as though her lungs might burst.

Rick's hands cupped her breasts, and she nearly cried out with the pain and longing that she knew would forever after be her constant companion. His mouth traveled the familiar path down her neck and across the smooth flesh above her breasts. When he took one of her nipples into his mouth and pressed his face into her breast Karla cried out her love for Rick, and he responded with a hunger to match her own.

Their control disappeared in their aching need, and they joined in an urgency that destroyed all rational thought. When release came, it was not the naive joy they usually shared, but a poignant ending.

Afterward they lay side by side, their flesh touching from shoulder to hip to thigh. Rick's arm was flung over his face so that it covered his eyes, and when Karla reached up to touch his cheek, she found it moist with tears. Rick pulled her to him, resting his face against hers. Their tears joined in a river of sorrow for what might have been. If only. . . .

CHAPTER TWELVE

THE NEXT MORNING dawned as a reflection of the sorrow that held Rick and Karla in its grasp. The sky was a cold gray that trapped a layer of mist earthbound. Periodically a whispered breath of wind would stir the fog, and the water droplets would cling to everything, making the world as wet as if it had rained.

Heedless of the chill Karla walked out onto the porch, wrapped carelessly in her terry-cloth robe. The branches of the firs were heavy with moisture and bowed as though in sympathy with the gloominess of the day. This was the kind of weather the region was famous for, the reason for the lush green colors found everywhere in western Washington. But to people who craved desert and sunshine, such days, frequently coming one right after another, could make them frantic.

The weather was in perfect harmony with Karla's mood. For endless minutes she stood on the front porch and stared down at the water, where tiny lapping waves played with the shore. She had no idea how long she had been standing there when she felt

Rick come up behind her. He slipped his arms around her waist, and she leaned into him.

"The weather certainly isn't giving you a very good reason to stick around," she said, trying to force a lightness in her voice and in her mood for this, one of their last mornings together. But the simple words barely made it past the band she felt constricting her throat.

She had lain awake most of the night fighting an almost overwhelming desire to beg Rick to stay with her. She knew she could make him stay—by telling him that she carried their child. But what cost would that revelation finally exact?

After months of denying, of refusing to recognize the truth, Karla could no longer ignore the changes in Rick. She was not enough for him. He needed to be a part of his old life, of racing, as much as he needed air and food. Those were all essential to him; without any one of them he would gradually wither and die. She had seen it taking place over the summer, and now she realized that he, too, had known what was happening. It was a testament to his love for her that he had stayed as long as he had.

She closed her eyes, not wanting to acknowledge the pain he must have suffered at the endless questions he'd been asked. The night with Michael Whittaker, the tourists in the shop, the school yesterday—all were wounds he had suffered for her. And now she must let him go, must even make it

easier for him to leave. He had suffered enough
for her. She couldn't ask for more.

But if she was brutally honest with herself,
Karla thought, hadn't she known all along that it
would end like this? Wasn't that why, when she
had missed her menstrual period almost three
months earlier, she had lied about it to Rick? She
had told herself she was merely waiting to be sure,
but that wasn't the real reason. She knew how
much he wanted a child, and that if she told him
she was carrying his, he would stay...wouldn't
he? Were her motives less honorable than she gave
herself credit for, she wondered. Did she really
fear that he would leave despite the child? Did she
want him to stay because of it? If Rick were going
to stay for any reason, shouldn't it be because of
his love for her?

Karla turned around and laid her face against
the soft wool of his cable-knit sweater. How simple it would be if she were only brave enough to
tell him. Then she would know.

She looked up into his eyes. Dark pools of
misery were gazing back at her, and she experienced an unexpected calm. No, she wouldn't tell
him. And it wasn't because she feared his answer,
it was because she loved him enough to let him go.
Deep in her heart she knew it was the only way for
him to become whole again.

"When will you go?" she asked.

"Today."

The word struck her with the force of a physical blow, making her close her eyes against the burning tears that blurred her vision.

"So soon?" she whispered.

"Would waiting make it less painful?"

She shook her head. "No," she said aloud, knowing that their days together would soon have become unbearable. It was better this way no matter how much it hurt.

Laying her cheek against his chest again, she felt the now familiar mound of her ring, a ring she now knew she would never wear again. Numbly she asked, "Shall I help you pack?"

Rick held her away from him. "Karla, oh, Karla—I love you so very much. I'll love you forever—there will never be anyone else. Please...." He struggled with the words as though he were afraid of them. Still he went ahead and asked the question. "Please...come with me?"

A lone tear escaped her dark lashes. "I can't, Rick."

He pulled her back to him and crushed her in his arms. "What will I do without you, my love?"

And what will I do without you, Rick, she echoed in her mind.

KARLA FOUND IT IMPOSSIBLE to help Rick pack. She had dipped into the well of her strength one too many times, and now there was nothing left in reserve. Her heart broke with each piece of clothing that was folded and placed in the suitcase. In a rush to get away from the pain, she told Rick she could stand it no longer and that she had to leave while he finished.

Grabbing her jacket, she went outside and climbed the hill behind the house. Unconsciously she headed for the small opening in the forest where she had come years ago to watch the sunsets.

Rick found her there more than an hour later as he walked back from Jeff and Maggie's, where he had gone to say goodbye. He came into the clearing and sat down beside her. "I've decided to wait for the last ferry," he said.

Karla looked at him, the obvious question in her eyes.

He tucked a strand of her long, golden hair back into her hood. "It would be easier if I left after the Remainder Party. That way you won't have to field a lot of questions until you're ready to."

Karla nodded in understanding. He was right, of course. Rick had become a favorite with the island people. They would notice his absence immediately, especially if she went to the party without him. If she herself stayed away, there would be phone calls of anxious inquiry.

Rick pulled her into his arms so that her back rested against his chest. He leaned his cheek against her hair "You use the same shampoo and soap and perfume as millions of other women, yet you always smell so special. It's a scent that makes me catch my breath every time I get the lightest trace.''

''Rick, don't say things that will haunt me forever. I don't think I can take it. I already have so many memories.''

''Karla, I will talk of my love for you and how special you are to me forever. If I thought there was a snowball's chance in hell of changing your mind about coming with me, I'd spend every breath I take telling you of my love for you.''

''Instead of telling me, why don't you show me? Make love to me, Rick. Here. Now. I need you to make love to me this one last time.''

''Are you sure?'' he asked, his lips brushing her hair.

His words echoed from another time. She smiled softly, sadly at how appropriate they were. ''I'm as sure now as I was seven years ago,'' she said softly. She turned so that she faced him. Her hands went to her jacket and when she'd taken it off, she laid it on the bed of ferns beside her. When she began to remove her sweater, Rick reached out to stop her.

''Karla, we can go back to the house.''

''No.'' Her eyes spoke as strongly as her words. ''I want to remember this moment always, and I want it to be here in this place. Please.''

Rick's hands left hers and went to her face. He held her gently as he gazed into her eyes. Slowly he drew her to him. The meeting of their lips was as explosive as the first time they had kissed, just as wondrous. But this time their pleasure and their passion were tinged with a terrible sadness. Both of them were painfully aware that each second of their lovemaking had to be stored like a treasure against future loneliness.

Rick's hands moved to the hem of her sweater and with a fluid movement slipped the amber lamb's-wool garment over her head and tossed it beside her jacket. With loving fingers, he stroked the softly rounded flesh above her bra. "I never grow tired of looking at you." He smiled tenderly.

"Did you know that I've been watching this since I first noticed it seven years ago?" He touched a small mole on her left breast. "Had it changed an iota, I would have had you to the doctor the next day." He raised her chin until her eyes met his. "I want you to look at it every day," he said. "You'll have to watch it for me." He pulled her to him and bent his head to kiss the spot he had shown her.

Karla entangled her fingers in his thick black hair and held him closer. She shivered with bittersweet desire, a wanting that would mean an ending. Rick deftly removed the rest of her clothing. When she lay naked on the bed he had made with their jackets, he covered her with his sweater, still warm from his own body. Then he removed the rest of his clothing and was soon protecting her from the cold with the cover of himself.

His hands traveled well-known paths of love,

stroking, caressing, eliciting moans of longing from Karla. Fiercely she clung to him, moving against him in ways she knew would weaken his self-control.

Rick's hands went from her breasts to the almost imperceptibely rounded flesh of her normally flat stomach. She held her breath as he touched the exquisitely sensitive skin of her inner thigh. Gently he stroked and teased until she moaned and arched herself against him.

Gone were her surroundings, lost in their building passion. The cold and their unyielding bed were forgotten in their burning need for each other. Karla's mind, her body, her senses floated in a sea of desire where only Rick's claiming mouth and body could reach. When finally he entered her, she cried out his name. That one word expressed the love and the sorrow she held inside, as effectively as if she had taken an hour to tell it.

When at last they lay spent, and their passion no longer provided a cloak of heat, Karla began to shiver. Rick drew her closer, but the cold penetrated even the warmth he tried to give her. It became evident that they had to get dressed.

Rick raised himself up on his elbow and looked down at her. "Little of the rest of the day will be ours...."

Karla reached for her clothes, now as damp and cold as the air around them. "Does that mean you think we should say our goodbyes now?"

"If there are any to be said," he murmured softly.

Karla slipped her sweater over her head, recoiling as the wet wool touched and clung to her skin. She pulled her knees to her chest and wrapped her arms around them, blinking her eyes to clear them. He must not see her cry. Not now. "Rick," she said, barely above a whisper, "do you think I'm going to change my mind and follow you? Is that what makes it possible for you to leave?"

He sat up and raked his hand through his hair. "It's so little for me to cling to, Karla. All I have is the hope that you'll eventually change your mind."

"You've never understood," she said, determined to once more try to make him comprehend. "It has nothing to do with changing my mind. What I feel and how I react are as much an unchangeable part of me as whatever it is that makes you return to racing." Bitterly she added, "Something you know very well may kill you."

Karla leaned her head against her knees. "I can't understand what devil drives you to suicide, Rick. I only know that I cannot, that I will not, watch."

Rick was quiet while he put his clothes back on. His voice was hard when he turned to her and said, "You once told me you didn't believe that garbage about racers and suicide. What made you change your mind?"

She knew that arguing was futile. They were in a deadlock, and nothing would change either of their minds. Still, she went on, "Sitting in a hospital room on a death watch and seeing instead a miraculous recovery. And then learning that the person has so little respect for his life that he intends to try to snuff it out again." The tears that she had vowed not to shed spilled over her eyelashes. "Don't call me to watch you die a second time, Rick," she sobbed, turning away from him.

Rick put his arms around her and pulled her back into his embrace. Softly he said, "That's something I can't promise you, Karla. I might die tomorrow, or I might live to be a hundred. Either way I would speak your name with my last breath."

She put her arms around his neck and painfully admitted, "And you know that I would come to you."

"Then come with me now."

"No," she shouted, violently pushing him from her. "Don't ask me again. Don't make me suffer any more than I already am. You didn't listen to me when I told you I can no more change than you can. My God, Rick, do you think I'm playing some game? That only stubbornness keeps me from going with you?"

"No, that's not what I think. It's just...I can't seem to let you go. I can't extinguish that small candle of hope."

"Then stay with me!" The words came out of nowhere. She hadn't planned them, had only felt them. She saw the answer in his eyes before he spoke a word.

"I can't," he breathed. "I tried, Karla...I honestly tried."

She pressed her fingers to his lips. "I know, Rick. I know."

They gathered up their jackets, brushing off the loose madrone leaves and bits of clinging bark and then putting them on. Before they left Karla's special place, Rick held her to him as though he would never let her go. To anyone passing, it would have seemed as if they were vowing never to part.

They walked down the hill in silence. When they entered the house and Karla saw Rick's suitcases standing by the door, she felt her heart breaking all over again. She leaned against the wall, seeking support for her shaking legs, as Rick went into the living room and started a fire. Karla watched every movement he made, carefully cataloging it and filing it away in her memory for the nights she would sit alone in this room.

Enough, she chided herself. She mustn't let their few remaining hours be spoiled by maudlin thoughts. There would be time enough later.

"Would you like some coffee?" she asked.

Rick glanced up. "Yes, thank you."

Karla went to the kitchen and started the coffee. While it perked, she slipped into the bedroom to change her clothes. She glanced at the bed, then stopped to stare at it, at the bright yellow comforter she had bought in Seattle. She used to get so cold in that bed before Rick came! And now she would know that cold once again. But it would be worse. Now the chill would come not only from the cool sheets but also from her empty heart.

This house, which had been refuge from Rick, would become a constant reminder of him. There wasn't a room where they hadn't made love, where they hadn't professed their love for each other.

After hanging her wet things in the bathroom, Karla went back into the bedroom and automatically reached into the cherrywood dresser to get clean clothes for Rick. The empty drawer mocked her, and sitting down on the edge of the bed, she covered her face with her hands. She must not lose control now. There was so little time.

Rick came into the room, glancing at the empty drawer and then at Karla. Obviously guessing what she had in mind, he said, "I'll get something out of my suitcase." He held out his hand, and she let him lead her out of the bedroom.

They spent the rest of the afternoon in front of the fire. Few words were spoken, but the air was charged with messages of love and fear and regret. When the clock chimed four, Rick rose from the couch to scatter the fireplace embers and secure the glass doors. He turned to Karla.

"It's time," he said gently.

She nodded mutely. The steps she took to the door were acutely painful, but she walked as though it were only another trip into town. She smiled her thanks as Rick helped her into her coat.

"Do you want me to send your wet clothes later?" she asked.

"No, I'll take them with me to Phoenix."

She hadn't even asked where he would go first. "Your condominium there is beautiful," she said inanely. "I think you'll find that everything is pretty much as you left it. Steve and I packed only some of your things and gave away the perishables. We didn't. . . ." She couldn't go on.

"Don't, Karla," Rick pleaded with her.

She pinched the bridge of her nose, blocking her tears. Then she looked up and forced a smile. "You're right. I'll be more careful in what I say and what I think. I really don't want our parting to be worse than it has to be. We should be able to smile when we say goodbye. We've had so much."

They walked out to the truck. After Rick had loaded his suitcases he went back into the house for the twelve loaves of garlic bread that were their contribution to the Remainder Party. The bread would accompany the washtubs of chiapino and kegs of beer that would be consumed by the hungry crowd.

On the way Rick stopped by the ferry terminal in Marten's Cove and left his suitcases behind the

ticket booth. He didn't want anyone at the party to
see them and ask questions, he explained. By the
time they had made a quick stop at the gallery, they
were among the last to arrive.

The small beach was already ablaze with bonfires. The delicious smell of seafood stew mixed
with the smoke of burning driftwood and the crisp
salt air made an unforgettable autumn memory.
Shouts of welcome greeted them as they made their
way to the cooking area to drop off the bread.

Anyone who noticed Karla and Rick's subdued
mood was too polite to mention it. After the magnificent tourist season, which had brought an un-
usually large amount of money to Marten's Cove,
the favorite topic of conversation seemed to be the
new celebrity on Quiller Island.

*Sir Galahad had even managed to become a hit
at home,* Karla mused. It was too bad Jeff and
Maggie had to miss their charge's new notoriety,
but they were still on the uphill side of their flu.

Karla absently brushed her hair back from her
cheek. Facing the Himsons after Rick left was going to be difficult. She hadn't bothered to ask
Rick what they had said to him when he went over
to tell them goodbye. She didn't have to ask, she
knew. They would not be as circumspect this time
as they had been when Karla first arrived. They
had become good friends with Rick and knew too
much not to be personally involved this time. She
couldn't even hope they would understand.

As he delivered the bread, Rick exchanged a few words with Daniel Olsen, who, as usual, was in the middle of the kitchen area. Then he headed back to Karla, who was waiting for him beside one of the small fires. He took the blanket from under her arm and spread it out on the sand.

Karla looked at him, a panicky expression on her face. "I don't think I can do it. I don't think I can act normal while my world is collapsing around me."

"Do you want to leave?"

No! she wanted to shout at him. And she didn't want him to leave, either. What she really wanted was to crawl back to yesterday, to live their beautiful morning over again. It had been so special, and it had been over so quickly, a shooting star of happiness that had burned brightly and was gone forever.

In answer she shook her head. The moment of panic had passed. She sank to her knees on the bold plaid blanket. Rick put his arms around her, and to the world they looked like the lovers everyone thought them to be. Perhaps because of it, few people strayed over to interrupt their seemingly intimate moment.

They remained together on their blanket island lost in thought, staring into the fire until it was time to eat. As they waited in line for food, engaging in lighthearted conversation with those around them, Karla noticed a new face in the crowd. Rick told her the beautiful brunette was the reason for Daniel's healthy glow.

Karla smiled when a picture of Rick flashed through her mind. He had been so furious when he'd first met Daniel! Who would ever have guessed that the two men would become such good friends?

She wondered if Rick and Daniel would ever see each other again. Would they maintain their friendship? A macabre thought flashed through her mind. What if Rick visited Daniel on the island some time in the future and she came into town and accidentally saw them as they sailed into the harbor? A mirthless laugh accompanied her thoughts. How easy it would be for Rick to casually stop by to see his friend, how impossible it would be for him to do the same with her.

Karla wasn't sure she would be able to stand seeing Rick again, even on a casual, supposedly friendly basis. No, she absolutely knew she would not be able to have him anywhere near her. Even the slightest chance that they would cross paths would be more than she could bear; that was probably why she had come to Quiller Island in the first place. And now he was a part of her life here that could never be exorcised. What was she going to do? How would she ever live with the pain? Her island, her home, her friends had all been indelibly stamped by Rick.

She laid her hand against her stomach. Even the

child would be a daily reminder. But the child would also be a joy. . . .

Rick and Karla took their food back to the blanket and sat cross-legged in front of the fire. Every time Karla took a bite she found that it was almost impossible to swallow, so she finally gave up and put her nearly full bowl next to Rick's untouched one. He looked into her eyes and started to tell her something, but she put her fingers across his lips to stop him.

"Please, just one more minute," she said softly.

She wanted to memorize how he looked with the orange glow of the fire dancing in his eyes and creating soft highlights in his hair. He was breathtakingly beautiful, even more so now than when they had first met. Time had matured his features, making the strong lines of his face almost craggy. Someone seeing Rick for the first time would think him incredibly handsome, but also cold and aloof—until he looked up. Then it was obvious how special Rick Fleming was. Karla had seen him melt the hearts of teenagers and matrons alike with only a glance. And yet, oddly enough, perhaps because of the spark of mischievousness in their depths, Rick was what the sports writers liked to term "a man's man."

Karla leaned over and lightly pressed her lips where her fingers had been. "I'm not going to the ferry with you, Rick," she whispered as he held her. "I've thought about it, and I know that I

can't watch you leave. Take the truck; I'll have
Daniel drop me by to pick it up later. He's going
to know you've gone sooner or later. It might as
well be tonight.''

Rick touched her cheek and she could feel his
hand trembling. "I won't believe that it's over,"
he said.

They were oblivious to their surroundings as
they kissed one last time. Then Rick stood up and
walked away into the blackness of the night.

Karla waited for fifteen minutes, until she was
sure the ferry had gone. Slowly she cleaned up the
area around her blanket and prepared to leave.
She knew that if she had told Rick she intended to
walk into town for the truck he would never have
agreed to take it. So she had made up the story
about Daniel without ever intending to ask him
for a lift. She couldn't face questions tonight.
Tomorrow would be bad enough.

She managed to escape from the party without
anyone's noticing. The roads were deserted, and
most of the homes she passed were boarded up
against the fierce winter storms that sometimes
whipped through with near hurricane force, hurl-
ing huge pieces of driftwood onto the shoreline as
if they were twigs.

Once she was away from the crowded beach,
not even a barking dog broke the silence. It was a
fit background for her abject feeling of aloneness.

Rounding the last curve in the road that hid the

town from her view, she stopped in stunned surprise. The ferry was still in its slip! She cried out
against the unfairness of it. All she had asked was
that she not have to watch Rick leave. She didn't
want her last image of him to be such a final one.

But she stood and watched as though transfixed, and her heart wrenched when she heard the
distant sound of the mammoth boat reversing its
engines. Tears she had promised herself she would
not shed began to flow unheeded down her cheeks
as, without further ceremony, the brightly lighted
ship pulled away from the dock and swung past
the channel buoy on its way out of the harbor. The
departure was silent, without the usual blasts on
the horn to mark the occasion. And Karla was
sure that only she, a solitary figure on the side of a
hill in Marten's Cove, even cared that the ferry
had been late.

CHAPTER THIRTEEN

KARLA WENT TO THE GALLERY the next day and with a vengeance threw herself into the work that still needed to be done. She cataloged all the unsold art and wrote a letter to each artist, asking which pieces to store on the island for the winter and which to ship on to one of the other galleries he or she did business with.

Although many of the shops in Marten's Cove were already closed for the year, the gallery and several of the larger stores and restaurants were still open for the small crop of tourists who came for the brief Indian summer. It was more of a goodwill gesture on the part of the townspeople than anything else, as few of them did much more business than it took to break even.

This year Karla was immensely grateful for the excuse to keep herself busy, even though she knew the chances were good that the shop probably wouldn't earn enough to pay the utilities.

At the end of the fourth day, with even the books in perfect order, Karla was having trouble finding things to do. It was almost with a sense of panic that she roamed through the shop seeking something that would occupy her for yet another day. She was in one of the upstairs rooms when she heard the bell over the door tinkle and came down in a rush, hoping it was a long-winded customer. She stopped on the landing when she saw who it was.

Maggie stood in the middle of the room, her hands on her hips, her short hair disheveled from the gusting wind outside. She glared as Karla made her way down the last stairs.

"I've given you four days, and believe me, it hasn't been easy," Maggie said sharply. "Now I want you to tell me what the hell is going on."

Karla met her gaze with an angry stubbornness of her own. "No, I won't," she said evenly.

"That's not going to work this time," Maggie raged. "You and Rick have become part of my life as surely as if you had been born into it, and I absolutely refuse to stand idly by and watch you destroy each other."

"It's done, Maggie. It's a fait accompli. There is nothing you or anyone else can do. Let it be."

"That's not good enough. Dammit, Karla, someone doesn't have the greatest love since Gable and Lombard and throw it away as though another will come along at any moment."

Karla mentally flinched when she remembered how the great love Maggie spoke of had ended.

Clark Gable had never been the same after Carole Lombard died.

"Nothing was *thrown* away," Karla said wearily, "it was torn apart."

"You can play with words all you want, but the result is still the same."

"Why are you doing this to me? What makes you think Rick isn't the one to blame?"

"You're here, he isn't. And I didn't say I thought anyone was to blame."

The lack of sleep and the meals she'd missed suddenly caught up with Karla. She felt as though her legs would no longer support her. Like a puppet whose strings had been released, she collapsed on the bottom step, where she sat hunched over, hugging herself. "We tried, Maggie. We honestly tried."

"Not hard enough, or you would still be together. Accept it, Karla—I am not going to let go of this."

Karla stared at her friend, who was still standing defiantly in the middle of the room. "You'll have to sooner or later," she said. "You'll also have to decide if pursuing it is worth the price of our friendship."

Karla could see how devastating her warning had been by the sudden change in Maggie's posture. "I would be sorry for the rest of my life if I lost your friendship," the other woman said slowly, a catch in her throat, "but I would consider the sacrifice worth it if it brought you and Rick back together.''

Karla went to Maggie and put her arms around her. "I'm sorry," she whispered. "Forgive me?"

"Me, too, and yes," Maggie said. She looked at Karla critically. "Why don't you go home and let me finish here? You would probably scare away a prospective customer, anyway. You look like hell.''

A feeble smile curved Karla's mouth. "Thanks, I needed that. Just the words to build a woman's self-confidence."

"Have you eaten anything or slept at all since Rick left?"

"Yes to both."

"I knew you'd lie."

"Then why did you ask?"

Maggie took her by the arm and led her to the back door. She pulled Karla's purse from the roll-top desk and handed it to her. "Go home and eat the soup Jeff put in your refrigerator, take a bath and go to bed. I'll run the shop for the next few days. I want you to do nothing but sleep and eat." She opened the door and stood beside it as Karla meekly prepared to leave.

"But let me warn you," Maggie called out as Karla opened the truck door, "I'm going to camp on your doorstep in one week's time, and I'm going to stay there until we figure out a way to resolve your and Rick's differences. And I mean that camping out stuff literally. Jeff and Galahad are going to be in Oregon for three days and I have nothing else to do.''

Karla went home and did as Maggie had suggested, only in a different order. After she had bathed, she took her warmed soup to bed with her. The empty bowl was still on her nightstand when she awoke almost twelve hours later. She got up for a few hours and tried to read a book, then went back to bed again and slept until morning.

Feeling close to her old self, Karla spent the morning getting ready for winter. She packed away her summer blouses and brought out her heavier sweaters, checked the windows for air leaks and surveyed the wood supply.

Since she had first realized that she was carrying Rick's child, she had congratulated herself on obviously being one of the lucky women who had no trouble with pregnancy. She seemed to be carrying it off as though it were merely a temporary weight gain.

But now the full list of symptoms hit her, as if she were a textbook example of everything miserable that could possibly happen. Her breasts became swollen and so painful that she winced every time she accidentally touched them. The mere thought of food made her queasy. Huge magazine ads for food, which *always* seemed to be in living color, actually sent her stumbling toward the bathroom. She held water until her fingers and toes felt like fat little sausages, and the rest of her looked like a blimp.

After three and a half days of misery, Karla made an urgent phone call to the doctor who had confirmed her pregnancy. He assured her that her symptoms were normal and that her body was not getting ready to miscarry. He said that he was only surprised that she had been so comfortable for so long, since most women became ill earlier. The reassurance did nothing to stop her constant gagging, but it did ease Karla's mind.

The child she carried became more precious to her each day. It was the salve that made the wound of her loneliness bearable. Although its reality was still very much in her mind and not yet the physical manifestation it soon would be, she had no trouble visualizing the child she carried. Each time she thought of the baby inside her, Rick's words guided her.

She tried to decide whether she hoped for the girl he had described or for the boy but was unable to choose. She only knew that she wanted the child to have Rick's eyes. . . .

A knock on the door interrupted Karla's daydreaming. True to her word, Maggie stood outside the door with a day pack in her hand. They stared at each other for a long minute before Karla broke down and began to laugh.

"I suppose you have a tent in there, too, just in case I don't let you in?"

"Just a small one."

Karla stepped aside and Maggie entered with a flourish. She set her pack on the floor and slowly started to remove her gloves, one finger at a time, as she stared at Karla. When the gloves were off and lying on a chair, and her jacket had joined them, she matter-of-factly said, "So you're pregnant."

Karla blanched. She couldn't deny how ghastly she looked, but perhaps she could sidetrack Maggie. "What makes you think I don't have the flu?" she said weakly.

"Oh, I don't know. Perhaps it's because someone's checkbones don't disappear when they have the flu. Or perhaps it's that I've known you for three and a half years and in all that time I've never once seen you sick."

"Did it occur to you to keep your mouth shut until I decided to tell you myself?" Karla's tone betrayed her exasperation.

Maggie smiled. "Not once."

"I don't suppose there's anything I can do to get you to change your mind about staying here?"

"Nope."

"Well, come in by the fire then and sit down."

Maggie followed Karla into the living room. She took Jeff's favorite chair and pushed it closer to the circle of warmth near the crackling blaze. She slipped off her shoes and tucked her feet comfortably under her, reminding Karla of a nonchalant lioness who was trying to convince a wary herd of zebras that she really wasn't on the prowl.

"I have to warn you," Karla said, "that this will not be the most pleasant visit you've ever had. See that?" She pointed to a plate containing three half pieces of dry toast. "I've been working on trying to get that down all morning."

Maggie's face reflected her sudden concern. "Is that normal?" she asked.

"The doctor says it could last throughout the entire pregnancy, but he assures me it usually doesn't. He says I've been lucky not to get sick until now. It seems to me that lucky should mean not getting sick at all."

"I'm glad to hear that you're seeing someone." There was a pause in the conversation while Maggie went into the kitchen to get herself a cup of tea. When she returned, she looked Karla directly in the eye and began to pursue her reason for coming.

"Something tells me Rick doesn't know about this."

"Why do you say that?"

Maggie leaned back into the chair and sighed. "Listen, Karla, I know you don't want me here. . . ."

When Karla started to protest, Maggie stopped her. "All right, let's say you don't want me prying into what happened between you and Rick. Fair enough?"

Karla nodded.

"Still, I'm here and I'm not going away, so let's not play games."

Karla stared into the fire. "I'm just not ready for this, Maggie."

"It's been almost two weeks since Rick left. It's not going to get any better."

A sudden burst of anger shot through Karla. "How about if I tell you it's none of your business?"

Refusing to let Karla intimidate her, Maggie softly said, "We've already been over that."

"Dammit, Maggie!" she cried, then, in a voice only slightly lower, she said, "I don't think I've ever met anyone so stubborn."

Maggie's eyes flew open. She laughed aloud. "I can think of two people who outshine me in that category without any trouble at all."

"All right. Since it's obvious you're not going to go away, get on with it."

"Let's go back to where I said, Rick doesn't know about this, does he?"

Karla shook her head in answer.

"Why didn't you tell him?"

"Because he would have stayed."

"That doesn't make any sense. Isn't that precisely what you wanted him to do?" Maggie blew on her tea to cool it.

"Yes, but not that way. Any chains I put on Rick would eventually destroy him."

"Rick would never consider a child to be a chain. I've watched him around kids. He loves them. That's why Jeff and I didn't hesitate for a moment before asking him to take Galahad to Seattle."

Karla's face grew ashen. She stopped looking at Maggie and stared again into the fire, feeling tears come into her eyes.

Obviously concerned and puzzled over Karla's strange reaction to her seemingly innocent statement, Maggie leaned forward in her chair and asked, "What happened in Seattle, Karla?"

Karla waited until the painful tightness in her throat eased. She sighed deeply before she answered. "Nothing really—yet everything. It was only a little thing that happened, but it was the drop of water that made the cup overflow."

She swept her hair away from her face, absently tucking a stubborn strand behind her ear. "I don't know why it didn't occur to any of us...but then maybe it did occur to Rick, and he never mentioned it. Anyway, I can't imagine how we failed to realize that junior-high-school kids are old enough to realize who Rick is, and that with all the fuss made this summer about his retirement from racing, they were bound to bring it up. Of course it didn't help that the principal introduced him like a long-lost friend and opened up the subject of Rick's racing at the very beginning. After that I'm afraid poor Galahad took a back seat."

"I'm so sorry, Karla," Maggie breathed. "Jeff and I had no idea something like that would happen."

"If it hadn't occurred then, it would have later," Karla said more philosophically than she felt. "It was only a matter of time." She picked up a piece of the hard toast and began to nibble on the corner.

"The worst part was as we were walking out. We overheard a boy saying that his father thought Rick had quit racing because he had lost his nerve. I think the way he put it was that Rick had turned chicken."

Maggie flinched.

"But, as I said," Karla went on, "it was only the final drop of water. The cup had been filling all summer." With her fingers Karla wiped away the tears perched on her eyelashes. "Now do you understand?" she said softly.

"Yes. I understand why Rick left but not why you didn't go with him."

"So that I could be there when he kills himself?" Karla said tonelessly. "Is that what you think I should do, Maggie? Consider it for a minute. Picture Jeff in Rick's place. Racing isn't something he does once or twice a year. You would have to spend week after week after week praying that nothing happened while he was on the track qualifying. And then there are the actual races.

"Have you ever seen a car like Rick drives when it gets in a wreck?" She didn't wait for Maggie to answer. She didn't even look to see if she had nodded. Karla was lost in a world of remembering, where Maggie was unable to go. "Pieces fly in every direction. It's not uncommon for spectators to be killed or maimed, but most often only the driver is involved.

"How do you think you would feel, Maggie, watching on the sidelines while the fuel tanks rupture and burst into these really spectacular balls of flame? And all the time you're watching, you're aware of the fact that the man you love is in the center of that inferno. You watch as the yellow flag comes out, and the caution light begins to flash, and you listen for the sounds of sirens telling you that the track's fire crew is on its way. When you see the other racers slow down and pass, your mind screams at them to stop and help, but they don't. Everything moves in slow motion except the flames.

"And then you see clouds of white powder suffocate the fire and the rescue people crowd in to take the limp figure of a man out of the pathetically small and unrecognizable remnants of a race car. They rush him into an ambulance and take him to the infield, where the track doctors look and poke and prod and then send him on to another hospital.

"Before you leave to go with him, the cleanup

crews have come out onto the track and have quickly dispatched all signs that there had even been an accident. In a very short time the race starts again, and the missing car and driver are forgotten as easily as last night's dreams.

"At the hospital people come up to you...they say the strangest things. 'It was just an accident, not anyone's fault....' 'Don't worry, the driver's group-insurance policy will cover this....' 'My brother, father, uncle, cousin was in a wreck just as bad and he made it.' And you listen to every word even though the only thing you want to hear is the doctor telling you that the man you love isn't going to die and that he isn't going to be a vegetable, forever tied to a machine." Karla's voice faded to a whisper. "But sometimes he doesn't tell you that." She looked up to see tears in Maggie's eyes.

"Imagine how you would feel if someone handed you an article from *Time* magazine that had photographs of the wreck, and you could see a helmet that had been strapped into place at the beginning of the race now flying through the air? The photograph is so clear that if you looked closely through the flames, you could see hands reaching out for help. And after reading the article you felt as though you had been a very real part of the accident, and a factor in the death, because you had never said, 'No, don't race.' Instead you look back and you remember how many times you had cheered and smiled and joined a wild victory party when the competition was over, and never once did you consider what you were doing.''

Karla flung the half-eaten toast back on the table and excused herself. She barely made it to the bathroom in time.

When the siege of nausea passed, she placed her hand against her stomach. "I'm not sure whether you were responsible for that one or not, little one,'' she murmured. She started the water running in the sink and washed her face and rinsed out her mouth before going back to rejoin Maggie.

"I didn't mean to go on and on like that,'' Karla said, sitting on the couch again.

"Have you ever told Rick how you feel?''

"In bits and pieces. But it's something he can't understand any more than I can understand his compulsion to go back. Rick needs someone like Mary Davies, who has been around racing all her life.'' The words, because of their stark truth, hurt even more than she had thought they would.

"I take it Mary Davies is someone Rick once knew?'' Maggie asked.

"He dated her for a while when we were separated. She is everything I'm not and everything that Rick needs in a wife.''

"But obviously not what he wants, or he would have stayed with her.''

"It is to both of our sorrows that in each other we picked the wrong person to love.''

Maggie rubbed her hand across her forehead. "I was so sure that I would be able to help. I feel like such a fool."

"As hard as I fought against telling you, I'm glad now that I did. If it's possible to feel better about all this, I guess I do." Karla leaned her head against the cushion. "You're a wonderful friend, Maggie. You were right to want to help. I only wish there had been something you could have done."

"I'll tell you one thing for sure," Maggie said, a determined gleam in her eyes. "Jeff and I will make the best godparents, or uncle and aunt or whatever it is you might want us to be to your baby, that any child ever had."

Karla smiled. "Of that I have no doubt. And it will be godparents."

Each drifted into her own thoughts. After a while Maggie said, "You know you'll have to tell Rick about the baby sooner or later."

"Yes, I know. But there's time yet. It isn't something I have to decide on right away."

"He would want to know...." Karla's look stopped her. "All right. I'll back off. I only need to learn one lesson a night."

BY THE END OF THE WEEK, Karla's morning sickness had begun to confine itself to the mornings, and she was able to go back to work. She still suffered terrible depressions when she constantly felt on the verge of tears, but she was learning to cope even with those.

By now all the local people had heard the news that Rick and Karla were once again separated. Whoever she ran into would express sympathy, then quickly change the subject when they saw her eyes begin to moisten. Karla learned early that few people knew what to do with someone in tears, so she stopped fighting hers when they came and started to use them to her advantage.

Invitations began to come in as they did every fall, to open houses and birthdays and anniversaries, many of them celebrated a quarter of a year or more late because of the scarcity of time in the summer months. Karla refused them all, preferring to stay at home. Maggie fussed and argued but to no avail.

And then two days before the gallery was to close its doors for the year, Maggie came into town and insisted Karla accompany her out to lunch while Jeff ran the shop.

"I'm going to get you out and interacting with people again if it's the last thing I do," she proclaimed, pushing Karla out the back door. "I've decided that you're going to be my winter project. I won't relent until I've seen some color back in your cheeks, and you don't flinch every time you meet someone who might ask you about Rick."

With a sigh of resignation, Karla followed Maggie to her car. "Where are you taking me?"

"Can you face eggs?"

"No," Karla said too quickly.

"I have a feeling you can face the eggs, but not Daniel Olsen. Am I right?"

Karla nodded. It wouldn't have done any good to lie about it; Maggie was too perceptive lately for her to get away with anything. Or, Karla grumbled inwardly, she herself was too transparent.

She just wasn't ready for the questions Daniel was sure to ask...or to face the possibility that Rick had been in touch with him while he hadn't contacted her. How easily the coin had turned. She was the one jealous of Daniel now, jealous of his easy friendship with Rick. Jealous of the freedom that friendship gave him, while she was tied with rope of...of...of what, she wondered.

With a start, she realized that Maggie was staring at her as though assessing her mental strength. "All right, we'll skip the eggs. How does a nice greasy hamburger sound?" At Karla's immediate reaction she laughed. "Sorry. I guess you'd better pick the spot before I have you too sick to go."

By the time they returned from their leisurely lunch—a chicken-salad sandwich—Karla's spirits had improved to the point that she was actually laughing with Maggie over Galahad's latest exploits on the mainland. The wolf apparently had been confined for countless hours without anyone remembering his needs. With tears of laughter

Maggie told how Galahad had finally walked over to one senator's potted palm and delicately relieved himself. "Thank heaven," Maggie choked, "the senator was already on our side and took the episode with good grace."

They were both grinning widely as they entered the gallery, where they discovered a beaming Jeff waving a hundred-dollar bill. "In your absence, I have done what neither of you have been able to accomplish all summer long," he said grandly. "I have sold *the* paperweight."

"You're kidding," Maggie and Karla chorused.

"I am not! Marten's Cove has seen two great sales this season. One ghastly paperweight and the Whaler's Restaurant."

Karla's eyes opened in surprise. "I hadn't heard that the restaurant had been sold."

"It hasn't been announced yet. I know because the new owner cleared the debt over the bronze whale—with a check that didn't bounce."

"I'm impressed," Karla said. "Who is this person of such honor?"

"It isn't a person, it's a corporation."

Her face reflected her disappointment. "That's too bad. I hate to see the businesses in Marten's Cove taken over by corporations. Can you picture what kind of Remainder Party they would put on?" She barely managed to finish the sentence before the memories of the last Remainder Party came back to her.

"For crying out loud, Karla," Maggie said in exasperation, not realizing why she had become so emotional. "It's only one little restaurant, not Main Street. Stop looking for reasons to be depressed."

Karla smiled. "It did sound that way, didn't it?"

"Besides," Maggie crowed, "you know what this means, don't you?" When she saw Karla obviously didn't know what she was referring to, Maggie went on, "You owe me a tea at the Empress! And I can't think of a better time to go than next week on my birthday."

Karla's eyes narrowed. She had the distinct feeling she had just been cleverly manipulated. Instead of answering Maggie, she turned to Jeff. "Tell me about the person who bought the paperweight."

Jeff launched into a detailed description of a middle-aged man who had said his wife was a long-time collector of paperweights. Apparently this new acquisition was to be a Christmas present for the dear lady, and the man had gone on and on about how lucky he felt that he had found such a unique creation, unlike anything he had ever seen before and unlike anything his wife currently owned. And best of all, it was cheap.

Despite herself, Karla began to laugh. She could just imagine the look on a true collector's face at seeing that paperweight. Christmas would never be the same in that household. She wasn't sure whether or not she believed Jeff, but the story he'd told was so wonderful that she decided she didn't care.

On their way out, Maggie said, "We're going to spend the night in Victoria, so be sure to bring an overnight bag."

Now Karla knew she had been duped. "Hold on a minute. That was never part of the deal."

"I know," Maggie said in a rush, "but you could use the extra time to get some new clothes. The things you've been wearing lately are becoming a little snug, don't you think? As I remember, Eaton's has a lovely maternity department."

"How would you know that?"

Her friend shrugged. "All their other departments are nice, so why wouldn't their maternity be nice, too?" She smiled, waved and bounded out the door before Karla could say anything else.

Karla stood on the landing and watched the Bimsons leave. She would have to remember to give Jeff back his hundred-dollar bill. Better yet, she thought, letting the baser side of her personality have free rein for a moment, maybe she could talk him into giving the paperweight he had "purchased" to Maggie for her birthday. Karla smiled. That would rate right up there with the world's all-time dirty tricks. She would have to remember to talk to Jeff tomorrow.

By the time Maggie's birthday arrived, Karla had discovered she was looking forward to it with an eagerness that scared her. Without work to occupy her days, she found it increasingly difficult to function. Normally an early riser, she was now reluctant to get up at all. She tried going out on long walks, but there wasn't a path on the island where she could go without memories of Rick haunting her every step.

Although she tried to deny her reasons for doing it, she scanned the sports section of the newspaper every day for news of him. At the end of one long article about his return to racing, an article that was basically a rehash of his career, Karla discovered that he was entered in the Las Vegas Grand Prix as the team's number two driver. The article said that Rick had refused to bump his teammate from the number one position, which he had acquired when Rick retired.

It was only then that she realized Rick must have spent countless long hours on the telephone talking with scores of people when he had decided to retire. A man like Rick could not have quit easily. Sponsors would have to be convinced not to withdraw their money, or the team Rick left behind would have collapsed. No wonder he had become so restless.

Karla's heart beat painfully against her ribs. How could she possibly have been so naive? Had she hidden her head in the sand for the entire

summer? What other surprises were in store for
her?

She had known what a terribly difficult decision
it had been for Rick to leave racing, but she was
only now realizing how much he had sacrificed for
her. If only he could have held out a little longer!
It would have gotten better.... She bit her lower
lip. Would it have?

"If onlys" and "might have beens" echoed forlornly in Karla's mind until she thought she would
go crazy. It was a futile game, but one she didn't
know how to stop playing.

THE MORNING of the day they were to go to Victoria dawned with blinding splendor. An earlier
storm had washed away the last of the summer's
dust, clearing the air so that everywhere Karla
looked she had to squint against the brightness.
The island's clusters of maple trees had begun to
turn, making bold spots of color against the deep
green of the Douglas firs.

The air had a pleasant bite that forewarned of
winter and had the possibility of snow. Snow was
a treat to the island people, who never got enough
of it to cause the problems that it would have
made it a chore.

Karla met Maggie and Jeff at the ferry. Jeff immediately commandeered her overnight case, acting as though she had carried a cannon up the
walkway. Instead of arguing and pointing out that

she was perfectly capable of carrying her own luggage, Karla smiled her thanks. Her feminist instincts aside, she found she enjoyed being pampered. Pregnancy was doing strange things not only to her body but also to her mind. A latent nesting instinct had begun to make itself felt, and she found herself spending hours planning the changes she was going to make in the "nursery." Even the grotesque wallpaper had developed a certain charm that amazed her every time she thought about it.

Karla and Maggie settled into the lounge for the short ride to Sidney, while Jeff went off to get something warm for them to drink. A thought suddenly occurred to Karla. She turned to Maggie, who was thumbing through a magazine.

"What did you do with Galahad?"

Maggie smiled—her cat-and-canary smile. "Mrs. Pahlberg is watching him."

"How could you do that to Galahad?" Karla gasped.

"They've become bosom buddies."

"I find that hard to believe."

"It's true," Jeff said, handing Karla a steaming cup of hot chocolate.

"Chocolate?" Karla looked from the cup to Jeff.

"Drink it. The milk is good for you."

"But—"

Maggie laughed. "Unless you're sure it's going

to make you throw up, I'd drink it if I were you. Jeff can be very tenacious.''

Karla wrinkled her nose and sipped the strangely colored liquid. She had grave doubts about its milk content, but it didn't taste as bad as it looked. *Oh, well,* she sighed to herself, *it's just another inch on an already disappearing waistline.*

CHAPTER FOURTEEN

THE EMPRESS HOTEL, with its brick facade half covered in ivy, was one of the dominating landmarks in a city filled with charming buildings. It was the first thing visitors glimpsed when coming into the harbor from sea, and after that they were hard pressed to notice anything else.

As Jeff, Maggie and Karla drove into Victoria after taking the car ferry to Sidney, B.C., their view of the harbor was dominated by the Legislative Building, to the left of the Empress. A broad expanse of grass just above the sea wall held neatly trimmed beds with flowers planted to spell Victoria. This Canadian city had all the charm of an English village, while a hundred times that size.

Karla loved Victoria and rarely had to be prodded into going. But today, even though the baskets of flowers hanging from the light standards were still in bloom, the place looked less magical than it had before. Perhaps because most of the tourists had gone, Karla thought. They had abandoned the miraculously clean city and fled like migrating geese, seeking a warmer climate.

But perhaps the heaviness in her heart was because she had never gotten around to sharing the
beauty of Victoria with Rick. She had told him of
the horse-drawn rides through town, of the huge
storybook Legislative Building that was outlined
in white lights year-round except at Christmas,
when the thousands of white bulbs were replaced
with green and red. But she had never taken time
to bring him here.

Their reservations for the formal tea were at one
o'clock. They arrived early enough to have time to
wander through the lobby shops. After looking at
and commenting on the furs and jewelry, which
seemed obscenely expensive even after the rate of
exchange between Canadian and American dollars
was taken into account, they moved on to a shop
that featured work by Canadian artists. Karla was
irresistibly drawn to an unusual piece of scrim-
shaw. Instead of depicting one of the ordinary sub-
jects—whales or Inuit or walruses—the artist had
carved a lone man standing on a rock overlooking
the ocean. The longer Karla looked at the piece, the
more clearly she saw Rick. He looked so alone. . . .

Karla showed the piece of ivory to Maggie, who
dismissed it with the words, "Kind of sentimental,
don't you think? It's certainly not the artist's
finest work."

Not knowing what she would do with it when
she arrived home, knowing only that she had to
have it, Karla bought the yellowed ivory and care-

fully tucked it into her purse, avoiding Maggie's puzzled frown.

"We had better get going," Jeff announced, putting an arm around each of their waists. As they walked back toward the main lobby, where the tea was served, he bent his head toward Karla and said in a stage whisper, "Putting on a little weight, aren't you?"

Karla laughed. "Oh, that's a marvelous thing to tell someone just before you take her out to eat."

"Matters not, my lady. Seems to me, as I remember it, that you're paying for this little outing."

Karla looked at Jeff. His face was alight with a self-satisfied grin. She smiled sweetly and said, "That's right. And I just happen to have a crisp new one-hundred-dollar bill that should do the trick. By the way, I've been meaning to tell you that your gentleman friend must have had second thoughts about the paperweight. It seems he returned it." She frowned and shook her head as though terribly confused. "He must have been an odd one, though. Not only did he neglect to ask for a refund, he hid the paperweight in the back of my desk."

Maggie groaned. "Couldn't you have thought of someplace a little more clever than that, Jeff?"

"You came back sooner than I expected!" he yelped.

Because they were so early they were given seats by one of the two huge fireplaces that dominated the opposite ends of the lobby. Seated across from them was a young couple with twin daughters no more than three years old. The dark-haired girls were dressed alike in lavender pinafores and frilly pink blouses, precisely the type of clothing Karla had hated as a child. And precisely the kind she now grudgingly acknowledged looked beautiful on the little girls.

Karla let her gaze sweep over the room, stopping at the cream-colored columns and apricot ceilings as she tried to avoid looking at the dozens of couples, many obviously on honeymoons, who were scattered throughout the lobby. By the time the tea arrived, she found herself staring at potted palms and the bargello pattern on Jeff's wing chair.

It hurt more than she liked to admit to watch others so obviously in love. It was a painful reminder that she would forever be a third party, as she was today. Or alone, as was the woman sitting on the gold-colored love seat beneath one of the narrow, fifteen-foot-tall windows. Karla watched the woman for a moment. She seemed content, even happy. Perhaps Karla would be too...someday.

The waitress, wearing a black dress and starched white apron, brought them a silver container filled with crumpets, the first serving in their four-course tea. Karla watched the twin girls opposite her as they experimented with what was obviously new food to them. One decided it was grand and ate all that was given her. The other surreptitiously slipped her remaining portion over to her father's plate.

Jeff brought Karla's attention back to their threesome when he softly said, "Karla, I want to talk to you about Rick."

Karla glanced from Jeff to Maggie. Their faces reflected a seriousness that had been absent earlier. She realized the day had been even more carefully planned than she had first thought. A flash of anger coursed through her, so strong that she had to forcibly keep herself from getting up and walking out. "Did you bring me here to talk because you thought it would be less conducive to hysterics?" she hissed.

Jeff reached for her hand, which she immediately withdrew. "Don't be mad at Maggie, this was my idea," he said.

"She could have talked you out of it." Karla looked at Maggie. "How could you be a party to this? You, above anyone else, know why it's useless to keep rehashing what is past."

"I tried," Maggie said helplessly. "Jeff wouldn't be dissuaded."

Karla glanced at Jeff. "All right. Say what you feel you have to say. Then, if you want to remain my friend—" she forced the rest past a catch in her throat " never talk to me about Rick again."

"Karla," he said softly, "I don't want to hurt you. I want to help you to understand something. You once said you felt that if Rick had truly loved you he would have quit racing when your brother died. I can only assume that you still feel that way now, especially after what's happened.''

Karla didn't reply, she couldn't. She was afraid to trust her voice.

Jeff went on, ''I don't think Rick's racing has anything to do with his love for you. It's as separate as how I feel about Maggie and the love I have for my work. I've tried to picture myself and Maggie in your and Rick's position. I've tried to decide if I could give up what I do for a living if for some reason Maggie asked me to, and I knew I would lose her if I didn't. I have to be honest with you, Karla. I think I *could* give it up. I would miss my work terribly, and it would probably be a lifelong yearning, but I think I would survive.''

Karla bit her lip until she could taste blood on her tongue.

''But I'm not Rick, Karla. I've never been the *best* at anything, the way he is. I don't know how many people are involved in driving race cars, but there must be tens of thousands throughout the world. And that's only a fraction of those who would like to do it. Of them all, Rick is the unquestioned best. He has the gift, the talent—call it what you like. Whatever it is, it has made him better than anyone else, *ever*.

''To be truthful, I can't imagine what it would be like to be a Picasso or an Einstein. . .or a Rick Fleming. Few humans are so blessed. And until it nearly destroyed him, Rick was willing to give it all up for you.

"Rick will go on without you, because you have given him no choice. But I know that each day he's away from you a part of him dies. I've never conceived of a love as strong as what he feels for you. Do you have any real idea what he went through this summer?"

Karla could no longer look at Jeff, so she stared at the twins who were climbing onto their father's lap.

Jeff reached for her hand again, and this time Karla held on as though only contact with someone who cared would keep her from sinking into a hell of her own making. He squeezed her hand and when she looked at him, he smiled. "What if Lindbergh had had a wife who asked him not to fly the Atlantic? Or Hillary's wife had been afraid of mountain climbing?" he softly teased.

"Please believe that I didn't say any of this to hurt you, Karla, or to try to insinuate that what you've gone through isn't reason enough not to go back to a life so filled with tragedy. I only wanted to help you understand how Rick could love you and yet still leave you. I thought I could help to ease things for you, if only a little."

Incapable of words, Karla managed a smile that let Jeff know she was no longer angry.

They finished their tea in a comfortable silence. When it came time to pay the check, Karla's emotions were under control again. She told Jeff she would give him back his paperweight money if he agreed to pay the bill. She said it was fitting retribution for the subterfuge he had so gleefully engineered.

She glanced at Maggie. "You wouldn't believe how I had originally planned to get even. Remind me to tell you someday—someday when you're in a very good mood."

As they prepared to leave, Jeff declined to accompany Maggie and Karla on their shopping trip, saying that there was an exhibit at the provincial museum that he wanted to catch while he was in town. They separated with plans to meet in front of the Crystal Garden at five.

Karla grew increasingly quiet as they went from store to store. She let Maggie decide which items of clothing looked best on her, purchasing several practical slacks and tops as well as one beautiful bright red silk dress for the holidays. Finally she pleaded fatigue and asked to go back to the hotel. When they arrived, she announced her decision to go home instead of spending the night in Victoria. Maggie started to protest but Karla stopped her.

"I have a lot of thinking to do, and I would like to do it at home. . .and alone."

"At least wait until Jeff comes back. He can take you to Sidney."

"I would just as soon take the bus. I get a kick out of those double-decker monstrosities." Karla hugged Maggie. "Pass that on to Jeff, and tell him I didn't mean what I said."

"He already knows that," Maggie sniffed.

"Don't you dare start crying," Karla grumbled, fighting back her own tears. "If there's anything I can't stand, it's women who make spectacles of themselves in public. Besides, it gives every male chauvinist within earshot another notch in his gun."

At that they hugged each other again and burst into laughter, which brought its own form of tears.

Fumbling for a tissue, Karla said, "Do you suppose puffy eyes will ever be 'in'? I can't remember the last time my mascara stayed on for an entire day."

"I'm told weepiness goes along with being pregnant."

"Wonderful," Karla groaned. "Now I find out."

Karla made it to the ferry terminal in plenty of time to catch the last boat out on the abbreviated winter schedule. After a few cursory questions from the customs and immigration officials, she was allowed to board. Although there was a definite chill in the air, she stood outside as the ferry pulled out of the Sidney slip. She needed to be alone, and standing outside was the quickest way to assure that she would be.

Walking around to the stern to catch the sunset, Karla was struck anew by the pristine beauty of the area. Tourists came to Puget Sound and British Columbia in large enough numbers to keep the communities economically stable, but those towns were still so sparse in number and concentrated in such few areas that most of the land was still un-spoiled. Many of the islands the ferry passed on the way to Quiller Island were uninhabited.

Karla stared into the swath of smooth water that was their wake. With the setting sun reflecting off its surface, it looked like a section of gold icing that had been smoothed with a knife. She thought of the child she carried, and of Rick's description of the golden-haired boy of his dreams. She felt a warmth in her palm as she pictured herself holding a little boy's hand. She smiled when she remembered the twins she had watched earlier. How patient their father had been with them, how adoring. She felt a terrible sadness when she realized Rick would be denied loving moments like those with his own child.

Visitation rights, no matter how generous, never provided enough time to build a relationship such as those twins had with their father, she knew. Only day-to-day encounters filled with love and precious moments of sharing could produce what she had seen today. Karla's hands tightened on the railing. Would the child she carried become a torment for Rick instead of a joy?

She raised her eyes to stare at the now deepening purple of the sky overhead. Looking across the water she recognized Bradley Island and knew that if she moved to the bow, she would be able to see Mount Rainier already wearing a thin new mantle of snow over its year-round glaciers. She had started to walk forward when she heard the clear, sweet music of a flute drifting out of the lounge. After listening for a few seconds, she decided to stay where she was instead and watch the show nature was providing behind the rugged Cascade Mountains.

The flutist played several Simon and Garfunkel tunes, now and then adding his own interpretations. Karla thought about the music and wondered who the world's best flutist was. If there was such a person, was he or she torn between the demands of a career and a home life?

When Karla felt herself beginning to understand Rick's position, a panic tightened her chest and made her struggle to breathe. She would feel all the agony she had gone through, and she would know once again that it was real, not imagined.

She stared out at the rapidly darkening sky. The area just above the Cascade Mountains had turned a bright orange streaked with crimson, as though a fire raged out of control just over their peaks.

Homes, both mansions and cabins, randomly dotted the shorelines of the islands they passed. Slowly lights began to appear in them. Against the black velvet of the fir-covered dots of land, the lights looked like cat's eyes peering out of the forest at the passing ferry.

When they came at last to Quiller Island, Karla watched their approach with a pleased smile. It was obvious that Marten's Cove was a town asleep for the winter. Only the most necessary lights brightened the streets. Power was expensive here and thieves uncommon, so the residents felt little need to "light up against crime."

Karla was the only passenger to disembark. By the time she had climbed the hill to the gallery, the brightly lighted ferry was halfway out of the harbor on the day's final run to Anacortes. Lost in a bubbling caldron of thought, she drove home slowly, discovering when she arrived that she was unable to recall the journey. As she unpacked her overnight case, Jeff's earlier words echoed in her mind.

She realized that she had never thought about Rick the way Jeff had described him. Being the "best" at racing was a facet of Rick's personality she had taken for granted, never truly realizing what it implied. And there was no question, he was the best. Had he cared to collect them, Rick could have filled rooms with the articles that had been written about him in newspapers and magazines over the years. Articles proclaiming him number one, the praise backed up with statistics impressive even to fans not thoroughly familiar with racing. But Rick rarely read them. He accepted what and who he was with such casualness that Karla had learned to do the same.

She made herself a cup of tea and wandered from

room to room until she ended up in the bedroom, staring at the closet. For the first time in a long while she thought of the painful memories hidden there, packed away in an old cardboard box.

Rick had been right—she was a coward. It was easier to try to bury the memory of Bobby than to face it. Why else would every physical trace of him that she still possessed be tucked into a dark corner?

Without giving herself a chance to reconsider, Karla set her cup of tea on the cherrywood dresser and reached past her shoes to pull the sealed cardboard box out into the light. She sat on the floor and ran her trembling hands over the edges. It looked so innocent, like any other packing box. There was nothing on the exterior to indicate the heartache Karla would find inside. She broke the seals and unfolded the flaps.

Lying across the top, cushioning the mementos below, was a navy blue turtleneck sweater. Karla lifted the wool garment out of the box. Burying her face in the soft folds, she closed her eyes and saw her brother as clearly as if he stood in front of her.

Vividly she remembered them as children, sharing their dreams while perched on the upper branches of a tree. Bobby had always talked in superlatives that were beyond the other kids in the neighborhood, but because she was older and she cared, Karla had tried to understand.

"I want to do it all, Karla," he would say. "I

want to hunt for buried treasure in the Caribbean, and I want to sail around the world all by myself. I want to look for life on Mars," and more softly he would say, "and I want to figure out some way to keep all those kids from starving to death right here on earth."

She had listened to and shared his dreams in their private treetop world, never comprehending what it was that drove him to such impassioned outbursts but accepting them because he accepted her need to break out of the mold their parents seemed intent on pressing her into. . . .

Karla put the sweater aside. Back in the box her hand traced the frame of a photograph. Slowly she pulled the picture out and turned it over. It was a frozen moment in time, showing Karla and Rick and Bobby standing in front of the race car that had killed her brother fewer than six months later. The click of a shutter had captured them forever in an instant of such happiness that it seemed to radiate from the print. There was no way Karla could prevent the tears that filled her eyes so she just ignored them, unconsciously reaching up to wipe them away periodically when they blurred her vision.

Tentatively she reached out and with the tip of her finger touched Bobby's face. "I'm so sorry, Bobby," she whispered.

The words, never spoken before, brought a strange comfort to her soul as though a crushing burden had been lifted. But they also brought a

frown to her face. Why had she apologized? Could
it be possible that she somehow felt responsible for
Bobby's death? The idea stunned her. She had
never been able to fully accept the idea that she had
subconsciously blamed Rick. But it had never occurred to her that her strange actions after Bobby
died could have been influenced by the fact that *she*
had felt responsible.

Karla stared at her smiling brother, and for a moment it was as if he once again stood beside her.

"Bobby?" she choked. "What would you have
done with your life if I had never met and married
Rick?" She leaned her head against the dresser.
"Where would you be today if I had not introduced you to racing?" she whispered. "It *was* my
fault that you died, wasn't it?"

But as soon as she said the words, she knew that
it wasn't true. She could no more accept blame for
his death than she could accept credit for the happiness she saw on Bobby's face in the picture. She
had not asked or encouraged him to drive, she had
only introduced him to the world of racing by
marrying Rick. The decision, the persistence had
been Bobby's own, just as the victories had been
his, not hers. If she could not take any credit, then
neither could she take the blame.

How long had she been punishing herself for his
death, she wondered. How had it influenced her decision to leave Rick, to refuse to go with him even
now? She held the photograph tightly clasped to

her chest and smiled sadly through her tears. "Oh, Bobby, if you only knew what I've done...you would be so mad at me. I've been such a fool."

Karla rose to her feet and stood in front of the tall, seven-drawer chest she had bought for Rick. Carefully she adjusted the stand on the back of the picture and placed it on top of the dresser. She stepped back and stared at the photograph.

"I will never stop missing you or loving you, Bobby," she finally said. "But it's time I forgive myself for your death and move on with my life." She pressed the tip of her finger to her lips and then to the photograph.

"Wish me luck, little brother," she whispered.

THE NEXT MORNING dawned with the promise of one of the storms the Strait of Juan de Fuca was famous for. A lulling wind, which only occasionally gave a hint of the fury the incoming storm contained, whipped through the trees, crackling the leaves and the loose bark of the madrone and mercilessly bending the branches of the firs. The dark blue sea was a paint-splotched canvas of whitecaps.

Karla stood for a while at the front window watching huge black clouds tumble across the sky as the storm increased in intensity. Then she curled her hands into determined fists and turned back to the dark living room, where she walked over to the television set. Last night she had made the decision to watch the Las Vegas Grand Prix, and before she could talk herself out of it, she wanted the prerace feature to numb her resistance.

As usual, for some unknown reason, the turbulent weather made the television reception beautifully clear. She could see every curve of the model who was draped across the hood of a car, incongruously advertising the durability of tires. Karla's hands went to her thickening waist and she realized with a start she had absolutely no urge to throw up. Not even the insipid model had made her ill. She grinned.

She was feeling rather smug when the advertisement abruptly ended and a photograph of Rick flashed on the screen. Her heart lurched, and she clasped her hand to her mouth to stifle a cry of surprise.

God, how she missed him! It had been such a long time since she had seen him in his own element. He looked so happy—so self-confident.

The announcer broke into her thoughts, telling his invisible audience that a camera crew had been allowed to follow Rick Fleming during the frantic week before his long-awaited return to racing. Because of his last-minute panic to make sure everything was ready, however, they had only been able to get one fifteen-minute face-to-face interview.

A lifetime of memories came crashing through Karla's mind as she lived with the camera crew, and with millions of other viewers, the previous week in Rick's life. Familiar faces that she'd almost forgotten during the three years of her exile from racing made brief appearances on screen, clasping Rick in bear-hug embraces of welcome, sporting huge grins of pleasure when they saw him. Even though the short film purported to be a closeup report of Rick Fleming's return to racing, it was a revealing portrait of the man he was. Other drivers might have felt animosity toward him for stealing the limelight; instead, they paid him glowing tribute. It was obvious that they were glad to have him back—and that he was glad to be there.

The second to the last scene had been shot the night before, with Rick in the garage checking his car over one final time—something he always did before a race. The camera panned across the select group that had been allowed inside the spotlessly clean building. Karla smiled when she saw Steve McDonald wiping the engine. She knew it was something he did from nervousness as much as from anything else, and that he would probably still be doing it late into the morning.

Karla paused long enough in her reminiscences to hear the announcer say, "Unlike many of the drivers who harbor superstitions about women and racing, Rick Fleming doesn't seem to mind them around the pits or in his garage. One beauty in particular—" here the camera swung around to Mary Davies, who was smiling broadly at something someone off camera said to her "—has been seen in the Fleming garage all week."

Karla recoiled as if somehow the storm raging outside had suddenly found its way into her heart. A coldness permeated the most protected part of her being and made her shudder. With blinding clarity, Karla remembered the pain that had been in Mary's face the last time she had seen her. Now it was gone. In its place was a glow that made her even more beautiful than Karla remembered. She seemed the epitome of happiness, the example to everyone else who still struggled toward that goal.

The camera pulled back, and it became obvious the man Mary was listening to with such love in her eyes was not Rick, as Karla had foolishly feared, but Steve, who made a final swipe at the engine before he looked up and winked at her. Karla was stunned—and delighted. Obviously Steve's shoulder had become more than something for Mary to cry on.

The screen faded to black before filling again with Rick's profile. His earlier smile was gone as he stood all alone in front of a brilliant orange setting sun and stared at the track.

The announcer's voice was a soft whisper as he said, "Only another racer might know for sure what could possibly be going through Rick Fleming's mind as he paces the track one last time before tomorrow's race. But if I were to hazard a guess, it would be that after the tragic accident six months ago that claimed the life of one of his best friends and almost claimed his, Rick Fleming wonders if he has lost any of the skill and nerve it takes to be number one. Has he lost that special something that made him just enough better than anyone else to become a living legend? Surely the thought has crossed his mind that it might have been better to remain in retirement than to disappoint his legions of fans with a poor showing today.''

The picture of Rick faded, to be replaced by a serious-looking announcer in a dark blue blazer. ''No doubt about it, folks, there's a lot resting on Rick Fleming's shoulders today. The question is, will he be strong enough to carry the weight? We'll find out right after. . . .''

Involuntarily Karla's hand reached toward the screen. The announcer's words had penetrated her mind like a scathing indictment. She should be beside Rick. If ever he needed her, it would be after the race, regardless of the outcome. How could she have been so selfish? How could she have thought only of herself, never once considering the mental torture Rick would go through over this race? Even if she never went to another, she should have been with him today.

When she heard the sounds of the car engines, Karla felt herself growing physically ill. But she forced herself to watch the race. It wasn't until it was almost half over that she realized she was smiling. Rick had lost nothing. His skill was as evident and as beautiful and as much a joy to watch as it had ever been. He maneuvered through the other cars and around the track with a grace that was all his own.

If he died on this track or any other track because of an accident, it would be just that. As much an accident as if it had happened on a freeway or at an airport or in a slippery bathtub at home.

Karla thought of the years she had wasted, time they could have been together. If something were to happen to Rick today, either on the track or on the way home afterward, there would be no way to make up the time they had lost. With sudden clarity she knew that, even if they were together only until the next race, it was time she wanted to spend with Rick. Each day, each hour was incredibly precious. She had been treating them as though there was an endless supply.

She looked at her watch. Five hours from now she could be on her way to him. She smiled and hugged herself as she pictured their reunion. She would put a call through to him as soon as the race ended, telling him that she was coming—telling him that she would never leave him again.

CHAPTER FIFTEEN

Before Karla could place her call, the storm broke, taking with it the telephone service, followed shortly by the electricity. In the rapidly disappearing remnants of daylight, she packed her new clothes, wondering how she would tell Rick about the baby and how long he would be angry because she hadn't told him before he'd left. It didn't matter. He could be furious with her as far as she was concerned, as long as they were together again.

Karla had already started out the door when she remembered Maggie and Jeff. They would be frantic if they came home tomorrow and couldn't find her. Leaving her suitcases by the door, she went to the kitchen and wrote a note.

"Going to find Rick."

The words were the most beautiful she had ever seen.

"Don't worry!"

She knew they would anyway, at least until they heard from her again.

"Love, Karla."

And they loved her back. Better than she deserved sometimes.

She taped the note on the refrigerator, secured the hood on her rain jacket, grabbed her suitcases and made a dash for the truck. Before she could get her luggage and herself into the cab, she was soaked. Any other time she would have paused a moment to watch the water falling from the sky in wind-whipped sheets. Tonight all she could think about was reaching Marten's Cove in time to catch the ferry. She only hoped Rick would still be at the track by the time she could get to a working phone. Now that she had made up her mind to go to him, each minute they remained apart seemed like an eternity.

Karla carefully maneuvered the truck along the road, trusting her memory of the deeper holes more than the quick glimpses her struggling windshield wiper afforded. When she had gone less than half a mile in almost fifteen minutes, she realized she would never make the ferry on time if she didn't speed up. She took the next puddle with enough speed to make it through without any problem, except the hole was deeper than Karla remembered. She heard something snap just as a flood of water splashed around her. After a few choking sputters, the truck died.

It took a minute for Karla to realize that it was not going to restart despite her efforts and pleas. She held her hands up in supplication as she stared at the dusty dashboard. "How could you do this to me?" she wailed. "How could you let me down now?"

When she finally had to acknowledge that she was still too far from town to make it to the ferry by walking, even if she left her suitcases behind, she laid her head against the steering wheel and sobbed in frustration.

Without the heater, Karla's wet slacks soon felt like sheets of ice against her legs. The cold prodded her into leaving the truck and heading back down the muddy road for home. Perhaps, she told herself as she stepped around puddles, the telephone would be restored soon and she could at least call. She knew better, but she needed something, some small hope to cling to, until she could leave in the morning and begin her search for Rick. It would be a painfully long night.

Once inside the house again, she began to shiver uncontrollably. She found she couldn't hold her hands still long enough even to light a lantern, so she peeled her wet clothing off in the dark. Her teeth chattered like bottles on top of a humming refrigerator as she struggled into her robe and went to start a fire.

When at last the kindling crackled to life, she imagined she heard her name being called in the sounds of the fire.

No, it couldn't be.

There it was again, rising above the howl of the

wind. Loud thumping noises came from the back of the house and the door flew open abruptly.

"Karla?" Rick frantically called out.

She was so stunned that she was unable to move or to answer.

"Kar..." He spotted her kneeling by the fire, her body hidden in the folds of her robe, her head covered by a towel, wrapped turban style.

"Rick?" she finally managed to answer.

He closed the door and stared at her as if suddenly unsure of his welcome. He wore a down jacket so wet that each quilted pocket looked as if it held a reservoir of water that was about to burst. His soaked jeans were no longer a deep blue, but instead seemed almost black. Water dripped from his hair in tiny rivulets that ran into his eyes and forced him to squint.

They looked at each other for what seemed like hours, as though each one was afraid to awaken and discover he or she had been dreaming. Finally the silence was broken and they both spoke at the same time.

"What happened to you?"

"How did you get here?"

What Karla really wanted to know, she was afraid to ask. Why had he come?

"I was on my way to the ferry..." she said.

"I came on the ferry..." he replied in harmony.

"Why?" they chorused.

Karla saw Rick shiver from the cold. "Come in by the fire," she said, still not believing that he was indeed with her, that she had not conjured him up in her need.

"I'm wet."

She smiled. Nothing Rick could have said would have more readily convinced her that he wasn't an apparition. She would never have dreamed the inane conversation that had just passed between them. She tried to swallow, but her throat constricted. "You're really here," she whispered finally.

Rick met her halfway across the room and pulled her into his arms. His mouth closed over hers, and in the depth of his kiss she knew the loneliness he had felt while they had been apart. He held her so tightly against him that Karla felt the moisture seep from his jacket into her robe.

"Rick, I don't understand...how did you get here?"

He cut her words off with another kiss that made her almost forget her question. "I pulled in a few favors and left right after the race on a sponsor's private jet. I made it to the ferry just as it was getting ready to pull out."

He reached up to hold her face between his hands. He looked deeply into her eyes. "But how I got here isn't important. I have something I want to give you...."

She saw fear in his face, and it frightened her.

"But this time, if you take it, it has to be forever." His words were hesitant, his voice cracked. His hands left her face and went to his neck. Slowly he pulled the chain he wore there over his head and unclasped the hook. Finally the gold band lay in his palm.

Karla held out her hand. "Will you put it on me?" She could see the turmoil in his eyes.

"Karla, do you know what it is I'm asking of you?" he said.

"To love you."

"And to be with me."

She smiled. "Always. Wherever you go, I will go."

"What made you change your mind?"

"Can I have my ring first and answer questions later?" she asked softly.

Rick took her hand in his and slipped the band on her finger. "I love you, Karla."

She gazed at her hand. How beautiful the ring looked, how right it felt. "And I love you, Rick." She put her arms around his neck and kissed him. She moved against him in a way that let him know how she felt.

But instead of responding, he pulled her arms from his neck. Confused by his behavior, Karla glanced up to see him glaring at her, his eyes now full of anger.

"We have some things to discuss," he said curtly. "But first I'm going to get out of these." He ran his hand down the front of her robe, feeling the wetness he had put there. "You'd better put on something dry, too. And do something with your hair. I don't want you to catch a cold."

Karla's eyes were wide in disbelief as she watched Rick disappear into the bedroom. She was still standing there too stunned to move when he came back moments later wearing an old robe of his that she had commandeered when they were first married. He tossed her a thick flannel nightgown and watched her closely as she slipped out of the robe and into the green gown.

When she was dressed, Rick pulled a chair closer to the fire and told her to sit in it. He tucked a blanket around her and tossed several more small logs onto the fire before turning and staring at her again. "You owe me an explanation, and it had better be a damn good one," he said.

"It might help if I knew what you were talking about," Karla said, stalling for time.

He moved the chair that matched hers closer to the fire in turn, so that he was directly across from her. He didn't say anything, just sat back and glared.

"How did you find out?" Karla finally sighed.

"Does it matter?"

"For some strange reason, it does."

"I figured it out for myself." Rick rested his chin on his folded hands. "I couldn't stop thinking about the last time we made love and how. . .

how rounded you felt. Your breasts were different, and where you should have been concave from not eating, you weren't. We hadn't done anything to prevent a pregnancy...." He shrugged. "Now answer my question."

"I don't have an answer."

"Then make one up."

Karla knew how stupid the truth would sound, but she was too tired and confused to think of anything else. She stared into the fire. "I knew that if I told you, you would stay."

Rick rubbed his temples. He sighed. "That's what I thought."

"You did?" Karla asked in disbelief.

Rick smiled with his eyes. "Do you remember the O. Henry story about the woman who wanted to get her husband a Christmas present? She didn't have any money, so she cut her beautiful long hair and sold it to buy a chain for her husband's prized watch?" Rick asked.

"And she discovered that her husband had sold his beautiful watch to buy her combs for her hair," Karla added.

"I've sold my watch, Karla, and you've cut your hair."

The confusion she felt was mirrored on her face.

Rick reached for her hand. "I officially retired from racing today. It's all over."

"But you didn't have to—"

"I know," he interrupted. "I saw your suitcases in the truck."

"You can still go back. I meant what I said—I will go with you." Karla reached over to brush the still-damp hair from his forehead.

"I know you will. But everything is different now. It's not just the two of us anymore. I've done a lot of thinking since I left, about us and about the baby. It's a wonderful thing to know that there will be a child of ours born in a short time, but it's also frightening in a way. I have to earn the right to be called daddy by a bright-eyed little girl or to be hugged and kissed by a honey-haired boy. And that means being here for the good times and the bad. I don't want to be a drop-in father—and if I continued to race, for most of the year I would be just that.

"I don't want to do to our child what my parents did to my sister and me." Rick smiled sadly before he went on. "It's amazing how creative I became at inventing reasons why they stayed away from us. I would tell the lies and Barbara would listen as though she believed every word. I've often wondered which of us it did the most good."

Rick reached out and pulled Karla over to him as though he could no longer stand not being touched by her. She snuggled into his lap, resting her head against his shoulder. His hand touched her face. "Did you know," he said softly, "that you are the only person whom I've ever said, 'I love you' to?''

No wonder he had fought so hard against loving her, Karla thought. How especially cruel her own abandonment of him had been. How would she ever make up for the pain she had caused him? Overcome with an indescribable sadness, Karla thought of the scores of people who had filled her life with loving joy from the moment of her birth. She had been surrounded by adoring brothers, cousins, grandparents, aunts and uncles. She couldn't imagine a childhood without them. She wished she could reach back to the little boy Rick had been and share some of the love that had been lavished on her.

Rick ran his hand along her arm. "Do you understand why I had to go back? Do you know that it had nothing to do with the way I feel about you?" Before she could answer, he continued, "It's important that you realize I didn't choose racing over how I feel about you." He seemed desperate that she comprehend.

"Over the summer, I began to doubt my reasons for leaving racing. I questioned whether I'd left because you wanted me to or whether it was simply an easy way out for me. I *had* to know whether racing had won or I had. It almost became an obsession with me that I walk away a winner, if only in my own mind."

Karla suddenly remembered she hadn't seen the

finish of the race. "And did you?" she asked. She could feel the muscles of his face pull his mouth into a smile.

"Yes," he said simply. "In more ways than one."

Karla smiled, too. She shared his pleasure and now, finally, she understood his pride. "How will you survive without that excitement, Rick? It took me a long time to understand how much a part of you racing is. Now that I do, I'm afraid you will change...that eventually you'll be terribly unhappy that you didn't stay with it."

"You needn't be. I've made my peace, and I'm leaving because I want to."

"But...." She didn't want to say what she'd been thinking because in her heart she knew it would mean saying goodbye to Quiller Island and the life she had grown to love. Softly she finished. "But what will you do now? What will *we* do now?" she amended.

Rick drew her closer and pressed a kiss against her hair. "Karla, sometimes I feel such an overwhelming love for you that I'm afraid it would terrify you if you could see it. If unleashed, I think my love would suffocate you. I know how much you are willing to sacrifice for me, too. However, I would never ask you to leave here."

"And yet, even though I tried to ignore it, I know how you suffered this summer with nothing to do," she replied softly. "How can we possibly stay?"

"But now I have something that will keep me busy." He laughed when he saw the confusion on her face. "From all the research I've already done concerning my little project, I think it may keep me even busier than I want to be."

"Needless to say, I don't understand what you're talking about," Karla said.

Rick's eyes twinkled as he kissed her on the nose. "Our child will not only be raised with the cultural stimulation of an art gallery," he said, "he or she will also be familiar with a first-class gourmet restaurant."

Karla's puzzled frown changed into a pleased smile. "So it was your corporation that bought the Whaler's Restaurant."

He nodded. "Daniel Olsen checked everything out for me and recommended it as the steal of the century. How could I pass it up?"

"But you don't know anything about—"

"I agree. And what a hell of a challenge to make a go of it. I'm going to need every bit of your business talent to help me get started." Rick grew serious again. "I'm not fooling myself, Karla. I know how much racing and all the attendant excitement has meant to me. Some would probably say that in a way I've thrived on it. I hope the restaurant will ease a few of the transitional pains. I'll still be in a business where I'll be meeting people, and after listening to Daniel talk about the problems involved in running a top-notch restaurant, I think I'll even enjoy some of the headaches. At least for a while. After that, who knows? I can't give you any guarantees, only a promise. Whatever it is that we do, wherever we go, from now on it will be together. And it will be something we can both live with. If nothing else, we'll learn to compromise.''

"It sounds as though you planned on coming back here all along.''

"Didn't I tell you when I left that I refused to believe it was over between us?''

"Why didn't you let *me* know? It would have saved me a number of sleepless nights.''

Rick caught her chin in his hand. "We both had a lot of things to work out. I didn't know how the race would end or how I would feel about it until it was over. To say something before then would have been wrong, somehow.''

Karla looked down at her lap. "Do you have any idea how infuriating it is to be married to someone who's always right?'' She felt a low chuckle begin to rumble in his chest, and knew she had just played straight man for him again.

"No,'' Rick said, unable to resist, "tell me how it feels to be married to someone who is always right.''

Karla glanced up to see him smiling at her. "Okay,'' she conceded, "that's one for you.'' She reached up to brush a lock of hair back from his forehead. "What about during the winter?'' she asked. "People have been known to develop cabin fever around here, you know."

Rick grinned at her wickedly. "I can think of all kinds of things to do during the winter. I'm amazed at your lack of imagination."

"I'm serious." She was afraid he would see the effect his words had on her, and they would abandon their conversation before it was finished.

"If the restaurant isn't enough to keep me busy, there's another offer I've been mulling over since midsummer. One of the networks wants me to become a racing commentator for them—but I wasn't sure how you would feel about spending even that much time around a track."

"I'm certain now that it wouldn't bother me." When he looked at her questioningly, she grinned sheepishly. "Well, maybe a little, but I'll work on it. You've given so much, Rick. It's important that I give some, too. But what about you?" she went on. "Wouldn't it be terribly difficult for you to be on the outside looking in?"

Rick hesitated before answering. "Before this last race, I would have said yes. But not now. I've worked racing out of my system and it's a good feeling to know I'm leaving on top, and because I want to." He thought for a moment. "No, it wouldn't bother me. I think I would enjoy it, as a matter of fact."

"Then tell them you'll do it. We might have to juggle schedules every once in a while, but we can work it out. Daniel could help with the restaurant, and Maggie and Jeff can take care of the gallery." She smiled. "And the baby will just have to learn to like traveling."

He kissed her lightly. Their lips met but a second, yet stirred the embers of their long separation into a sudden fire of longing. Rick's hands went to Karla's face. He held her gently as he gazed into her eyes.

"I love you," he said softly. His hands moved to her throat, then to the back of her neck and he pulled her to him. He teased the corner of her mouth with his tongue, exploring her mouth with a suppressed passion.

"I have dreamed of being with you again until it forced every other thought from my mind." She felt his lips curve into a smile. "Steve could hardly wait to get me on the plane after the race. He said I was driving him crazy. Oh, by the way, he also said to tell you that we're invited to his and Mary's wedding next month." Rick dropped the information casually and waited for her reaction.

"I'm not surprised," Karla said, refusing to rise to his bait.

"You're not?"

She laughed. "That's one for me. I watched the prerace special they did on you. There was a particularly telling moment when Mary and Steve exchanged loving looks." Karla shrugged. "I put two and two together."

Rick ran his finger down her jaw. "I told them that I hoped their love was as strong and as enduring as ours." He smiled reminiscently. "Steve thanked me and said that if I didn't mind, he would forgo some of the problems we've had."

Karla leaned forward. Against his lips she murmured, "What problems?"

Rick pulled her questing tongue into his mouth. He moaned his pleasure at her aggressiveness as she slipped her hands into the fold of his robe and massaged his chest. This time it was her turn to bite and tease, and she covered his face with quick kisses.

He captured her mouth again and held her there with the sheer power of his need for her. "Let me see you, Karla," he said against her lips. "Let me touch your new body. I want to know the differences our child has brought. I want to share every moment with you of the changes that will come."

With infinite tenderness he undid the dark green buttons that held the flannel over her breasts. When he'd finished, he moved the material aside, letting his hands brush lightly against flesh that throbbed for his possessive touch. The time for words had passed. Now they were lost in a need that could only be assuaged by their physical union. Words could no longer express what Karla wanted to say or what Rick wanted her to know.

Gently he moved her to a cushion of blankets that he had arranged in front of the fire. Almost reverently he touched her swollen breasts, cupping them with his hands before lowering his head to take one nipple into his mouth. Karla sighed her yearning as he moved lower to caress her rounded stomach. He laid his face against her womb; then his hands and his lips continued to travel over her body, relearning some curves and indentations and exploring the new ones that their tiny child had created.

"Each time that we're together is intoxicating," he told her. "I've become so addicted to the feel of you that even though I knew we would be together as soon as the race was over, I almost went out of my mind waiting for the day to come. I couldn't have stayed away this time, Karla. I would have followed you to the ends of the earth."

"I think I must have known all along that our separation was only temporary." Karla was hardly aware that she had spoken her thoughts aloud. "But there was something I had to work out before I could come to you a whole person again. I had to find a way to say goodbye to Bobby and to get on with my life."

"And did you?" Rick asked slowly.

Karla looked into his eyes, so filled with love for her, so anxious for her happiness. "Yes," she said. "At long last."

Rick kissed her, and everything but their desire for each other disappeared in the passion of his embrace. Their lips, their bodies sealed and renewed a promise that they had made to each other on their wedding day. A promise that had somehow been lost in the turmoil of pain-filled years but was now once again bright and strong. They would live, they would love, they would remain as one for the rest of their lives.

"Love me..." Rick murmured as he took her mouth in a crushing kiss.

And she did.

About the Author

Restless Tide is Georgia Bockoven's first romance, but she's no stranger to a typewriter. A professional writer for years, she's had countless nonfiction articles published in newspapers and magazines across North America.

One day in *Time* magazine she saw a color photograph of a race car exploding in flames. "How would I feel if I were in love with the driver of that car?" she asked herself. *Restless Tide* was the result.

With her father in the military, Georgia went to at least fourteen different schools while she was growing up, in as many different places. Her nomadic childhood gave her her love of travel and of people, she says, but she always found it hard to leave the friends she'd made. Her father's last post was Sacramento—and she and both her brothers have lived there ever since.

Georgia is married to a marvelous man and has two sons. Her boys, both quarter-midget racers, taught her about the special frenetic world of racing, which is almost as thrilling on the junior levels as it is in the Grand Prix circuit.

ANNE MATHER

The world-renowned author of more than 90 great romances,
including the runaway bestseller *Stormspell*,
continues her triumph with...

WILD CONCERTO

Her second blockbuster romance!
Big exciting trade-size paperback!

A bizarre twist of fate thrusts the innocent Lani into
the arms of a man she must never love. He is Jake
Pendragon, a brilliant concert pianist romantically
involved with a beautiful international opera star --
who just happens to be Lani's mother!

**A searing story of love
and heartbreak,
passion and revenge.**

Wherever paperback books are
sold, or send your name,
address and zip or postal
code, along with a check
or money order for $5.70
(includes 75¢ for postage
and handling) payable to
Harlequin Reader Service,
to:

Harlequin Reader Service
In the U.S.:
2504 W. Southern Ave.
Tempe, AZ 85282

In Canada:
649 Ontario Street
Stratford, Ontario
N5A 6W2

WC-N

HARLEQUIN
PREMIERE AUTHOR EDITIONS

6 top Harlequin authors — 6 of their best books!

1. JANET DAILEY Giant of Mesabi
2. CHARLOTTE LAMB Dark Master
3. ROBERTA LEIGH Heart of the Lion
4. ANNE MATHER Legacy of the Past
5. ANNE WEALE Stowaway
6. VIOLET WINSPEAR The Burning Sands

Harlequin is proud to offer these 6 exciting romance novels by 6 of our most popular authors. In brand-new beautifully designed covers, each Harlequin Premiere Author Edition is a bestselling love story—a contemporary, compelling and passionate read to remember!

Available wherever paperback books are sold, or through
Harlequin Reader Service. Simply complete and mail the coupon below.

- -

Harlequin Reader Service
In the U.S.
P.O. Box 52040
Phoenix, Ariz., 85072-9988

In Canada
649 Ontario Street
Stratford, Ontario N5A 6W2

Please send me the following editions of Harlequin Premiere Author Editions.
I am enclosing my check or money order for $1.95 for each copy ordered,
plus 75¢ to cover postage and handling.

☐ 1   ☐ 2   ☐ 3   ☐ 4   ☐ 5   ☐ 6

Number of books checked_____ @ $1.95 each = $ _____

N.Y. state and Ariz. residents add appropriate sales tax $ _____

Postage and handling $ _____ .75

I enclose $_____   TOTAL $ _____
(Please send check or money order. We cannot be responsible for cash sent through the mail.) Price subject to change without notice.

NAME_____
(Please Print)
ADDRESS_____ APT. NO. _____

CITY_____

STATE/PROV. _____ ZIP/POSTAL CODE_____

Offer expires April 30, 1984   31056000000